GIRL
FEVER

GIRL FEVER

69 STORIES OF SUDDEN SEX FOR LESBIANS

EDITED BY
SACCHI GREEN

CLEiS
PRESS

Published in the United States by Cleis Press, Inc., 2246 Sixth Street, Berkeley, California 94710.

Printed in the United States.
Cover design: Scott Idleman/Blink
Cover photograph: Celesta Danger
Text design: Frank Wiedemann
First Edition.
10 9 8 7 6 5 4 3 2 1

Trade paper ISBN: 978-1-57344-791-1
E-book ISBN: 978-1-57344-803-1

Contents

INTRODUCTION

Sudden sex is what you crave when your need is too great to wait. For this collection, I asked writers for short, hot, intense writing to satisfy this kind of hunger, and they gave me all that and more. These stories are concise yet fully rounded, just right for a mouthful or a handful, and always delivering the Full Monty. Quick to read, best savored in single doses, they pack intriguing characters, stimulating action and even food for thought into small packages bursting with sensuality.

The authors sweep you along for sex not only in planes, trains and automobiles, but on roller coasters, carnival rides, elevators and ferries as well. If a grassy knoll or traditional bed is handy, that's fine too. You can find sex in zero-G, underwater, in a canyon, in a closet, even in the kitchen. Shanna Germain's "Answering the

Call" shows us games EMTs play in an ambulance, while Victoria Janssen's "The Airplane Story" crams us into the metal-walled bondage of an airliner restroom. Sommer Marsden makes the very best use of "An Hour," Allison Wonderland gets it "Off and On" in under ten minutes, and Tigress Healy offers "Six Minutes or It's Free." But there's more to it than speed, and the sixty-nine pieces in *Girl Fever* by skilled writers such as Cheyenne Blue, Rachel Kramer Bussel, Delilah Devlin, D. L. King, Anna Watson, Jean Roberta and scores of others offer characters you'd love to fuck, evocative settings and sizzling stories that can captivate and surprise you, as they did me, all the way to seduction.

Sacchi Green
Amherst, Massachusetts

LOOK AT ME NOW, YOUR HOLINESS!

Cheyenne Blue

If only the pope could see me now.

My face is mashed so far into Christie's pussy that my world consists of curls of hair and bitter salt. I am falling so far into her, entering her body face-first, a parody of rebirth. Juice on my face, glistening lips. I lean into her, bite gently.

She gasps, returns the favor. My thighs clasp around her head and she pushes a stiffened tongue up into my cunt. The outward spiral sweeps me in and I explode in an indigo wave.

My lover, my partner, my life, I chant in my head.

Deviant, sinner, the morally fallen, the pope chants in return.

Christie and I lie together, sticky thighs entwined in love.

She reaches for the bedside table, pulls out the purple dildo. "Has the pope issued a statement on sex toys?"

"Not yet," I say. "But I'm sure he'll get around to it eventually."

"Want to fall farther from grace with me?"

In answer, I take the toy and rise up, straddling her legs.

Look at me now, Your Holiness.

ANSWERING THE CALL

Shanna Germain

The back of the ambulance is no place for fucking. It's small, for one thing. It smells like cleaning fluid, latex gloves and sticky tape. It's clean, sure, but it's clean for someone else. Namely the patient-to-be. And illegal? We won't even go there.

But Barrie and I can't help ourselves. Every single time.

For me, it's that goddamn uniform she wears, navy blue to match her eyes, the way she's always buttoned all the way to the very top and you can still see the hollow of her chin, the beat of the pulse at her neck. Her belt too—black leather, wrapping her hips, the way it carries so much. Med scissors, knife, beeper, a single rubber tourniquet. I dream about her taking that belt off, the scissors, the rubber. I dream of her beating me black and blue, angling the scissors along the inside of my thigh, wrapping my wrists with the pale rubber tube. But that's not the way Barrie does things.

I let Barrie fuck me because I want her so much. I let her fuck me in the ambulance because every damn time she gets in the back wearing that uniform, it's like I have no choice.

I don't know what her excuse is. I'm just a driver, in my blue slacks and my white button-up. My mouse-brown ponytail. Maybe she just gets bored. You can only sit in a parking lot so long, waiting for a call, before you're itching for something to do—all that pent-up energy with no place to go.

Like this morning. We'd spent four hours waiting, half our shift with not a single beep, not a single call across the radio, not even a false alarm over at the old folks' home. Barrie had her legs on the dashboard, some thick-ass book on her lap. But she wasn't reading it. She was singing to the radio, some song I didn't know. Barrie's older than me, almost a decade, and she likes those old hippie folk songs, the kinds of things my parents used to listen to, way back when.

I thought were going to go through one whole shift without getting in the back. I thought I could roll back to the station without smelling like sex for once.

Then the song ended, and Barrie started smiling like she does when she's got a dangerous idea.

"You know the best way to get a call?" she asked.

I was afraid to even guess, especially since I figured I

knew the answer. Didn't matter—she was already taking my hand, slipping through the little doorway between the front of the ambulance and the back, dragging me with her. And who was I to resist, with that round ass leading the way?

"Down," she said, giving me a shove onto the stretcher. So wrong on so many levels. And maybe that, and not boredom, was the appeal for her.

I was already down the stretcher on my back though, and hardly about to argue. All Barrie had to do was start ordering me around and I was wet. Which wasn't a problem now, but it was starting to be a problem on calls. Barrie would say, "Help me get him on the stretcher," and I'd instantly be soaking through my uniform. Even a simple, "Turn right" from her gets me going these days.

I wanted to touch her, but I knew better. That isn't the way Barrie does things either. She's *touch*, but not *be touched*. There's probably something important in that, but when she starts touching me, I can't think about it too much.

I wrapped my fists around the straps used for patients, tried to keep myself still. Barrie had one leg on either side of the stretcher.

"They really…" she said, pulling open my slacks and then tugging them down over my hips, "…need to let drivers wear skirts."

"That would be…" I started to say *dangerous*, and then her fingers slipped under my underwear, touched the already wet space between my thighs, and I forgot the word.

She has good fingers, sure fingers, the kind of fingers that should only belong to piano players, emergency paramedics and mythical lovers. Into me, out of me, the same rhythm, the same surety I'd seen her sew people up with.

Sometimes I just look up at her when she's finger-fucking me, at those blue eyes staring down, at the sly half grin on her face, at the concentration with which she sinks her fingers inside me. But mostly it's too much, watching her watch me, and so I just close my eyes and feel everything.

This time, her two fingers searched out my G-spot, thumped up against it, rhythm like music. Her thumb on my clit, twitch-twitch-twitch. Her breath was quick and sweet on my face, her growl in my ear. Her breasts almost touching me, their curves behind the fabric, the nipples that I've never seen. She knew just how long to tease me, how long it took until my clit did that aching, throbbing, on-the-very-edge thing it does.

That's when she leaned down even farther, driving her fingers into me harder, faster, her thumb hard-circling my clit.

"Come for me," Barrie commanded.

And how could I not obey?

I went off at the same time the radio did, both of us blaring nonsense into the air. Mine were swearwords and god words and Barrie's name and a hundred other things that didn't have any meaning beyond pleasure. The radio's were *Rig 118* and *MVA* and *priority 1* and *What's your ETA?*

Grinning, Barrie pulled her fingers from me, sucked them clean just like she did when we got cream-filled donuts, the same look of quick pleasure on her face.

"Told you," she said, laughing, excited, already making her way to the front seat. "Best way to get a call."

It took me longer to get back up front. It's hard to pull your pants up in the back of an ambulance, especially when your legs are wobbly and your insides are still churning. The whole ambulance smelled like sex, like me.

"Sirens, lights! Let's roll, baby!" Barrie slapped her hand against the dashboard.

And me, I respond to her need. Because it's what I'm built for, because it makes me wet and wanting, because it's Barrie and hers is the one call I cannot resist.

A WET PUSSY

Rachel Kramer Bussel

G o over there and tell her you want a wet pussy,"
Meri whispered in Eva's ear.

"What?" Eva screeched, taken aback. She was still
getting used to being out in public with a woman, let
alone being surrounded by hundreds of women intent
on fucking each other by night's end. It wasn't so much
the lesbian thing that threw her, as the public displays of
affection. Before meeting Meri, Eva'd been on the shy
side, the kind of girl who hid behind her brown waist-
length hair and freckles. Meri had laughed the first time
she dangled all that hair around her naked body.

"A wet pussy. It's a drink. I want you to go ask
for one. It's good. Trust me." Meri winked, knowing
exactly the effect her words were having on her girlfriend. She was enjoying the process of corrupting Eva,

of turning her from a proper sorority girl into a dyke willing to boldly go places her former self didn't even know existed.

If Meri had had any doubts about whether Eva was truly responding to her, about whether Eva really was a lesbian waiting to be discovered, about whether her pussy really did get wet, she'd have taken things slower. But Eva was the one who'd whimpered and sobbed and begged when Meri had taken her home that first night. Her voice was so twisted in its desire, Meri hardly had to ask whether she was a virgin. It was clear that Eva had never given sex much thought, probably because guys didn't do it for her and the idea of being queer had never occurred to her.

But she'd responded when Meri had made the first move at a campus lecture a month before, sitting next to her, nudging Eva's bare arm with her leather jacket–covered one. The past four weeks had passed in a blur, and now Meri knew exactly what Eva wanted, even if Eva didn't quite know it herself. Meri's nipples hardened as she watched Eva walk slowly, tentatively toward the bartender with the short dreadlocks and easy smile. Eva didn't need to know until later that Meri had spoken with Sherry earlier, had given her a heads-up that here was a new girl on her arm, and she wanted to show her exactly how they did things in girl world.

Meri inched close enough so that she could hear their conversation. "I want a wet pussy," Eva practically whispered. Meri didn't need to see her to know how red

Eva's face was.

"What did you say, darlin'?" asked Sherry. "You'll have to talk a little louder." There was a hint of impatience in Sherry's tone.

"A wet pussy," Eva said a little louder.

"A wet pussy?" Sherry shouted back over the bar.

"Yes. Please," replied Eva.

Meri smiled, knowing that she planned to reward Eva for her boldness. She knew that there was a cause-and-effect response going on right now; saying the words "wet pussy" was causing Eva to have exactly that. She'd bet on it. Eva took a nervous glance behind her, then reached into her tight jeans pocket to pay for her drink. Meri hoped the denim was pressing against Eva's pussy—her wet pussy. Eva handed Sherry a ten, for the six-dollar drink, and told her to keep the change.

"Thanks, darlin'," Sherry said, gazing deep into Eva's eyes and making her blush again. When Sherry had mixed the cold red concoction in a martini glass, she held it aloft for Eva to try. Eva leaned forward and positioned her lips over the chilled rim, then took her first taste, followed quickly by another. When Eva stood back, Sherry placed the drink on the bar, then ran her cool fingers over Eva's. "Any time," she said flirtatiously.

Eva stammered her thanks, then took the drink and moved back toward Meri. "Want a sip?" she asked.

"Oh, no; my pussy is plenty wet already." Eva almost dropped the glass, but she kept sipping, getting more and more used to the drink, the bar, the women seemingly on the verge of getting naked all around her. And yes, the wetness that was clamoring between her legs, demanding her full attention. Meri stepped in front of Eva and slid her leg between Eva's. "What about you? Are you wet yet?"

Eva felt tears race to her eyes, and she blinked them back. Why was she so sensitive, all over, when it came to Meri? Why did everything Meri said to her make her want to go totally wild? When Meri slipped her hand between Eva's legs and pressed her fingers against the damp, hot fabric covering Eva's core, Eva shut her eyes entirely. She wanted to put the drink down but there was nowhere to put it, so she clutched the glass tightly and let Meri's fingers tease her.

"How bad do you want me to fuck you?" Meri asked, her breath tickling Eva's ear, sending shivers down her neck. "Will you let me do it right here, where anyone could see us? How much of me do you think you can take?" The words should've sounded foreign, wild, extreme; no one had ever talked to Eva the way Meri did, not even in her dreams—at least, the dreams she'd had before Meri. But Meri made her want all the dirty talk the more experienced girl could dish out and then some. Meri made Eva want so many things she could hardly contain them all in her mind.

"I want to take all of you," Eva said, "your entire hand." She meant more than simply Meri's fist; she meant all of Meri: mind, body and soul; but that was too much to convey in the middle of a sweaty, loud bar.

Besides, Eva had a feeling Meri could read her mind, from the way she kept her hand in just the right sensitive place and stared probingly into her eyes.

"I can't wait, Eva. I want you now," Meri told her. "Come in the bathroom with me." For a moment, Eva thought of what her best friend back home would've thought. Sex in a bathroom? How tacky! How unsanitary. Eva would've thought that once too, but now all her body was telling her was: *How soon can we get in there?* The ache was overwhelming.

Soon they were in a stall and four of Meri's fingers were deep inside Eva. Eva's teeth were clenched, her body straining, while Meri simply melted into Eva, feeling like she was being given the greatest gift of her lesbian lifetime. For some reason, Eva got to her like no other girl ever had. Instead of telling her that, Meri leaned forward and bit Eva's lower lip, just enough to feel the corresponding tightening, then opening, below. "Give me your wet pussy, Eva. Give it to me," she coaxed softly, and Eva did, letting Meri all the way in. Just for a few moments, her fist was there, inside. Those moments were more than enough for them. They both knew there'd be more of them, infinitely more of them.

They returned to the bar. "Wet pussies all around," Meri said, and smiled.

AN HOUR

Sommer Marsden

As she was halfway through the bedroom door, the arm reached out and grabbed her. Amy hit the bed, facedown, body shaking.

"Hey—"

"Don't move a muscle, lady," said the voice.

"But—"

"Don't say a word."

Amy tried to shake and tried to cry but all she could do was laugh. Even as the firm hand slid up the inside of her thigh. Even as the stiff fingers plunged into her without knowing if she was ready.

"Come on, baby, play with me." It was Joyce's voice in her ear. She sounded like she was smiling too.

"Sorry," Amy gasped. She gasped because that finger pressed her clit and soft, warm lips slid down the back of

her neck the way she liked, making her nipples spike—
hard and sensitive.

Then came the nudge and bump of the strap-on
between her thighs. Along her crack.

"Get up on your knees for me. I just want to play.
You work from home but I'm a slave to the time clock.
I only have an hour," Joyce said.

Joyce yanked her by the waist and Amy found herself
on hands and knees, ass high in the air, legs parted to
accommodate the body pressing her from behind.

She glanced in the mirror: Herself, naked and damp
from the shower. Joyce, larger than she was, dyed black
hair standing on end, firm naked body strapped with
leather. Wielding a cock.

Their eyes met in the reflection and Amy grinned.

"An hour? We can do an hour."

And then the smooth silken glide of silicone pressing
into her moist cunt. Fingers that she loved gripped her
hips with an almost painful grasp. Slim hips she liked to
trace with her tongue undulated and the payoff was the
fullness and the goodness and the blips of pleasure.

"Stay right there." Joyce grabbed her by her wet hair.
Amy watched as the other woman wound the long locks
around her hand twice and used them as a rein. "Good
girl. Good, good, good fucking girl," she was chanting.

Big brown eyes shiny with lust, body moving with
force, filling Amy with her cock. And Amy knew that
nubbin on the inside of the harness was kissing and
flicking and working her lover's clit.

Between the hank of hair in her fist and the friction of the toy, Joyce looked nearly possessed.

"Touch yourself for me," she demanded. And still they stared each other down in the mirror.

Blue eyes meeting brown. Soft, curvy body accepting cut, toned body. Amy worked her clit with slippery trembling fingers, bit her lip, tried to wait, but when Joyce rammed deep and made that sound—that half growl, half sigh sound—deep in her chest, Amy lost her battle.

She came, eyes forced wide, hair tugged back, neck exposed, body bowed. Watching the whole scene play out as she took a few more strokes, saying, "Please, baby, please."

And Joyce came. Bowing her head to her lover's back, her lips pressed to damp skin.

She laughed, a long, low laugh. "There's still time left in our hour."

"So there is. You hungry?" Amy asked, meaning lunch.

Joyce's eyes came up again and stared her down. Amy shivered and blushed when Joyce said, "I am. Roll over on your back."

They really could do amazing things in an hour.

GOOD MORNING

Emily Moreton

Hey, baby."

Rebecca rolled over onto her back, checking the alarm clock. "You're late." She heard Enid's boots hit the hall floor, the rustle of her coat coming off. "Good night?"

"Yeah." The bedroom door opened and Enid wandered through, pulling out the pins holding her bun in place. "Just long."

Rebecca sat up, letting the covers pool at her waist. When she reached out, Enid took her hand and sat on the edge of the bed, leaning in for a kiss. "Too much coffee."

"Probably." Enid's hands were cool, not cold, when they brushed Rebecca's bare arm. She must have been inside a while, even though she was still in her uniform.

"Stopped by Steph's, she snuck us a free cup."

"PC Watts, illicit coffee, what's next?" Rebecca ran her hands through Enid's hair, her nails catching slightly.

"You gonna put me in handcuffs?" Enid snuggled in closer. "You're warm."

"I've been in bed all night. In this nice warm flat, curled up under this duvet…"

Enid groaned. "You think I wasn't thinking about that while I was dealing with drunken fools at three in the morning?"

"I wouldn't like to speculate." Rebecca wrapped her arms around Enid's waist, tipping them both back onto the bed. Enid's belt dug into her stomach, the buckle cold against her skin where her T-shirt had ridden up a little, but that was easy to ignore as Enid kissed her again. "Tell me," Rebecca said against Enid's mouth.

Enid shook her head. "Can't. You'll be late."

"I'm in charge, I can be late."

"Tell that to Mrs. Betts when she's on the phone at nine thirty wanting to know about, I don't know, whether she gets a mint on her pillow during her Highlands coach tour."

"She doesn't." Rebecca started on the buttons of Enid's shirt. "Lavender soap though, new every morning."

"Stop talking. Or stop undressing me, pick one."

Rebecca ran her hand over the curve of Enid's breast, dipping inside her bra to stroke her nipple. "I like undressing you. But you did ask about Mrs. Betts."

Enid caught Rebecca's upper arms, tucked one leg behind her knees and rolled them so Rebecca was on top. "I thought about you like I am now," she said firmly. "On your back in this bed."

Rebecca unfastened the last button, pushing Enid's shirt open, then off when Enid lifted her upper body slightly. "Tell me more," she said against Enid's collar-bone.

"I thought about you just like this, in your flannel pants and your old T-shirt. With your hair a mess and pillow marks on your cheek."

"Sexy," Rebecca said dryly. Enid's cotton bra tasted faintly of washing powder, but it was familiar, and anyway, she loved the way Enid's breath hitched as she bit gently at Enid's nipple through the material.

Enid stroked her hands down Rebecca's back, cupping her ass. "I like you like this. You're my girl like this."

Rebecca would swear, if asked, that the reason she shivered just then was the feel of Enid's hands on her ass, but the truth was, she loved the way Enid's voice sounded when she said, "My girl." Loved hearing it applied to herself, and that was why she raised her head, kissed Enid hard on the mouth, tongue thrusting inside, her hand tightening on Enid's breast without her entirely meaning it to. "What else do you think about?"

"Put your mouth on me again and I'll tell you."

Rebecca trailed one hand down Enid's perfectly smooth stomach—foot patrol, swimming every morning, an hour at the gym three times a week, and it showed, the effort she put into her body—then tickled across the waistband of her trousers.

"Your mouth," Enid repeated, sounding mildly impatient.

"Trust me, you'll like where I put my mouth." Rebecca sat back on her heels, needing both hands to open the stiff leather of Enid's belt and ease it free. It didn't hurt that sitting up meant she got to look at Enid, topless but for her bra, unreasonably sexy for being from Marks and Spencers; her hair spread dark across the pillows, her eyelids heavy with lust. Rebecca shifted slightly, getting just a tiny bit of friction where she needed it. "You're so hot."

"You're so procrastinating."

"Big word for someone who fantasizes about me in bed asleep."

"In bed in your pajamas," Enid corrected, then, when Rebecca started on the top button of her pants, she went on. "You were wide awake. Thinking about me."

That was true enough, though two years together had been enough for Rebecca to lose the unreasonable fear that something terrible would happen to Enid on every shift. She eased Enid's zipper down, then nudged her hips up so she could pull the trousers down. Enid was wet, her curls damp when Rebecca pushed her underwear aside.

"Thinking about what I'd do to you if I was in bed with you. How I'd—Becca, please, don't tease—how I'd get you naked, put my fingers inside you."

"Keep going," Rebecca said, and went down on Enid, licking at her just the way she liked, not too deep, but fast and hard, loving the way Enid tasted, the way her thighs trembled under Rebecca's hands.

"I thought about you touching yourself," Enid said, very fast, sounding breathless. "Stroking inside your thighs, pinching a little." Rebecca groaned, making Enid shudder. "And teasing yourself—over your pants, getting your pants all wet, smelling yourself on your fingers; I thought about how you'd close your eyes, your pretty mouth panting."

She broke off, breathing hard, rocking her hips a little in time with Rebecca, who eased up, stroking one thumb up the crease of Enid's thigh.

"I can't," Enid said, her voice tight. "I can't, fuck; I thought about you fingering yourself, trying to make it last, the way you look when you're nearly there and you keep—you can't keep still, the way your voice sounds when you say my name, I thought about you—fuck, Rebecca, please, please, oh—"

Rebecca pressed her hands firmly to Enid's hips, holding her down, scraping her teeth against Enid's clit. Enid trembled, her voice cracking on a stifled cry, her cunt fluttering under Rebecca's mouth as she arched her back and came.

Rebecca kept going until Enid sighed, said, "Enough," patting clumsily at her hair. Then she lifted her mouth away, resting her cheek on Enid's thigh as she licked the taste of Enid from her lips.

"I thought about you fucking yourself until you came on your own hand, shouting my name," Enid said, sounding remarkably composed for someone who'd just come.

Rebecca shivered. "You'd better be going to make good on that."

Enid pushed her relentlessly away, rolling to her own feet. "No time, alarm's about to go off."

Rebecca flopped onto her back, glaring up at Enid, who grinned back mercilessly.

"I hate you."

"You think I'm hot," Enid corrected, disappearing toward the bathroom and leaving the door open.

Rebecca followed. She knew an invitation when she saw one.

SHE WRITHES
BENEATH ME

Roxy Jones

She writhes beneath me, gasping and arching—my hungry fingers coaxing low moans and supplications, prayers to the god of hotel-room carpets and fluorescent lights. My hand is slick with her, bathed in her need, and my thighs are sore but greedy still—pushing, taunting, fucking in a daze of amazement at my luck to have such a handsome feast laid out for eager hands to grasp, darting tongue to discover.

When we finally venture downstairs, eyes blinking in the light, craving coffee and day-old pastries, we don't notice the glances of our shocked, sleepless neighbors at first as they pick at their Frosted Flakes, but then it swells up behind us like massive waves of jealous whispers, and their hollow eyes betray the hours they lay still, listening with cold, blue envy. They wonder, I imagine, how we were entwined, whose sweaty skin slid on sheets, whose knees were spread and held, whose face met the sky with a growl and a whimper as we arched up off the bed like we had learned to fly. They're desperate to ask, to guess at which of us lay back to receive and which dealt it out, those hours of savage recklessness, the audacious pounding that drove the bedpost into plaster walls over and over throughout the Sweet. Silent. Night.

I smile at them with a wicked pride, like a lion in the sun, because I know. I know the color of her thighs, the shape of her belly when we dance tight, the smile that belongs to me and no one else. I know her smell, her touch, the look in her eyes when I slammed her up against the cold, dirty, brick alley wall and we melted together in the darkness.

They're all guessing, but I know.

I know the sound of her thirteenth orgasm, begging for release. (I count them like wanton rosary beads, head bowed in prayer, devoted lips mouthing my zeal.) I know the sweet, salty thrust of her hips, tense with desire. I know the woman inside the man, the clit behind the catalog cock that rocked between us, linking pussy to cunt like two massive steam engines racing recklessly together on the same track, headed for one glorious, shuddering collision after another.

So I smile again, sweetly, and broader than the first, and they turn away, suddenly red.

I wonder if it's the knowing in my eyes that makes them look away, afraid of what would happen if they asked, or what they would hear if I answered. Terrified to know that all their shocked and horrified hand-wringing, their frenzied, frantic dreams of bodies entwined, coiled and bent in feverish passion, didn't come close to the fiery, fierce heat that burned between us all night.

They sit, frozen but for fluttering hearts, afraid of what they're guessing at, afraid of what they'd ask, and desperately, but politely, afraid of what they'd hear.

Because they know in their guts, from the sparkle in my eyes, that I might just tell them.

Everything.

OH CAPTAIN, MY CAPTAIN

Cha Cha White

W hat we need," said the captain, her ass testing the twill fabric of her pants as she strode down the corridor, "is some girl-on-girl action."

"Come again, ma'am?" Lieutenant O'Hara struggled to catch up as the captain neared the engine room of the alien craft they'd captured when their own ship was destroyed.

O'Hara wished the captain would wear the regulation uniform jacket, instead of the black muscle tee that showed her sculpted arms, set off her brown skin and emphasized her perfect, braless tits. Combined with the snug pants hugging toned legs and that wonderful ass, the sexy tee was a major distraction.

"You heard me, Lieutenant. Assemble the crew. Our hostage is dead, we have no way home but this hijacked craft and we have forty-five minutes to charge that fuel cell before the star we're orbiting goes nova."

Mystified, O'Hara rallied the crew of the former Lesley-Ann IV in the alien craft's control room.

"Gentlemen," the captain began. This was her idea of humor; most of the crew were female. "When we captured this alien craft, we had no idea how its drive worked. Now we know the aliens relied on electrical activity in the brain to charge the fuel cell. Our hostage was charging it for us, but that hostage has died."

A collective gasp ran through the room. The captain held up a hand.

"Apparently a suicide. This is no time to panic, gentlemen. I've studied the electroencephalogram from the alien's brain activity and compared it to a human readout, and I've made a discovery that could save our sweet asses."

Some sweeter than others, thought O'Hara, with an involuntary glance at the captain's posterior.

"There is a process that creates similar activity in the human brain," the captain continued. "Anyone want to guess what it is?"

No one spoke.

"Orgasm. Specifically, female orgasm. So what I need now are two volunteers. Preferably two highly orgasmic ones."

A snicker from the audience. The captain brought her fist down on the console.

"This is not a joke, people. I need two volunteers.

You can do each other, or you can get off by yourselves, I don't care. I need two brave women to stand and deliver. We need this done and we need it done now."

Feet shuffled. Female crew members exchanged glances. O'Hara felt a rosy blush creep up her cheeks.

"No volunteers? Fine, I'll get the ball rolling myself." With one swift gesture, she stripped off the black muscle tee that had maddened O'Hara since the start of her tour of duty. O'Hara's mouth fell open as she took in the sight of the most beautiful pair of naked brown breasts she had ever seen.

Hands shot up all over the room. O'Hara blushed harder, her own hand in the air, fingertips tingling with excitement.

The captain scanned the room, a glint of amusement in her eyes, a slight smile curling her lips.

"That's more like it. O'Hara!"

O'Hara jumped, then elbowed a random ensign out of the way. "Yes, ma'am."

"You know how to operate this contraption. Since you also volunteered, you may as well stay. The rest of you, prepare the ship to leave orbit as quickly as possible. I'll give the order as soon as the fuel cell is charged."

As the crew filed out, with a few curious backward glances, O'Hara attached the electrodes to her own temples and the captain's. She thoughtfully observed the captain's smug smile, her arrogant posture. *With all due respect, Captain,* she thought tenderly, *I'm going to wipe that smile right off your beautiful face.*

The setup finished, the captain stepped forward, and O'Hara sensed her uncertainty. The captain, always cocksure in front of a crowd, had no idea how to make the first move. Instead she compensated, assuming a stern, swaggering air.

"You up for this, O'Hara?"

"Oh, I'm up for it, Captain," O'Hara replied. She slid her hands under the waistband, undid the button and pushed the twill pants down with one gesture. At long last she could cup that magnificent ass in her palms.

"Nice initiative, Lieutenant," said the captain. Her breath came fast; her voice trembled slightly.

"If there's one talent of mine that goes wasted around here," said O'Hara, kissing the captain's exposed throat, "it's my talent for eating pussy. Now sit down and shut up."

The captain's brows drew together. Clearly, she was not accustomed to being told to shut up. O'Hara gave her no time to vent her displeasure. Pushing the superior officer down on the console, she found the small, shocked clit and warmed it with her breath, moistened it with the point of her tongue. At the same time, O'Hara's right hand slid down to find her own pussy, already soaking wet, and she teased her own clit without mercy.

"Insubordinate—aunhhhhh…" gasped the captain, burying her hands in O'Hara's red curls. Her clitoris promptly swelled and began to throb under the deft strokes of O'Hara's tongue.

With expert pressure, O'Hara brought the captain

to the brink. Blindly, with her free hand, she stroked the lovely dark breasts, teasing the nipples. But with practiced discipline she kept her attention focused on the captain's inner thighs; her warm, wet pussy; and her clitoris, now engorged almost to the point of pain. *Ever the good lieutenant*, she thought. If orgasms were needed, then orgasms she would provide.

But despite the urgency of the situation, O'Hara couldn't resist pulling back when the captain's rushed breathing told her orgasm was imminent. Panting, wiping her mouth with the back of her hand, O'Hara regarded her captain with all the coolness she could muster.

"Good?" she inquired.

The captain's head was arched so far back that O'Hara couldn't see her face, only her gorgeous, strong throat—but she straightened up when O'Hara stopped.

"Hunh?" she half gasped, half sobbed, looking at her lieutenant in dismay. "Wha... Why did you stop?"

"I want to be sure that my execution of your orders meets with your approval, Captain."

No trace of the smug smile, she noted with satisfaction. This was a woman on the verge of begging for more. To her credit, however, the captain snatched at the vestiges of her authority.

"Yes," she moaned, thrusting her shapely hips forward. "More, Lieutenant. That's an order."

"Yes, Captain," murmured O'Hara. She sank her tongue deep in the captain's cunt, drawing two, three, four lazy upward strokes to her clit to finish the job.

AT THE HIP

Anna Watson

Two weeks post-op, I'm about to get my period and my leg feels like a sodden log. Like it doesn't even belong to me. The incision slices down my thigh and I'm supposed to be massaging it with vitamin E oil, but I don't like touching it. Sometimes I let Chelsea do it, but I don't like her touching it, either.

Our bedroom is bright and clean, lots of flowers in vases and get-well cards pinned up. A spring breeze floats through the curtains and I can hear a mockingbird yelling his head off from our apple tree. Everything is saying new beginnings, growth, beauty, blossoms and baby lambs and all I can think is, *Fuck, fuck, fuck, I hate my life!*

"Earl Grey. Hot." Chelsea sets a tea tray down on my bedside table and pulls up a chair. We both grew up with

Trekkie parents, and time was we wrote slash together, nerds that we are. Feeling too sorry for myself to crack a smile, I grab my cup and spill tea onto my chest.

"Shit!" I pull my nightgown away but can tell I've been burned. Chelsea gallops to the kitchen for an ice pack and helps me out of my nightie. She leers when my breasts are revealed, something meant to cheer me up. It doesn't.

"I feel crappy!" I snap. She drops the leer and starts mopping up the bed. I sit there with the ice pack over my titties, eating one Fig Newton after another. She looks at me.

"What?"

"C'mere." Her eyes are lustful. I get angrier.

"Come where? I can hardly move! I just had an operation, you know!" I cram another Fig Newton into my mouth and point to my leg, propped on its pillow.

She kneels beside the bed.

"No," she murmurs, her voice filled with longing. "C'mere."

My breath stops and starts again. For the first time in over a year I feel a little something down there that isn't related to my fucked-up hip. She can do that to me, I remember, warm my pussy until it feels like molten honey.

"Daddy," I whisper, just letting it slip out. Lately, that word has become just another utilitarian endearment, but saying it now I feel its full sexy power. I reach out a hand.

"Angel," she says.

I caress her face and run my fingers through her buzz cut. My perfect butch husband. Carefully she leans closer and holds me against her chest, her strong arms encircling me, her breath starting to come faster. I can tell she's getting hard. We kiss, softly at first, then with more passion, and my pussy continues to wake up. I start thinking about something other than my pitiful condition and allow her to pull me back into my body, which, it turns out, has just been waiting for the right moment. The right moment on this perfect spring day.

I mew and squirm under her as she takes my mouth. My burned titties feel glorious, the good, stinging pain reminding me of all the times we played with hot wax.

"That's right, good girl," she says into my ear. "Come back to me. Come back to your Daddy."

A few tears leak out of my eyes, and then a few more. Chelsea keeps on kissing me, steady, unafraid. She never has been afraid of my emotions. I grab on tighter, pressing as much of myself as I can against her body. My leg comes dislodged from its pillow and I give a yelp. Chelsea helps me get it settled again and takes up where she left off, her tongue and lips demanding my full attention. I pull her closer and try to get at her dick, but she holds my hands away.

"No, baby," she scolds. "You let Daddy finish his work."

I sink back into the pillows and offer myself up.

Chelsea lowers her mouth to my sore nipples,

nipping and sucking, worrying them until they're throbbing with delicious pain. My pussy swells, yearning for her touch, and I start talking the way I do when I'm so turned on it's like I'm a little crazy. "Open for you, Daddy, so wet for you, need you, Daddy, fuck me, take me, yours, Daddy, take what's yours."

Chelsea angles her arm across the hip of my good leg and gives me some steady pressure, something I can move my pussy against. I'm still crying, still talking, "Give it to me, Daddy, fuck me with your dick, do it to me."

Both of us know it's too soon for Chelsea to take me with the cock she keeps in her boxers, to lie on top of me and plow me, but there is more than one way to fuck a femme, and Chelsea is a master cocksman. Grabbing a fistful of hair, she holds my head still, moving back up to kiss my mouth, kiss the tears from my face as the fingers of her other hand dip into the moisture seeping from my cunt, smearing it on both thighs, on my belly, in both of our mouths, and then she's driving herself into me, performing some magical butch feat, fucking me as hard as I need without hurting my hip. I get louder and louder, telling her my pussy is hers, that she's nasty, a dog, a fucking dog, and then she puts her mouth on my clit, her breath fast and warm, her tongue in all the right places, her finger-dick moving in a frenzy, exactly right, exactly as if we'd been doing this yesterday instead of over a year ago, and then I'm screaming and coming and we're both crying, holding on to each other so tightly I think I might stop breathing.

"Baby, lover, sweetheart," Chelsea speaks softly into my ear. I can feel her tears on my cheek and all the love I'd pushed back in pain, in fear, comes welling up into my heart.

"I'm your girl, Daddy," I whisper, the words coming easily. I almost always say this after we fuck, but this time I can hear a question behind the old, familiar words.

"Oh, Patricia," says Chelsea, hands framing my face. "You are my girl, baby. Forever and ever."

Later that night, Chelsea moves to the couch because I'm so restless. I send her off with my blessing—she always feels guilty about leaving the conjugal bed—and lie in the dark waiting for the pain meds to kick in. A few years ago, a screech owl made his home on one of the trees in our little postage stamp suburban backyard; we were never sure where he'd come from or why he stayed. As the Percocet takes hold and I begin to feel all fuzzy and floaty, Chelsea comes creeping in to give me one last good-night kiss, and the screech owl begins his low, sweet, crooning call, sending his love out into the night.

CLEAN SWEEP

Fran Walker

Kat shifted her cleaner's cart to the corner of the elevator when a young woman wearing a maroon suit stepped in and pushed the button for the top floor. Kat nodded to herself. Another new almost-employee about to face the last hurdle. Lord only knew why the company owner insisted on seeing every selected candidate and making the final hiring decision himself.

The elevator clunked, shuddered and stopped.

"Oh, my god!"

Kat smiled at the woman. "Don't worry. This happens about once a week." She pushed the emergency button.

"Service," said a man's voice, tinny and muffled through the speaker.

"The north elevator is stuck again," Kat said.

"Twenty minutes ETA."

"Twenty minutes?" The young woman's lips went taut. "But I have my interview with Mr. Colehatch at ten twenty-five."

Kat glanced at her watch. "The service guys will be here in twenty minutes, and they usually get this beast going again within a couple of minutes. It's only ten now, so you've got plenty of time."

The woman shook her head. "I was hoping to get up there early. I wanted to spend a little time…"

"Checking your hair and makeup? Panicking? Don't bother. For one thing, you look fine." Kat smiled. That much was certainly true. "And for another, Mr. Colehatch is nearly blind. No one knows how he decides whether or not a new candidate gets hired, but it's not on looks."

"I heard…"

Kat raised an eyebrow.

"A friend of mine, she works here in HR. She said that, well, that maybe Mr. Colehatch chooses people on…"

Kat waited.

"Smell."

Kat laughed.

"No, I'm serious. Oh, I'm Marina. I'm going to be— that is, I might be the new lobby receptionist."

"Kat. Housekeeping. So, tell me more about this smelling thing."

"My friend did a survey. Informal, you know. Private. With each woman who got interviewed by Mr. Colehatch.

Those he accepted, and those he turned down. And she found one thing in common. All the women he accepted?" Marina's voice dropped. "Had sex that morning, or the night before. Jennif—I mean, my friend, she said that he must smell it on them. She told me he's often said that employees with a happy sex life are good workers."

"How very odd," Kat said. "Still, you could be right. Colehatch is an odd man and practically senile."

Marina looked at the elevator's control panel. "When will they be here?"

"Soon." Kat found herself trying not to laugh. "So you were going to go into the ladies' room on Cole-hatch's floor and—"

"Make myself smell sexy," Marina said defiantly. "Yes."

"Jack off. Masturbate. Bounce the bunny. Tweak the twat-hole."

Marina flushed.

"Poke the pussy," Kat said. "Naughty girl."

"I..."

"Very naughty. Naughty, but nice. I bet you have a nice...pussy." Kat pulled the feather duster from her cart and slapped it lightly, repeatedly, against her denim-clad thigh.

Marina sagged against the wall of the elevator.

Kat waited.

"I am naughty," Marina said.

"Should you be punished?"

The long, dark eyelashes swept down. "Yes."

Kat's breath caught. Oh, she was lovely! Hair long and dark like the eyelashes, rich warm skin, even richer curves beneath that prim maroon suit.

"Drop your skirt," Kat said.

Marina unzipped the maroon skirt and tugged it down. Now it covered her from knees to ankles, instead of from waist to thigh.

"Pull down your panties."

Marina shoved her underwear down to her knees.

"Bend over."

She bent over the cleaning cart, one hand grasping the rail of the elevator.

Kat turned the feather duster around so that she held it by the feathered end. The long, round wooden handle with its little leather loop at the end jutted out from her hand. She swung it, tapping it lightly against Marina's ass.

Marina gasped and leaned forward, jutting her ass up into the air.

Kat tapped the duster handle against Marina's ass again, harder this time. Her buttocks jiggled, and a faint red strip appeared.

"I'm a very naughty girl," Marina said. "Very naughty."

Kat smiled. "Then you'll need to be taught a lesson." She smacked the duster handle across Marina's ass, first one side, then the other, then straight across the middle. Marina panted. Kat squeezed her free hand down the front of her jeans, rubbing herself in rhythm to the strokes she applied to Marina's ass.

Marina let go of the elevator rail and slid her hand between her thighs.

"No!" Kat pulled Marina's hand away. "I did not give you permission to do that."

Marina whimpered. Kat slapped the duster handle against Marina's ass, hard enough to leave a bright red line.

"Please. Oh, please," Marina whispered.

Kat dropped the duster and grabbed Marina's hips, pulling the woman's bare buttocks against the front of her jeans. Then she slid one hand around and forward to Marina's clit. She rubbed herself hard against Marina's ass while she rubbed the woman's swollen clit. The thick denim of her jeans bunched, creating a fold of cloth that pressed against her own clit. The two panted in unison as Kat squeezed and rubbed, harder and faster.

Marina cried out. Kat felt her own orgasm gather, squeeze and explode.

They both lurched forward against the cleaner's cart when the elevator shifted.

"Good timing." Kat straightened up.

Marina tugged her panties and skirt up. "Oh, my god."

"If your theory is right, you'll probably get the job, a promotion and a pay raise all at once," Kat said, winking.

Marina smiled. "I sure hope I get the job. I wouldn't mind working in the same building as you."

The elevator chimed, and the doors slid open.

TASTE OF MY WOMAN

Giselle Renarde

I pressed number one on my speed dial: *Monique Cell*. She picked up on the first ring. The phone bill was going to be astronomical this month.

"I only have a minute," I whispered, glancing around the office to make sure nobody was hovering too close. "Sid just got up to grab lunch, and he won't be gone for long. How's the conference going?"

Even over the phone, I could hear Monique shrug her shoulders. My woman was beautifully predictable with that sort of thing. "This city's full of politicians. I never know what to believe and what's spin."

Yes, I'd started it, but I realized right away I didn't want to talk about work or spin or politics. "What are you doing right now?"

"Just ducking out of the lunch line to talk a little

more…" Her voice deepened to satin gravel, shimmering and gorgeous and gritty all at once, "…privately."

A moan slipped through my lips before I could catch it. I looked around the office, but no one was about.

"Are you eating?" Monique asked. Not what I'd anticipated as an opening gambit; I found the question jarring. "You don't eat enough, Jackie. I worry about you."

I sighed. "Well, *don't* worry—I'm eating," though it wasn't true. I hadn't called her for a lecture. Monique hadn't been away twenty-four hours, and already I was craving her presence, her body, her taste in my mouth.

"That's good," Monique replied. "I'm eating too. Here, I'll put a bite of this in your mouth and you tell me what it is."

Closing my eyes, I focused on the pleasured moan Monique released into my black Nortel phone receiver. Warm sweetness caressed my taste buds, and I knew precisely what she'd place on my metaphysical tongue. "You're eating dark chocolate. I can taste it." I peered down the hallways to make sure Sid wasn't on his way back. The coast was clear, and I was going all in. "Now, you tell me what I'm eating."

Monique gurgled, but answered without pause. "I know exactly what you're eating. You've got your face all up between my thighs, and you are just devouring my pussy."

"Yes I am, babygirl, and your pussy is delicious." There was a throb between my legs, like a drumbeat, at the sound of those words from her mouth and from mine. We didn't do this. We didn't talk like this.

"Oh, you are sweet," Monique cooed. "Sweet as chocolate."

My eyelids fluttered closed. I wondered where she was, if she was alone now, if she was reaching down inside her panties to play with her clit. God, I loved the image of my woman with her hand down her pants, slowly rubbing that sweet spot. I loved the image so much I was half tempted to slip my own fingers down between my pussy lips and play in that liquid heat. But I couldn't do that...not at work...not sitting at my desk in my wide-open office...

"I'm kissing your mouth," I told Monique. Her little panting noises were getting the crotch of my panties incredibly slick with juice, but I wanted her words in my mouth. "Can you taste your pussy on my tongue?"

"Yes I can," she replied in a sizzling whisper. "It's mingling with the chocolate, like a dark-chocolate pussy."

My breath hitched and I wanted so badly to slip a hand beneath my top, inside the cup of my bra, and pinch my nipples until they were as hard as little pink pebbles. All I could do to resist was close my eyes and lick the picture Monique had planted in my mind. "Oh, your dark-chocolate pussy is melting in my mouth... *and* in my hands." My head buzzed with sugarcoated arousal. "It's all over my fingers. The juice is running down my chin. Oh babygirl, your chocolate pussy is dripping all over me."

Monique gasped, and the sound sent a shock wave from my tits to my clit. "Tell me where," she begged. "Where's that chocolate dripping, Jackie?"

My name on her tongue was sweetest of all. "It's dripping all down my naked tits and you're sucking it from my nipples." I could feel my thighs squeezing together of their own volition, applying pressure to my fat clit peeking out from between two wet lips. I stifled a squeal.

"You lick it from my lips," she whispered. Her voice was a secret. "It's everywhere now. You suck the chocolate from my tongue and then sink right back down to suck it from my clit. My chocolate body is all over your skin, babydoll."

"My tongue is all over yours." I could see her now: the chocolate of her flesh melting with the heat of my lips on her engorged pussy lips, the warmth of my hands on her smooth, dark thighs. She's all over my face. I'm messy with the taste of her.

"Lick me," she begged.

"Yes." My hand snuck up my thigh, pressing the seam of my neat gray slacks against my throbbing clit. The sensation was so startling my hips bucked forward before I could quell the motion. "God, babygirl, I'm getting off just imagining the taste of you."

"Me too."

And the idea that Monique was every bit as aroused as I was turned me on even more. It didn't take long. My

imaginings had my clit thick and throbbing, just waiting
for those little touches, one finger stroking over the top
of my slacks. That's all I needed—I missed her so much.
Her breath in the phone seemed sweet with chocolate,
and my pleasure caught in my chest, a suppressed sound,
thumping right there next to my heart, right there next
to Monique. She was everything to me.

Sid cleared his throat and my pounding heart jumped
out of my chest. When I pried my eyes open, he was
standing in front of my desk with a grin plastered ear to
ear. My skin prickled like it was breaking out in hives.
Embarrassment didn't even begin to describe what I was
feeling in that moment. My face must have been glowing
crimson. "I have to go, Monique." I didn't want to tell
her why.

"Tastus interruptus?" Her lustful giggle spoke
volumes, and I stared down at the keypad on the phone
to keep Sid out of my field of vision. I wanted just this,
just five more seconds alone with my woman before we
had to hang up.

"I love you," I said. It came out as a whimper.

"You too, kid." The smile in Monique's voice made
me flush all over again. "Now get yourself some food.
You need more for lunch than a single helping of long-
distance pussy."

OFF AND ON

Allison Wonderland

Y ou're late, sweetheart."

Blazers.

"It's four according to my watch."

Shirts.

"It's five after four according to mine."

Bras.

"Five comes after four according to mine, too."

Shoes.

"Really? Then explain why you're late."

Belts.

"My watch keeps perfect time and yours is five minutes fast."

Slacks.

"We'll have Brody settle the matter when he gets home from school, which should be sometime in the next five minutes, give or take five minutes."

Panties.

"It's better to give than to take. Well, except when I take you."

Mouth first, shushing, rushing.

Hands then, scaling, flailing.

Bodies next, crashing, thrashing.

Moans now, unbidden, unhidden.

"You give good headway, sweetheart."

Panties.

"To be honest, I wasn't sure we were going to make it."

Slacks.

"Think we have time to run through it again?"

Belts.

"Watch yourself."

Shoes.

"That reminds me—what time did you get here?"

Bras.

"I arrived at five after four."

Shirts.

"Thank you."

Blazers.

"But I came at four fifteen."

CLOTHES MAKE THE WOMAN

D. L. King

"You can't just rifle through my closet." I sat on the bed while my sweetie pulled hanger after hanger out of the closet, flinging dresses, skirts and blouses everywhere.

"No, but it's perfect, we're the same size. What're you going as?" she asked.

My Chloe, who probably hadn't worn a dress since her sixth-grade class picture, had gotten the notion to go in drag to Sid and Meg's Halloween party and she was using my closet as her costume store. "You know I wear that stuff to work. You could give it a little more respect. Maybe I'll go through your closet."

She looked at me. "No, really, what are you going to wear?"

Why not? If she was going to wear my clothes, why

couldn't I go butch? I wear pants. Not often, because
Chloe likes me in dresses, but I have some.

"I know: you could go as a harem girl. You'd look
great in harem pants and a skimpy, 'I Dream of Jeannie'
top."

"Maybe I could go as Cat Woman," I said.

"Yeah, in a skintight…well, maybe not. What do you
think about this?" She held up a light-blue baby doll
dress. I'd bought it a few years ago when they were in
style and didn't like it even then.

"Not a good look for you," I said. "Here, get out of
the way." If she was determined to wear my clothes, the
least I could do was try to make her look good. And save
my wardrobe in the process. I handed her my brides-
maid dress from my sister's wedding to try on while I
picked up some of the mess she'd made.

"Tada," she said. It was so not her, but she looked
beautiful in it. "This is too funny," she said, pushing up
a strap and looking at herself in the mirror.

"First rule: don't make fun of my clothes," I said,
"not if you ever want to see me in them again."

"Yes, ma'am." She gave me a peck on the lips.

I studied her. "You need a wig and you're going to
have to practice walking in heels. Here, put these on."
I handed her my bronze sandals. "We should practice
makeup, too. I want to try a couple different looks on
you." She was starting to get that look; the *maybe this
isn't such a good idea, after all,* look.

"Want me to take you to the costume shop to look

for something sexy for you?" she asked.

I told her I'd take care of it; it was going to be a surprise. I figured what was good for the gander was good for the goose, and what the gander didn't know wouldn't hurt her.

The day of the party came and her wig looked great. I finished her makeup and she was getting dressed when the phone rang. "What? Really? But I have a... Yeah, I know. When?" Chloe came back into the bedroom, dressed but still barefoot, and gave me a questioning look. I covered the phone and mouthed, *My boss.* "Okay. Okay," I said and hung up.

"What was that?"

"He needs me to participate in a conference call with our Japanese client. He's going to call me here when they're on the line. He said it would be in about an hour."

"Did you tell him you had plans?"

"I tried, honey, but it's a million-dollar deal. He said it probably wouldn't take that long."

"All right, I'll wait for you."

"No, you go ahead," I said. "I promise I'll be there just as soon as I can. I don't want you missing the party because of my work. I'll grab a cab and meet you there." I gave her my *I won't take no for an answer* look and she grudgingly agreed.

Once she was out the door, I went back into the bedroom and took the suit I'd chosen from her closet.

Our friend, Gwen, who'd called earlier, impersonating my boss, rang the bell just in time to help me get into my new black silk corset. My take on drag was slightly different. I slicked my long black hair into a low bun, put on some dark liner and smoky shadow and Chloe's gray, wool pin-striped suit, slipped my black stocking-clad feet into a pair of black alligator pumps and checked out the look. Kind of a cross between Madonna and Dietrich.

"Damn, woman, you look hot," Gwen said. She put the finishing touches on her Wonder Woman costume and we were off to the party.

The clothes made me feel powerful. In fact, I breezed through the door with just a kiss and a "Dahling" for Meg, the hostess, grabbed a martini and breezed out the back into the yard to scan for Chloe. I spotted her, in the far corner, talking to a couple of butch friends. She was slouching and her legs were spread. The dress looked great but she had no idea how to carry off the look.

I vamped my way over to where she and her buddies were standing and saw Sid elbow Chloe. "Dude, your girlfriend's here."

I took a leisurely drink of my martini. "Is that any way to behave in a dress like that?"

Sid, who was dressed as a gangster, plastic machine gun and all, started to chuckle. "Yeah, she's got you there, man." Chloe shot her a look.

The two other butches stared at my breasts, threatening to spill from the top of the corset. It was obvious they'd already had plenty to drink, otherwise they would have been able to maintain in front of Chloe.

I knocked back the rest of my drink and grabbed her arm. "Come with me, Missy," I said and dragged her toward the opposite corner of the garden.

Still feeling empowered by the clothes, and slightly drunk from gulping that much vodka, I backed her against the fence and grabbed her crotch with my free hand. She started to say something but I smashed my mouth against hers, kissing the words into oblivion. Moving my hand up to her breast, I ground my own crotch against hers and gave her nipple a hard pinch.

Chloe melted into the pinch and then straightened up. "What are you doing? You're not a t—"

"Squirmy. I'm going to have to take you home and tie you down before I fuck you," I countered.

She kissed me, this time, and smiled her big butch know-it-all smile. "It's not that I mind, or anything, but what's gotten into you?"

"Noisy, too. Yeah, tie you to the bed and stuff my panties in your mouth," I muttered, kissing her again. "Clothes really do make the woman," I said, rubbing my body against hers, knowing the boning in the corset was attacking her still-hard nipples. "At least this woman. Time to go home and strip 'em off."

She followed closely behind me as I headed toward the house and home.

YAB-YUM

Sacchi Green

Sometimes, when it hadn't been too long, we would focus with yoga-like intensity. She scissored her legs across mine and we sat erect, mound not quite to mound, breast so close to breast that the whisper of space between shimmered with the tension of our nipples. We swayed slowly, movements exquisitely precise, our breathing just barely in control.

A fine and poignant torture, worth prolonging; the moment came too soon when flesh demanded the press of beloved flesh, and the fire mounted so high it threatened to consume us. But not quite yet.

"Yab-yum," she would say, or I said, or we chanted as one; and all around us shadows took shape and voice from our shared memory.

Poetry, doggerel, curses, laughs; flashes of brilliance, wine-slurred philosophy; a place and time and voices that live on in millions more minds than ours, yet in memory are still ours alone.

We were wannabe Dharma Bums, not-quite-jailbait chicks high on the Road and the Beat, hanging with Kerouac and Cassady and Ginsberg on the fringes of their world. Brought to their parties by others, we were swallowed up, instead, in the urgent mysteries of each other. In dim corners we echoed their game of Yab-yum, silent, still, close, closer, fighting not to touch while breast swayed nearer to breast, cunt edged toward cunt, tight nipples sought nipples. Hunger pulsed hot and slick between damp thighs.

We seared each other with blue-hot sparks of longing, need rising in a tide that swept away the will at last, the game well-lost, while our bodies clutched at joy with hands and mouths and limbs as fierce in their hunger as any savage tooth and claw.

She thought she heard cheers across the smoky room. My ears were still ringing with glory.

Fifty years later that glory still swept us, memory only a brief distraction. The same lightning crackled through the vanishing space between until bodies had their way—hands, tongues, thighs, my lean hands, her divinely heavy breasts—knowing each other's flesh and hearts so well that every joy, every cry, transmuted into poetry known to us alone.

We will remember. Always.

LOVE *LAS MUERTAS*

Kirsty Logan

I haven't been scared of ghost trains since I was ten years old, but this one looks different in the fading sun. Even the *Día de los Muertos*–themed illustrations, highlighted with green neon paint, look creepy when the wind is tugging at my hair and the ground is pebbled with candy floss. The odd tape-recorded cackle or groan of machinery still echoes from behind the doors. But my heart is thumping in my throat, and the heat between my legs shows no sign of fading.

Like most stupid decisions, my choice to dawdle past closing time at the carnival is because of a girl. I've been thinking about her ever since I first saw her, the sun warming my shoulders and my mouth full of candied peanuts. Her skin was powdered bone-white, roses nestled in the curls of her hair, and the parts of her body that weren't covered by her ruffled red dress were painted with intricate spirals and swirls. According to the lurid illustrations of her face on the ghost train's walls, her name is Encarnación. I wouldn't have stopped, but she ran over and presented me with one of the flowers from her hair; even under the paint, I could see the gorgeous dimples on each cheek when she smiled.

I live close by, so I told my friends I'd walk home by myself—but really, I'm just here to get Encarnación's number. Now that the sun has faded it's too cold for my strapless summer dress, and I move in closer to the ghost train to get out of the breeze. My nipples feel hard as thumbtacks—though I couldn't say whether that's from the chill or the thought of how Encarnación could warm me up.

This is ridiculous. The girl is long gone and I am making a fool of myself. I turn to leave.

Boo, grunts the devil in my ear as he wraps his arms around me. All my muscles stiffen and my throat closes around my scream. But already the devil is laughing, releasing me from his grip. It's Encarnación in her ruffled dress, her face wiped free of makeup. Her skin is the color of acorns and she smells of sugar and sunlight.

"We're closed, *señorita*. Perhaps tomorrow?" Her accent is heavy on her tongue; already she has turned toward the ghost train doors. "Unless"—she turns back to me—"you'd like *una aventura?*" She holds out her hand to me, grinning wide, and I try very hard not to stare at the way her cleavage peeps over the top of her low-cut dress. "I think you'll enjoy," she says.

I grab her hand, plant a kiss on her palm and let her lead me through the door.

The ghost train car is just wide enough for two and Encarnación's thigh is pressed against mine. In front of us a ragged black curtain ripples in the breeze, blocking my view ahead. The air smells musty, like clothes in vintage shops. Encarnación pulls down the barrier over our knees, then twists to check something in the back of the car; her breasts press against my arm and it's everything I can do not to dip my head and kiss them.

"It's Encarnación, right?" I say, just to say something.

She twists back round and leans in close to me. "Emma, actually," she whispers. "I don't even speak Spanish; I'm from Laaahn-daaahn." Her accent has gone; she sounds just like me.

"I'm from London too," I say. "Camden. Whereabouts are…"

The car shudders forward, cutting off the rest of my small talk. It shakes and burrs along the track, juddering the bones of my hips and thighs, making my teeth chatter.

The ragged curtain wipes over our faces and we're through to the other side. Chipped neon skeletons jerk from every joint, their Ping-Pong ball eyes rolling in their sockets. Beautiful girls with painted faces smolder from the walls. A trio of bone-men strum guitars, candy-colored skulls flash in strobes, yellow petals scatter to the floor, cobwebs brush against my hair. Under the soundtrack of ghostly shrieks and cracks of thunder I hear the judder of machinery as we turn a corner. Emma is expecting the hairpin bend, but I'm not; I fall into her lap, my face practically down her dress.

"Fuck!" I say, righting myself. "Sorry, the car…"

Emma's laughing, her face close enough that I could press my tongue into her dimples. Lit by the strobe, each movement a photograph, she tugs down the hem of her dress so that her breasts press out at me. "Better?" she asks. It is better, obviously, because there's nothing I want to do more than pull off her dress and drop to my knees between her legs. But I can't say that.

"Um…" I say. I'm sure the quivering of the car is making my voice come out funny. Emma doesn't seem to be listening; she's wiggling on the narrow seat, lifting a hip and putting one foot up on the cutout side of the car. Then her head tips back and her eyes roll shut, a smile slipping across her face.

"Move two inches to your right," she says, nudging my leg. "Riiiight…there."

And I understand. Oh fuck, do I understand. The thick vibrations of the car are perfectly centered on my clit, making my heart beat in double time. A groan slips out of my mouth and I shift in my seat so the angle is just right. Emma's murmuring deep in her throat, her hand sliding up my thigh and then slowly, teasingly, her fingertips nudge at the two layers of thin cotton over my clit.

I shift closer to her so that my leg drapes over hers, sharing vibrations. Emma's breathing hard, her breasts straining at her dress, her thighs tensing with each throb from the car. I feel a pulse in my neck and lights are flashing in my eyes and my hand is guiding Emma's farther down, pressing her fingers against me, and oh god, oh god...

The car emerges from the ride, just as we shout out our orgasms to the scratchy soundtrack of tape-recorded ghouls.

We're outside in the dark and Emma's busy flipping off switches. I stand on the litter-strewn ground, unsure. What's the polite thing to do after you've just reached simultaneous orgasm on a fairground ride with a hot-as-fuck stranger? I turn to leave, then stop. Usually I'd be running scared, but it's like I left all my fear back in the ghost train.

"Do you want to come round?" I call over. "I could cook..."

Emma tucks the keys into the pocket of her dress, swaying over to me. Without thinking, I press a kiss to the dimple on her cheek.

"I'm hungry," she says, with a laugh.

I blow a kiss to Encarnación on the side of the ghost train, then take hold of Emma's hand and lead her back to my place.

SYSTEM

Jeremy Edwards

The first thing Gail did was show me the crotch seam of the peach shorts she wore under her employee apron—making me juice my panties right there in aisle 14B.

It wasn't intentional, though I later learned it's the kind of thing Gail *would* do intentionally. It was simply that she was squatting down and bending forward to crack open a case of soup when I came up behind her.

Soup happened to be the next item on my shopping list, so hovering in her vicinity to await access—to the soup, I mean—was perfectly legit.

As she resurfaced and stepped aside, she smiled invitingly, and her eyes flickered a barrage of messages: *Oops, I didn't realize you were waiting for me to get out of the way... You were checking out my ass, weren't you? But don't apologize, honey—I like girls too, and you can check me out any time you want... You do like girls, don't you?*

I'm pretty good at processing unspoken conversation, but it was all I could do to keep up. Finally, she brought her voice into the mix—while still keeping those sassy eyes flickering—by honoring our interaction with a brief, cheerful giggle while I logged her name tag info.

Then she rounded the corner into another aisle, while I just stood there with my clit twitching in my shorts.

If I'd been at home in this condition, I would have had my pants down and my fingers up my slit in five seconds flat; but this was errands-and-client-meeting day, and jilling in a public restroom wasn't really my style. So I embraced the alternative, namely, squirming my way through the afternoon until I could be back home—which, for a woman who could always get down with the lazy, viscous tension of anticipation, was an erotic pleasure in its own right. In my opinion, nothing brightened a weekday like the ever-present thought that there was a big, fat masturbatory orgasm in my future. *Just you wait*, I promised myself seductively.

When I returned to the supermarket two hours later, still riding the simmering libido that I'd been husbanding—if you'll pardon the expression—between my legs since my previous visit, I encountered Gail again. Amazingly, though her naughty eyes and her creamy peach butt had been with me all day in spirit, it hadn't occurred to me that I might actually see her when

I returned for my cold foods.

Her face lit up when she caught sight of me: I read approval, mischief, flirtation, employee courtesy...and a smidgen of surprise. Though my primal instinct was to drop my shopping basket and paw hungrily at the T-shirted breasts that bubbled under her apron, my social instinct was to account for my repeat engagement.

"You must think I'm the slowest shopper in the world," I said with a self-deprecating laugh. "But, honestly, I haven't been wandering the store this entire time. This is a separate trip."

"Yeah, I was wondering," said Gail with a teasing grin.

"You see," I explained, "I have a system."

Her eyebrows went up inquiringly.

"I only come into town once a week, for errands and a regular meeting. And whenever I'm running early, I get as much grocery shopping out of the way as I can before seeing my client."

"You run *early?*" Gail seemed genuinely impressed.

I shrugged modestly before continuing. "But then when I do the pre-meeting grocery run, I have to come back afterward. The proactive shopping trip is great for nonperishables, but there's no way it would work with frozen food and the like. So I stop by after the meeting to snag those items, before I rush home to my cold-air appliances. It does mean two visits, but the net result is I get home a lot sooner than if I left all the food shopping for last."

"Very clever."

"Thank you."

I could feel my upper thighs perspiring with erogenous alertness, like a quart of orange juice sweating en route to the fridge. And my nipples were stiffening like they were already there.

Gail was looking me up and down. "If there's one thing I admire, it's a woman with a system."

Oh, fuck. Was she blatantly coming on to me?

"And, yes, I'm coming on to you."

That did seem to settle it, I noted, as my knees began trembling and my bottom cheeks started tingling.

"May I suggest you hold off a little longer on the frozen food? I have a feeling you're going to be delayed for a few minutes."

"Nnnn." I was nodding frantically and nibbling the tip of my own finger like I always did when I was very nervous or very aroused—or, as in this instance, both.

"You can say that again," quipped Gail. She looked at her watch. "Would you like to join me in the customer service office? This is a dead shift—people will cover the counter if anyone needs customer service, but the office will be empty."

I swallowed, still nodding, before finding my voice. "*I* need customer service, Gail."

"And I will cover *that* personally."

I felt a small, surreptitious slap on my derriere as she followed me into the office, pulling the door tightly shut behind her.

I turned to face her.

"A woman who runs early, huh?" She grinned. "Well, then, let's see how early you can be for the dinner party in my pussy."

She licked her lips. Then she went all elbow-awkward as she tried to untie her apron at the back.

After hours of low-idle fantasizing, I was now aflame with the thought of getting my tongue all over the meal nestled in that peach crotch seam. "Here," I said breathlessly, reaching around to take hold of the straps. "Let me do that."

"Of course," Gail acceded.

She abandoned the apron to me and mirrored my embrace.

"After all," she murmured in my ear—squeezing my ass so hard now that I squeaked with desperate excitement—"you probably have a system, don't you?"

PROJECT RUNWAY

Sharon Wachsler

t's you, babe! It's you!" Marla turns from the mirror where she's buttoning her pressed, white shirt.

Modeling the new red dress and spiked heels I bought for her fortieth birthday party, I execute a careful twirl. The short rayon skirt billows up around my thighs. Marla catches me at twirl's end, sliding her hand up to squeeze my ass.

"I guess you like it, then?" I bite her earlobe, tonguing the silver stud. She's got on her dress shirt, black slacks. A silk tie with delicate pink petals lies on the hamper, waiting.

"I'd like this"—she slaps my ass—"in anything—in a trash bag."

"Like on 'Project Runway'?"

"Exactly like that."

"Well, then, I guess there's no need for finery." I make to slip away, but she pulls me in tight.

"Finery is good, too." She kisses down my neck to the V of the dress, her hand sliding under the fabric, gliding to my breast.

I gasp. "I need to sit down."

Marla hoists me off the toilet lid, plants herself on it then pulls me back down onto her lap. She rolls me over onto my belly, with my forehead resting on the cool floor, my thighs across her lap.

"This isn't exactly—" I start. Oh. Um. Fingers run up and down the backs of my legs and ass, making scratchy-nailed spirals on each upturned cheek.

"Don't start a run in my nylons," I mumble. *Rip them off.*

"Are you telling me what to do?" Marla's hand smacks my ass; my clit reverberates against her thigh.

"Oh, no, I'm just not sure this is the time—" I say. *Please, please, hit me again.*

Her hand whistles down. *Thwack! Thwack! Thwack!* I scream and moan and wriggle. All I see is red, a tent of red around my head. *The dress,* I realize, *she's pulled up my dress.* My head is swimming in it. I'm so wet. *Too wet.* "Your pants," I moan. "They'll stain."

"Fuck my pants," she grunts. And I do. I hump against her leg. Her hands, my ass, all has turned red; I can feel it. I see it in the red around me. Whistling smacks, shrieks piercing air, her hand coming down, coming down, coming down. *I love you,* my mind whispers. *I love you, Marla, I love you, love you.*

"Uhn!" It's her—her voice, sweating out the sound, muffled by my dress.

And a rip. There go my panty hose. And the high keening, is that me, like a siren as she pushes two fingers in? No matter. I writhe and ride, wailing, to the rhythm of her slaps and thrusts.

"Come now!" Her voice, suddenly rough, pushes me over. I howl, pulsing against her fingers. I hold her inside me, letting her feel my power, my inner strength, squeezing. Finally, opening.

My throat is raw. My cunt is raw. My ass burns. I feel fresh and spent, together. I can still hear the screaming.

"Ups-a-daisy," Marla calls from somewhere above. She's trying to pull me up to her, but I just want to be a puddle on the floor.

"The floor," I try to unstick my tongue. "The floor is soft." *Soft? No, that's not what I meant.* I giggle, but Marla understands and is lowering me, on my side, to the bath mat.

"I need to turn off the kettle. It's a terrible thing to burn out a bottom!" Her voice retreats, the pounding of her feet shaking the floor. Suddenly the strident call is interrupted with a sharp chirp that fades into a hiss.

Marla's face, puffing, appears above me. "Just in time. That's why I decided to hurry things along a bit. Sorry about that." She collapses with her back against the sink cabinet, her legs across mine.

"Oh, I didn't notice," I murmur, feeling hair in my

mouth. The updo I'd spent an hour creating has come undone. Her pants have a huge cum stain on both thighs. My nylons are shredded. My dress is crumpled.

"What didn't you notice? The kettle? Or me hurrying things along?"

"Either. Neither. It was so fast!" I shake my head, "You were in, I was coming, you were out!"

"Well, you know what Heidi says." She puts on a nasal, high-pitched German accent: "One day you're in, and the next, you're out!"

"True," I answer. "But you know what you did back there, under those 'tough time constraints'?"

We laugh together on the way back to our closets. "Made it work!"

I DO

Catherine Paulssen

Cautiously, I opened the heavy antique door and peeked inside. A huge gold-framed mirror was propped against the green wall, and, gazing into it on a plushy Louis XVI chair, sat the woman of my dreams.

She looked amazing.

Maybe it was the dramatic contrast of the sheer white silk and chiffon of her robe against her melted chocolate skin.

Maybe it was the way the sleek dark strands of her hair, adorned with small silk roses, curled on her naked shoulders.

But most likely, it was the happy glow on her face.

Now she adjusted the necklace I had given her for our five-year anniversary, and my eyes wandered down to where her V-neckline revealed the soft rounds of her apple-shaped breasts.

I breathed a sigh.

Olivia turned around. "What are you doing there? Out! Out!"

I smiled, shook my head and entered the sumptuous hotel room, locking the door behind me.

"But it's bad luck to see the bride before the wedding!" She giggled, coming toward me and wrapping her arms around my neck.

"Who says *you're* the bride?"

"Either way, it's bad luck."

I pressed a kiss on her plump lips. "It can never be bad luck with you, baby."

She purred. "Likewise, Mrs. Jewell."

"I wish it were that time already," I breathed against her lips.

"Only"—she glanced at the grandfather clock in the corner—"fifty-five minutes." She fiddled with the buttons of my high-collared cheongsam. "Alva?"

"Mm?"

"You know what'd be great?"

I kissed her again. "What?"

"If it were our honeymoon already." She peered at me from underneath her full lashes.

I bit my lips and lifted her onto a nearby mahogany table. The months of preparations for our big day had been strenuous and crazy. Some nights, exhausted and faced with a to-do list that didn't ever seem to get shorter, we had fought hard to remember why we were doing this.

But no matter what, she was and always would be the most wonderful woman I had ever kissed, and nothing could ever make me forget it.

I traced the outline of her silk gown from the shoulder straps down to her breasts. I could feel her stiffen though she didn't seem to move. I traced the shape of her breast over the material of her dress and lingered on her nipple, which poked out so enticingly that the certainty of having to wait another day to touch it, tease it and lick it consumed me with a yearning that needed immediate fulfillment.

Olivia's eyes followed my fingers as they tugged the chiffon aside. "What are you doing there, hm?"

"I'm giving you a little taste," I said, slipping the dress gently off her shoulder and running my fingers over the white bra underneath.

"A taste?" she said, then held her breath.

"Of our honeymoon."

I bent down and kissed her neck, her shoulder and the lace that shone against her dark skin. I took it between my teeth and nipped at it. When I got her erect nipple into my mouth and rolled it between my lips, she threw her head back.

"Alva, baby... You're scandalous," she said, a wicked grin on her face.

I placed little kisses along her necklace and licked at her naked skin until finally finding her lips again. "*You* brought up the honeymoon," I mumbled.

I nudged her mouth with my tongue, and she obediently parted her lips. I showered devoted caresses on her tongue and her lips.

"I can't even remember the last time you did that to my pussy," she sighed between two kisses, then grasped the nape of my neck and gave me an ardent look, followed by a quick kiss. "Don't leave me hanging like this." She kissed me again eagerly, encouragingly.

"You want me to...?" I looked at her with disbelief.

"Yes." She nuzzled at my lips. "Go down on me, babe."

Her sassy voice made my body tingle. "Say that again," I whispered.

Her eyes glimmered. "You like to hear me talk like that, don't you?"

"And it's even hotter when you're wearing that dress."

She drew me closer to her. "Eat me out, babe."

I knelt down and parted the layers of chiffon. She gathered them in her fist and watched my fingers follow the lace-top stockings up her thighs and gently nudge her legs apart. I traced the small birthmark on the inside of her thigh and pressed my nose against her skin. Running its tip up her thighs, my eyes closed, I inhaled her scent, that peculiar, bedazzling blend of rose oil, the starch of her crisp petticoat and the spicy musk of her arousal.

I tugged at her thong, a delicate garment she had bought specially for the occasion. Her breathing quickened as my fingers traced the roses woven into its thin mesh. I could feel her wiry curls beneath the thin material.

"Do it," she panted and propped herself up so I could strip it past her thighs. "Please."

I kissed her pussy and spread its folds with my tongue. Olivia leaned back and moaned my name.

Her cries spurred me on. I pulled my tongue away and licked every inch of her skin aside from her clit. Despite her pleading, I ignored that small pearl and instead laid my finger on top of her slit and ran it down very gently, evoking little gasps from her cherry-red mouth.

Her clit was exposed to me now, and I could sense her need just by the way her thighs trembled at my touch. Savoring the moment, I teased her with the tip of my tongue, sliding it over her most sensitive spots.

Olivia shivered. "Yes, oh…yes, taste me…" She stroked my cheek with the back of her hand. "Too bad I'm not allowed to mess up your hair," she complained in joking desperation.

I pushed my tongue farther between her folds, puckered my lips and sucked on her clit. My thumb rubbed her opening, and Olivia pulled away as the sensations overwhelmed her. I grabbed her legs and steadied her, knowing she wouldn't last much longer.

Her fingers clenched around the edge of the table, and she rocked her body back and forth. Her moans grew increasingly high-pitched, a sound I had missed for far too long. With a long groan, she collapsed onto the table panting. "Baby…"

I gently stroked her naked thighs and watched her body quiver as my fingers brushed her skin, still so sensitive in the aftermath of orgasm. Sighing happily, I slipped her thong back into place and rearranged the folds of her dress.

"You're so beautiful," I sighed, overwhelmed by her rosy cheeks and radiant eyes.

She cupped my cheek and mouthed, "I love you," as her breath grew steady again.

The grandfather clock chimed twice.

"Twenty minutes until the wedding march begins," she said, stretching herself along the table. Her glossy lacquered nails tapped the silk of my cheongsam, right below my hips. "Want me to...?"

I felt incredibly naughty. "I do."

SHANE

Jessica Lennox

S hane had never been good at keeping in touch, so you can imagine my surprise when I received a phone call out of the blue.

"Hello?"

"Hey. It's me."

Well, you could have knocked me over with a whisper, and suddenly it was as if I had lost the ability to speak. Finally I managed to croak, "What do you want, Shane?"

"Oh, now it's 'Shane'?" the voice asked.

"Well, I could call you asshole, but I thought you might prefer your given name," I replied smartly.

"Okay, okay, relax. I just called to see how you're doing."

"Really," I said, more as a statement than a question.

"In what way?"

"Are you seeing anyone? How's your sex life?"

Uh-huh. Well, if I'd had any doubt up to that point, I certainly knew now where this was going. Shane and I had a long history of quickies via the telephone. I swear, sometimes phone sex with Shane was better than live sex with whomever I was dating at the time.

"Yes, I am, and it's great, thank you," I answered, tersely.

Liar! my inner voice screamed in time with my pussy. Why did it feel as if my body and brain were ganging up on me?

"Hm," Shane replied, "well, if you ever get bored, you know how to reach me."

"Yeah, I do," I said. "Good night." I didn't wait for a reply. I hung up immediately and then furiously masturbated myself to orgasm. I dreamt about sex most of the night and woke up feeling frustrated and unsatisfied.

When my phone rang the next night, I didn't have to look to know who was calling.

"Hello?"

"Hi, doll."

Yep, there was that voice again. "Twice in one week?" I asked, sarcasm dripping from my voice.

"Yeah. Aren't you happy to hear from me?"

Now there was a loaded question. Parts of my brain simultaneously screamed *Yes!* and *No!* My pussy seemed to be agreeing with the *Yes!* side. I tried to ignore them all as I attempted to calculate what damage would be done by me giving in.

"Well?" the voice insisted.

Gawd, I could actually feel the cocky attitude and I couldn't decide whether to hang up, or come. Who was I kidding? There was no way I could resist.

"Okay, yes. I'm happy to hear from you," I admitted. And just like that, as if my body needed permission, I felt everything heating up, my pussy getting wet.

"You know what I want, don't you?" Shane asked.

"Yes," I said, whispering.

"What do I want?"

"You want me to come for you," I answered, feeling my nipples harden.

"That's right," Shane said. "Are you wearing panties?"

"Yes, red lacy ones," I replied, spreading my legs apart slightly.

"Mmmmm," Shane moaned. "Slide your hand down slowly until you're touching the outside of your panties."

Truth be told, I probably didn't even need to touch myself; Shane's voice was enough to make me crazy. A few minutes of squeezing my legs together would probably do the trick, but obeying Shane's commands was so much more enjoyable. I did as she said, moving my hand ever so slowly until my fingertips came to rest on the very wet spot that now adorned my panties.

"Now, close your eyes and imagine that it's my fingers touching you there, making you wet."

I was already doing that, but I wasn't going to break the flow of things, so I just continued to do so while my breathing turned shallow.

"Does that feel good?" Shane asked, her voice deep and inviting.

"Yes," I whispered, touching myself lightly, waiting for the next command.

"Good girl. Now slip your fingers into your panties and put one finger inside your pussy."

My clit twitched as soon as those words were spoken, and I quickly obeyed, not wanting to wait another second. I bent my knees slightly and slid my fingers underneath the elastic band and without hesitation slid my index finger inside my very excited pussy. I drew in my breath waiting for that voice to spur me on.

"How does that feel, doll?" Shane purred.

"Really good," I sighed.

"Mmmm... I bet your pussy is nice and tight. Put another finger in. I want you to stretch your pussy for me."

With no hesitation I pulled my finger out and replaced it with two. "Ahhhh," I said, my pussy throbbing and contracting around my fingers.

"I bet you really want to come, don't you?"

"Yes, please," I said, almost begging.

"I know you do. I want you to. Come for me. Move your fingers in and out of your pussy. Think of me fucking you."

I was doing exactly that. Shane continued, "Use your

other hand to pinch your nipples; imagine my teeth on them, biting them, sucking them while I fuck you harder and faster."

Oh, I remembered. I remembered exactly the way Shane's fingers felt inside me, her mouth on me, her voice in my ear as she fucked me, making me crazy, making it impossible not to come. I could hear her breathing turn to panting and I couldn't hold back any longer. I clamped down, trapping my fingers inside my pussy, and let out a scream as Shane's moans took me over the edge.

A few seconds passed. I was barely finished, my pussy still throbbing, when Shane said suddenly, "I have to go."

Yep, some things never change. "Whatever," I said with an irritated sigh. "Good-bye, Shane."

I hung up the phone, tossed it on the bed, then squeezed my legs together until I came again, the memory of Shane's voice still lingering in my ear.

SIX MINUTES OR IT'S FREE

Tigress Healy

Melanie was frantic when I picked up. "You're making us lose clients!"

"How?"

"You're making the wives *come*!" she scolded.

"That's not my fault!"

"I just took a call. Karin's hold-out time is getting shorter by the week. All of the women's hold-out times are."

"And...?"

I turned onto the client's street and drove slowly so I wouldn't end up sitting outside of the house talking on the phone.

Melanie continued. "So even though you had fifteen to thirty minutes when you first started fucking her, it needs to be about five to seven minutes now. Rick's been monitoring it. This is an investment for him."

"So?"

"Ira, this is business! I know you enjoy the pussy, but the *husband* is paying for it. *He's* the one married to a wife who is really a lesbian benefiting from heterosexual privilege, so—"

"You're passing judgment."

"Look, *he's* the one paying us, so get her hot and wet enough to not mind fucking him and get the hell out of there. Nothing extra!"

"Well, what do you think I do, paint her toenails afterward?"

"No, but you *do* get into it."

"I'm pulling up to the house."

"Ira!"

"How about you get off the phone and get us a merchant account so we can take credit cards instead of cash? We should already be paid before I come out to the homes."

"I'm working on that."

I turned off the car and looked into the rearview mirror, wondering how many households needed our services but didn't know a business like ours existed.

Mel started in again. "Ira, don't ruin this. We have a foolproof business. A profitable niche: we help men who are married to lesbians get their wives hot enough to fuck them, so they can have sex every week. This is a no-brainer, but we lose clients if you make her come and he ends up not getting any."

"Got it," I said, pulling down the visor to apply my pink lip gloss in the mirror. I ran my fingers through my black hair and popped a stick of Big Red into my mouth.

"I gave him a guarantee," Melanie said.

"What kind of guarantee?"

"That if Karin comes, which means he won't get any pussy, he doesn't have to pay."

"What the hell?" I couldn't believe that shit. "I enjoy my work, but I don't do this for free! I do this for the money! And as *partners*, you should never make an agreement without me, especially one that concerns me! *I'm* the one out here fucking while *you* sit in the air-conditioned office!"

"You poor thing," she sneered. "He was gonna cancel today. What could I do? I could only draw on my business knowledge."

"What business knowledge?" I scoffed. A couple of courses to get her associate degree and now she was an expert.

"About how Domino's turned their business around and changed the industry with their 'thirty minutes or it's free' policy," Melanie said.

"What does that have to do with...?" I took a deep breath and said, "Bye, Melanie."

So I wouldn't be paid upfront. I'd aim to work on Karin for six minutes, since Melanie had said she could only hold out for five to seven minutes before she came.

I spit out my gum, checked my reflection on the side of the car and approached the house. Karin came to the door dressed in an oversized men's shirt and worn khakis, probably getting ready to work in the garden. Her curly brown hair was unruly, but I liked it.

When Rick came to the door as well, Karin turned to him and asked, "Again?"

Her tone held surprise, and for a moment, I wasn't sure how she felt, but she broke into a smile and pulled me in, slamming the door behind me.

I fumbled to get my cell phone out as she groped me. I had to tell her to wait while I set the timer for six minutes, but I didn't tell her why.

I held the phone so I could keep up with the countdown.

00:06:00

I pushed Karin against the wall and unbuttoned her shirt. She fondled my tits as we kissed. She moaned when my lips met her neck and earlobe. She lifted my skirt and slipped her fingers into my Lycra thong. I sighed in pleasure when I felt her middle finger inside me and her thumb rubbing my clit.

Rick stood nearby stroking his hard-on through his jeans. It didn't bother me since company policy says he can't say anything, touch his wife or me, or pull out his dick while I'm there.

Karin pulled my tank top down and sucked my tits hard. I unbuttoned her pants and grabbed her ass, pulling her close to me. My fingers played in her hairy bush until I placed two of them inside her warm, wet hole.

She was soaked so I probably should've stopped there, but I didn't.

00:05:00

Karin and I got stark naked. I pulled her into the kitchen and onto the floor, because it was her favorite place to fuck.

I rode her pussy as she caressed me, kneaded my nipples and kissed my tits.

I tried to ignore Rick squeezing his lump and watching his watch, because I loved tribbing, and the sensation of Karin's tongue on my nipples as we ground our pussies together was spectacular. However, my job was to please her, so I laid her down and slowly sucked her full breasts while I played between her legs.

00:04:00

"Eat me," Karin begged, spreading her thighs wider. I took in the scent of her hot twat and teased her clit with the tip of my tongue before licking her pussy lips.

"Yes, lick me, baby!" she shouted. She whimpered when I grazed her engorged clit with my tongue. I hadn't even had a chance to really suck her pussy and tongue-fuck her the way I wanted to when...

00:03:00

She shouted, *"I'm coming! I'm coming so hard and so good!"*

Rick scowled and shook his head.

I rushed out to get my clothes.

Karin got up and went down the hall, shouting for

me not to leave, while Rick followed me back into the other room.

00:02:00

I felt his eyes on my back, as I dressed, and when I faced him, he pointed to his lump as if it was my fault then left the room in a huff.

00:01:00

"Ira, I wanted to give you a tip," Karin said, pressing a check into my hand. It was for a thousand dollars—far more than Rick had ever paid.

Not knowing what to say, I kissed her and said, "Thanks," before letting myself out.

00:00:00

In the car, I called Melanie and told her it was time for a new niche: helping lesbian women who are married to men come quickly—in six minutes or it's free.

We would offer our current (male) clients the guarantee, but make the wives come faster than that so that *they'll* be the ones calling and paying us big money.

"You're a genius!" Melanie shouted. "We'll make business history! Six minutes or it's free!"

IN HOT WATER

Elizabeth Coldwell

If you really want to find the perfect woman," Carole tells me, "you only have to ask, and the universe will send her to you."

She believes in all this cosmic nonsense: crystal healing, feng shui, the works.

Needless to say, I don't. The safest thing, I've learned from experience, is to humor her. "So what do I ask for?"

"Whatever you desire the most. Whatever will make you happiest."

So I reel off a checklist. "Okay... Long, dark hair, big tits, likes to take control in bed. Oh, and she's got to have a decent job. No more flaky actresses who are always broke."

Carole smiles. "That's it, Jasmine. It's out there. All you have to do now is wait for the universe to deliver."

Despite her assurances that this will absolutely, definitely happen, I don't give it another thought. Mostly because when I get back to the flat, it's to discover the boiler has broken down. Now, I can cope without lots of things, but hot water isn't one of them, so I'm straight on the phone to my landlord. Ray's a diamond. If there's a problem, he gets it fixed, and he says he'll find a plumber for me as soon as possible.

An hour later, there's a knock at the door and I open it. Standing there isn't the middle-aged, salt-of-the-earth bloke I'd expected, but a plumber whose brown hair is tied in a loose ponytail at the nape of her neck, and whose breasts push out the front of her baggy blue overalls.

Sometimes it's good to have your expectations confounded. This is one of those times.

"I'm here about the boiler." Her voice has a cigarette husk, low and appealing.

"Great. Come in." I lead her through to the kitchen, show her what I think might be causing the problem.

She gives her head a *leave it to the expert* shake and reaches for her wrench. I go back to the room that doubles as my office, but it's hard to concentrate on preparing a sales presentation when visions of her full lips and fuller breasts present a delicious distraction.

When she knocks on the office door, I almost jump out of my skin. Does she know I've been staring into space the whole time she's been working, thinking about her undoing those overalls to reveal she has nothing on underneath?

Flushing guiltily, I follow her out so she can talk me through the repair. She might as well be speaking Mandarin for all I understand of what she's done, but as long as I'll be able to take a hot shower later, I'll be happy. If only I could persuade her to join me!

But that's just fantasy—or so I think till I realize how close together we're standing, pressed between the kitchen wall and the temperamental old refrigerator. Her nipples are poking at the fabric of her overalls, and I wonder whether she really is bare beneath them.

She smells of oil and fresh sweat, but it's an intoxicating fragrance, the aroma of blue-collar babe. Breathing it in, I'm aware my panties are growing damp.

"Thank you so much," I say. "If you'd like to give the bill to my landlord, Ray, he deals with that side of things."

"And who deals with you?" she asks.

It's such a loaded question. I want to reply, "You, please, ma'am," but she doesn't give me the opportunity. Grasping both my wrists in one strong hand, she pushes me up against the wall.

Her lips mash against mine, tasting faintly of strawberry gloss, the only girly thing about her. This is so unlikely, such a porno cliché, to be seduced by the plumber, but it's real, it's happening, and I'm making no objections.

This will have to be quick; she's still on the clock. Calloused fingers pop open the button front of my dress. I want to respond, to free her of the unflattering overalls, but her grip is steady. She's in control, and I can't deny that's the way I like it.

She pushes a hand into my panties and smiles at the wetness there. All I can do is whimper as she explores my secret places, fingers roaming over cunt and asshole, before settling into a steady rubbing rhythm on my clit.

With almost embarrassing ease, she has me creaming around those persuasive digits. So much juice, soaking right through the cotton.

"Don't worry, hon," she purrs. "Dealing with gushers is all part of my job."

At last, she shrugs out of her overalls. Her tits, cradled in the sheerest of nylon bras, almost demand to be sucked, so I do. With her grip on my wrists released, I'm free to touch her pussy the way she's touching mine, fingertips skating over her slick lips. Our mouths meet again, kisses hot and frantic, tongues dueling as the tension rises.

Beside me the boiler, prompted by its automatic timer, whooshes into life, proof the plumber's done the job Ray's paying her for. But I'm only interested in the job she's doing on my cunt, the heat she's building in me with her relentless caresses.

Writhing against the wall, I come with a sharp cry. But my lover remains to be satisfied, so I hold it together long enough to take her to her peak, one finger deep in her tight hole as my thumb works in magic circles on her clit. Only then do I slump against her, panting into her bare shoulder.

Pleasure achieved, she's all business again. Brisk and purposeful, she fastens up her overalls, reaches for her tool kit and hurries off to her next customer—whose needs, I'm sure, will be very different from mine. Would I recommend her services in an emergency?

Absolutely.

"Call me," is all she says as we part at the door, pushing her business card into my hand. Her name is Lulu: so delicate for such a strong woman, but that's not what's making me smile. Carole will love this. You see, my gorgeous Lulu was sent to me by Universe Plumbers.

LOVE ON A
REAL TRAIN

Michael M. Jones

From the first time she saw it, Charlene was obsessed with the train scene from *Risky Business*. She couldn't explain why, exactly. It was the unforgettable combination of a young Rebecca De Mornay, the movie's hypnotic eroticism, and an exhibitionist streak aching to break free. Sometimes she watched it at home with Tilly, sometimes they playacted it out in the bedroom. And sometimes, they went out to ride the L.

Charlene would put on the little white dress and heels, Tilly would wear the sneakers and jeans and sport coat, and they'd ride along the Loop for hours, always waiting for the right moment, the perfect opportunity. They'd kiss slowly, fingers wandering, whispering desire-heated words against each other's lips. But the moment never came. Always foreplay, never the main event. Eventually, libidos raging and pussies soaked, they'd disembark, heading home to finish things properly. Once, they found an alley; Tilly shoved Charlene up against the wall and fingered her with quick, hard strokes, headlights strobing past them, finishing before they could be caught. That took the edge off. Still, the Holy Grail remained elusive, always a late-night group of students or club-hoppers or tourists making things unfeasible.

But tonight was perfect. Charlene nestled against Tilly, arms lightly looped around her girlfriend's neck, nibbling at her lips, breathing in her scent. Tilly had a few too many curves to play a passable Tom Cruise, but she butched up quite nicely with her short black hair and her "riding the train" outfit. Charlene, with her slight curves, lithe body, and long blonde hair, fit her role much better. They shifted together on their seat, fingers wandering whenever they could escape detection, whispering soft fantasies under the noise of the train. Hands brushed against breasts, dipped between legs, trailed over cheeks, leaving tingling nerves and growing arousal in their wake.

People got off the train, one by one, fewer boarding to replace them. And then they were alone. The doors hissed shut, the train jerked and swayed as it picked up momentum and Charlene exchanged a wicked look with Tilly. This was it.

Charlene swung to her feet, chest heaving with anticipation, eyes half lidded. Tilly, still seated, leaned forward to slowly run her hands up Charlene's legs, gliding up silky-smooth skin, vanishing under the little white dress. Up, and then down they came again, taking Charlene's panties with them, the skimpy white thong she only wore when she wanted to play out this fantasy. Charlene stepped out of them, gasping as cool air swept right up her legs. She bent down to undo Tilly's belt buckle and unzip her jeans. Tilly was packing tonight, wearing her favorite strap-on, the one with the thick purple fake cock, and Charlene pulled it free and erect through the undone zipper. All in silence, because they'd rehearsed this in their fantasies a hundred times.

With time being of the essence, they moved quickly. Tilly slid forward, and Charlene straddled her, lowering her aching pussy onto the shaft, hissing with delight as it filled her. Moaning, Tilly reached out to rake her fingers over Charlene's shoulders and back, while Charlene braced herself with her hands on the back of the seat, starting to rock up and down. Slow at first, but picking up speed, the dildo slick with her arousal, every movement sending a shock of pleasure against Tilly's clit as well. They moved together, letting the train do half the work for them, bodies jostling, quiet groans escaping parted lips.

Charlene suddenly ducked down, capturing Tilly's mouth in an eager, demanding kiss; Tilly tightened her grip, pulling her close. Charlene raised herself up and slammed herself down, taking the dildo as hard and fast as she could, feeling the orgasm rising within her until it finally burst forth. She screamed her release into Tilly's mouth, her entire body tensing and shuddering, and Tilly urged her through it with a fierce joy, hips arched upward to press into her.

Spent, Charlene broke the kiss, pulling back with shaky limbs and heaving chest. Tilly had to help her up and off the strap-on, supporting her until she could collapse onto the seat. There was some very hasty rearranging of clothing as they made themselves presentable again. The thong was gone, kicked somewhere under the seat; neither felt like retrieving it: a sacrifice to the gods for a night well spent. All too soon, the train hissed to a stop, and a crowd of semi-drunken frat boys boarded. The girls exchanged a wry look. Just in time.

As Charlene and Tilly exited the train a few stops later, ready to head home and clean up, Tilly grinned impishly at her girlfriend. "Have I ever told you what *my* favorite movie scene is?"

THE SECOND TIME AROUND

Sara Lynde

In my experience (not exactly staggering, but I know a thing or two about how to please a handsome, sexy butch,) nightly sex that lasts for at least an hour is the norm in a new relationship. So when the inevitable first sexless night with Danny came, I felt a huge letdown. Never mind that the situation couldn't really be helped. Let me explain.

Danny is a driver for Canfield Armored Car Service (guaranteed safe transport of cash and other valuables). It isn't like being a cop, where you drive to work in your street clothes and change into your uniform at the police station. Danny dresses for work at home. She wears a uniform, badge, gun, and a utility belt with a lot of contraptions on it. Although she isn't aware of it, every time she puts on her work clothes she turns me on to the point where I want to beg her to take me to bed and, what the hell, just show up a little late for work. But I never do that because Danny is very conscientious about her job. She wouldn't miss a shift, or even be a minute late, unless it was a matter of life or death. She keeps her uniforms and equipment in tiptop shape. She's always cool and in control—on the outside.

Oh, wait. I was about to explain about our first sexless night together. Due to an unforeseen crisis at Canfield Armored Car Service, Danny had to work a double shift. That night some guy on drugs or something tried to hold up Danny and her partner as they were loading the day's receipts for the local Home Depot. They subdued him, but in the process Danny's partner accidentally shot him in the arm, and that led to a trip to the police station to give a statement. Long story short, Danny finally got home at 3:45 A.M., exhausted. With only six hours until she had to leave for the morning shift, she crashed for what little sleep she could get before going back to work. So, no sex.

Anyway, I was about to describe the real Danny, the one that most people don't see. Under her "tough guy" exterior is a sweet, sensitive, tender person who is also a tiger in bed. She knows exactly how to give me the most mind-blowing orgasms I've ever experienced, and she does so regularly.

As far as her own needs, I guess the word to describe Danny is "clitoral," as opposed to me, maybe best described as "diversified." Even when she's not aroused, she has the biggest clitoris I've ever seen. It protrudes from her lips and if she doesn't wear jockey briefs to cover it firmly, the sensation of her clothing rubbing against it goes from stimulating to aggravating to painful in short order. The only time she wants that kind of stimulation is when I'm the source, and I can guarantee you that for me it's a pleasure like no other. Her response to my fingers, my tongue and the variety of toys we've tried is always the same: that gorgeous, sexy clit swells up and almost doubles in size. When she comes, it arouses me more than anything she does to me.

Oops—distracted from the story yet again. Sorry about that. I was entirely to blame for our second sexless night, which was two weeks later. Long story short, we went to a party and I drank too much. When we got home, the first thing I did was to pass out. The next morning I woke up two hours earlier than usual in a state of anxiety. I slipped out of bed, put on a robe, and started a pot of coffee. I downed two Extra Strength Excedrin with a large glass of water and then drank three cups of coffee while I contemplated the sad situation I had caused. I had planned a surprise for Danny when we got home from the party. It wasn't a big deal. In fact, it was a rather small deal—a miniature vibrator (one AAA battery required) that attaches to your finger and runs at the equivalent of about 3,000 rpm. I figured she would either love it or hate it. But sadly, thanks to me it was neither, since I'd passed out and left her with nothing.

I heard stirring in the bedroom, then the bathroom,

then the shower. A few minutes later, Danny came into the kitchen in her uniform. When I tried to apologize, she laughed and shushed me and said not to worry about it. She kissed me, harder and deeper than usual, and headed for the front door. I followed, unfastening my robe. I slipped my hand into the pocket where I had hidden the finger vibrator.

At the door she turned to me. She was grinning. Tonight, she said, we had a lot to make up for. I pressed closer and unzipped her fly. "And what if I can't wait for tonight?" I wondered. Well, I was assured, tonight would be here before I knew it, and then...and then her eyes turned cloudy as I slipped my index finger through the slit in her briefs and grazed the tip of her clitoris. She pulled me into an embrace and I felt it swelling quickly. She leaned back against the door, her feet several inches apart.

With my robe open, she was able to claim me in whatever way suited her. She massaged my breast with her right hand and held me tightly against her with her left. I moved my right hand so that the vibrator on my middle finger covered her clit, and my first and third fingers cupped her firmly. I don't know why, but I rested my left hand on the butt of her gun. She never took her eyes from mine. At first she moaned softly. Then her moans became the howls of a feral animal as the little vibrator worked its magic on her erect clit.

I felt her stiffen. There is nothing, nothing, *nothing* more exhilarating for me than bringing sexual fulfill-ment to a magnificent butch. I wanted this to last, but

I knew how much she craved release. Seconds later, she cried out in ecstasy. There was no thrusting or bucking or thrashing. She pressed herself against me, and I felt every part of her body as her orgasm reverberated through it.

I was almost insane with need. I told her that I would never, ever consider asking her to deliberately be late for work except in a life or death situation, and this definitely was one. I put her hand between my legs to prove it. When she felt the flood, her eyes widened and she broke into a huge smile. Yes, definitely an emergency, she agreed. She picked me up and carried me to the bedroom. What happened next was the greatest experience of my life, but that's another story.

Anyway, there's an old song about something being better the second time around. When it comes to sexless nights, I guess it's true.

ROUTINE

Jessica Lennox

I love Saturdays. Anyone who works an 8-to-5 job relishes Saturdays, but my love is more than that. I've perfected Saturday mornings with a routine that I look forward to all week long. Having a routine doesn't mean I'm boring or predictable; it just means I've guaranteed that every Saturday will be a happy one.

First—and this is the part that most everyone enjoys—I allow myself to sleep in. No alarm clocks, no appointments, no plans. I wake up slowly, allowing myself to languish in that twilight sleep—not quite awake, but not fully asleep either.

Here's the part that differs from everyone else's Saturday: once I feel like I've indulged enough in my laziness, I reach over to my nightstand and grab whatever erotic material I've placed there the night before.

Then I open the top drawer and free my vibrator from its hiding place.

I love my vibrator. It never lets me down. Let me rephrase that—as long as I have good batteries, it never lets me down. After years of experimenting with toys of all types, I have found the perfect vibrator—the silver bullet. I've tried others, high tech, expensive, fancy, different colors—nothing works for me quite like this model. The vibrating "bullet" is egg-shaped, and it fits perfectly between the lips of my pussy, nestled against my clit. Just thinking about how it feels makes me twitch. So, no more experimenting for me. When you find the perfect lipstick shade, the perfect hair color, the perfect vibrator, you stick with it.

Back to my routine: with tools in hand, I snuggle between the sheets, propped up by pillows, with just enough light to be able to read by, yet keeping the ambiance of the room sexy and inviting.

I begin with a story I've read a dozen times before—nothing too exciting, something predictable, but just enough to get me going. As I reach the first sex scene, I slowly nudge the vibrator between my pussy lips, which are already tingling with anticipation. I don't turn it on yet though—just the sensation of the cold, hard cylinder against my clit gets me excited. As the story unfolds, the details start having an effect on me—the strong hands on the girl's ass, the bulge of the cock seen through the jeans. I can feel it all as if I were part of the story. I'm in harmony with the main character—my excitement builds along with hers. As she submits to her partner's commands, I lazily stroke my breasts beneath the sheet, flicking each nipple to attention then gradually pinching and pulling them until I'm so hot, I have to kick the covers off and let the cool air travel over my naked body. The introduction of cool air against hot skin only increases my arousal, and finally, I turn on my vibrator to the lowest setting. The first burst of electricity shocks my clit, and I gasp with the suddenness of it.

Today, however, I will not be able to indulge myself at leisure. I have an early morning appointment that could not be avoided, so instead of languishing in pre-orgasmic bliss, I have to step up the pace. There will be no teasing, no holding back, no slow buildups.

Today I choose a story that I would normally save until much later in my routine, but I don't have time to mess around. I turn my vibrator on almost to full blast and flip to the middle of the story, reading at a furious pace. I am all too familiar with the feeling of sweet, delicious humiliation as the character in the story gets her ass spanked, then probed. The scene plays out quickly as my eyes speed past the paragraphs. I swiftly read the words that describe her emotional conflict between humiliation and arousal. I squeeze my legs together to create more friction between the vibrator and my clit as my hand travels downward to stroke my clean-shaven pussy. A few flexes of my thigh muscles along with some pressure from my fingertips, and I start to climax as our girl is getting fucked and spanked at the same time. I hold the vibrator in place with the palm of my hand, letting the tip of my middle finger squeeze its way in between my lips and dart just inside the opening until my orgasm has subsided.

I look at the clock. I have a few more minutes so I decide to go again, but I'll have to make it quick. This time I choose a story about two butches and a femme. There is something so hot about threesomes that usually I can't get through an entire story before losing it, and that's exactly what I need right now.

My eyes dart over the words while my vibrator does its job on my pussy. I squeeze my legs together as I live vicariously through the story's characters, imagining that I'm the girl: my mouth around some butch's hard cock while the other butch fucks me from behind. I thrust my hips upward, desperately grinding my clit against the vibrator. I make myself continue reading the story although I don't need the stimulation anymore; my clit is already starting to contract. I force myself to hold off for a few seconds until the femme in the story starts to come, and then I let go with a scream. I drop the book and press the vibrator harder into my pussy with one hand, while plunging two fingers inside with the other. I clamp down, feeling the contractions in my pussy over and over until finally the pulsing in my clit dies down.

Normally I would continue to lie in bed and stroke my pussy for several more moments, and maybe even go again, but today isn't a day for routines.

DEFENSELESS

Nat Burns

I looked at her handsome face and wanted to smash it.

"How could you?" I asked in a harsh whisper. "You butch bastard."

"Whoa!" She recoiled from my anger. "You said you didn't want the job."

"Well, I sure as hell didn't want you to get it!"

There's a lot of baggage between Willie and me. She'd dumped me a while back and taken off with my friend, Reese. Then, six months ago, she'd shown up at Mackie Brothers working in my department. We'd made some peace, as people do who have to work together, but this—getting the supervisory position that would make her my boss—well, it was treason.

"Why?" she asked, eyes keenly interested in my anger.

"You're just a snake, and you always will be." I turned back to the line.

"Come on, Saffron, give me a break. I need the money. That truck I'm driving is a pig, you know that."

"You don't have to drive that truck, Will. I told you before you bought it that it was gonna break you."

She shrugged and grinned that adorable butch grin that she knew melted me. It wasn't going to work. This time.

"Just get out of my face. I am so pissed at you. I may have to look for another job."

The lunch bell sounded and her smile drooped. "You wouldn't do that, would you?" she asked in a low, urgent voice. "Tell me you're not gonna do that, Saff."

I locked down the oven used to harden the epoxy we worked on then looked at her. I saw a weird pain in her face, something I'd never seen there before. "Will?"

"Saffron, we need to talk."

"About what?"

"About things."

"So, talk." I started toward the lunchroom.

"Let's go out to the truck," she suggested.

"I don't know..."

"Please?" She hitched her heavy work pants and shuffled her booted feet.

I sighed, never able to resist her when she was being shy. I motioned for her to lead the way.

Outside the sky was overcast and I knew it'd be raining soon. I breathed deeply of the grayness as we

traversed the big back parking lot. Fresh air is fresh
air and after a morning spent in the hot confines of the
factory, it felt mighty damned good. Willie strode next
to me with her usual swagger and I could tell she was
enjoying being outside too.

"Damn, Will," I muttered as we paused next to
her black Dodge, a ton and a half, with bright chrome
and oversized Tiger-paw tires. I ran my hand over the
gleaming front grille and shook my head. I spied her
childlike grin of pride. Will and her toys.

"I'd sell it in a heartbeat, if you wanted me to," she
said quietly.

Had I heard her right?

"Okay, what's going on?" I folded my arms across
my chest and leaned against the truck. "Talk to me."

"Inside." Her nod indicated the high truck cab.

We sat in silence for a moment and then I heard her
sigh my name. I sought her eyes and saw such pained
love there that it made my heart ache. Her lips found
mine, her tongue teasing, flicking, penetrating deeply.
The caresses tickled, aroused; I felt dizzy yet the kisses
continued. Heat grew inside me and when she pulled
me across the seat, closer, to gaze at me with darkening
eyes, I swooned into an intense ocean of want, of need.

I moaned as her lips traveled lower and teased the
swell of my breasts. My voice seemed to excite her and
she jerked up the front of my shirt so she could tug at
my bra with her teeth. She looked up at me, mouth
wrapped around white lace, and the desire in her gaze

brought me to the brink of orgasm. I hadn't realized how much I'd been wanting her until that moment. She twisted my bra and my breasts escaped to freedom only to be recaptured by Willie's ravenous mouth. When she latched on to one nipple, I cried out from the delicious torment. Willie broke the contact and pulled me into a new engulfing kiss that I felt all the way to my toes.

I needed her on my clit and whimpered the request. Obligingly, her hand was in my loosened trousers, frolicking in my sudden wetness. She moaned and I held her head, hands entwined in her short, soft hair. Her touch was tentative and I wondered if she was remembering how it had been between us. I certainly was, blending the two, then and now, into an all-consuming aphrodisiac. She studied my face while her fingers entered me. I kept my eyes locked with hers as pleasure rippled through me. Only with Will was I capable of such intimacy, such passion. Only Will.

She slid under me. Her right hand was still holding me intimately as her other arm steadied me above her thighs. I glanced around the parking lot and saw no one, only yards of empty cars. I closed my eyes and we moved together. She remembered how I like to be touched; gentle nudges at first then rougher as my clit tried to escape the trauma of orgasm. I pushed against her hand and I could hear her excited breathing as I mounted closer to coming. I opened my eyes and saw she was watching my face and realized how much pleasure this gave her. Damned butches; so defensive yet so soft. Embarrassed at being caught, she tucked her head and suckled each breast one after the other, over and over again, until I groaned and came in her hand, my clit, my whole body throbbing against her.

"Oh, Christ," I muttered against her neck. I slumped across her, awaiting recovery. Willie's breathing was heavy. In typical Will fashion, she would never say whether she'd come, but I knew. I knew.

"I came back here for you," she gasped, surprising me. "I need you to know that."

We straightened my clothing as I pondered her words. We had several wet spots that we studiously smoothed. She repositioned my bra, carefully tucking my breasts away. Her big damp hands, smelling of sex, paused on the bare skin of my waist and I thought I might stop breathing.

Still kneeling across her lap but fastened into the armor of my clothing, I felt I could focus. I grasped her face in my hands and stared deeply into her eyes. She didn't pull away and I could see all the emotion she ferreted away each day as she came out to face the world. I saw her defenseless and knew whatever happened from that point onward, I would love her.

"Let's keep the truck," I said against her lips. "Boss."

COASTING

Anya Levin

Y ou sure about this?" I asked.

The smile that stretched Sylvia's lips gave no room for argument.

The line moved slowly, a shuffling step forward, pause, another shuffling step. It felt like we were never going to get there. Ever ahead, teasing, was the screaming blur of the coaster making its round.

Sylvia didn't seem to notice the wait, with her attention fixated as it was. She'd told me that she loved coasters, that all she wanted was for me to ride with her. Sylvia, who never really asked for anything for herself, had asked for this one thing, and I was powerless to refuse her, despite the fact that standing in an endless line for a minutes-long ride—if you were lucky—was far from my favorite way to spend a weekend. So I waited, and stepped, and repeated the cycle over and over.

We finally reached the stairs to the boarding platform. Sylvia turned to give me another blinding smile.
She shifted restlessly from foot to foot and leaned
forward, clearly eager to get on the coaster.

"So why coasters?" I said, finally asking the question I'd been holding back since she first introduced the
subject.

Chocolate-colored brows lifted into the tumble of
her hairline. "What?"

"There's nothing wrong with it," I said quickly. "I
just never took you for an adrenaline junkie, so..."

She laughed, and slid an arm around me, leaning
against me in the tight line, lifting her lips to my ear
even as she pulled my hand down and pressed it against
the warmth of her cunt through the summer-thin material of her shorts. I curled my fingers against her without
thought. I barely heard her heavy whisper of "They get
me hot," as my attention locked on the heated look in
her eyes and the realization that I was in the midst of an
intense erotic experience, and hadn't even noticed!

My hand clenched against her again, this time with
purpose. Sylvia exhaled loudly against me, then pulled
free, taking two steps on the stairs to catch up with the
line, which had moved while we were "talking."

Head spinning, I was still digesting through the next
step, then two, and then we were on the platform and
Sylvia had my hand again, fingers tight against my palm,
and was leading me to the gates. The coaster rushed

away, laden with people, faces stretched in smiles that dimmed in comparison with Sylvia's.

I got an inkling of what she meant when the cars were set into motion—the rumble we felt through the soles of our feet and the vibrations in the air were body-shaking as we stood so close. Sylvia gripped the metal gateway and I was pushed against her as the people behind us waited for their turn to move forward. Her ass was hot against my leg, to onlookers probably nothing more than a casual touch, but I knew it was so much more.

Then a car pulled into place, and with a series of clacks the people who'd survived the ride pulled themselves free and stumbled away. In other circumstances I might have watched more carefully, but all I cared about now was that Sylvia was nearly panting in anticipation and that her nipples were rock-hard peaks against her T-shirt even through her bra. God, I loved it when she got excited. It got me wet, made me want to bend and push those shorts aside to touch her properly, to savor the smells and tastes of her, to hear her cry out with orgasm and look at me with those flushed cheeks and swollen lips....

I nearly fell getting into the seat, regained my footing and slid against her. Another rider, a stranger, pushed me even more tightly against her, and hell if I would complain! The bar came down, locking us in, and I turned to look at Sylvia. Her teeth touched her lip and her eyes were heavy. She shifted in her seat as I watched, her eyes locked with mine. The coaster rocked once, was set into motion, and she hissed, "Yes," between her teeth.

We climbed. I felt the bump of the coaster's motion through my body, deeper than I'd ever felt it before, reaching somewhere into my soul. My clit burned and ached, and all I wanted to do was come, hard and long. My eyes stayed on Sylvia. I didn't even notice when we reached the crest and were set free....

The stranger to my right was screaming in my ears, but I didn't care. All I wanted to hear were Sylvia's little sighs and breaths, her quiet "umms" as the wind rushed past and my stomach twirled and twisted. Up we went, and down, and even around, the sounds deafening as time passed, leaving my tunnel vision focused on Sylvia's face and lips. I felt her slide against me as we moved; her hand locked over mine, tight, on the bar, nails digging into the skin, and I clenched my thighs together and hissed my own pleasure.

Sylvia's giggle reached me even over the screams and the wind and the clack of the coaster's wheels on the track.

It ended too soon, in a rush that went too fast and left me panting and staring. We glided to a halt then stopped suddenly, the motion throwing us into the bar we both still clutched, hands twined together.

The bar loosened finally and we stepped free. I don't think she really knew where we were any more than I did. As we climbed free I slammed my lips on Sylvia's. She met me easily, her tongue tangling with mine, and then she was pulling me down a handful of stairs and sideways, into the shadowed alcove behind a maintenance building, out of sight. That was all I managed to process before she was hard against me, hand rubbing me through my jeans, sending sparks up and down my spine.

I didn't have much time before I came, and I knew it, so I was more ruthless than I might have been otherwise, thrusting my hand into the waistband of her pants, forcing her to pause, panting, to pull the button free so I had room. But I wanted—needed—her to come before I did.

I slid my fingers into her underwear, against the slickness of her labia and clit and then into the scorching heat of her cunt. She cried out, a mewling moan more than a scream, and shivered and came with two rubs, and the sight of her, the sound of her, sent me off too. I bit my lip and rode the surge of pleasure, burying my face in Sylvia's shoulder and leaning against her. She put her arms around me and we shivered together until she pulled back, tucking flyaway strands of hair into the remains of her bun, and buttoned up her shorts.

"Roller coasters get you hot, huh?" I asked, narrowing my eyes as I wondered aloud, "Are you ready to go again?"

FRONT-DOOR SEX

Zoe Eagan

We've been teasing and taunting each other on the phone for two weeks. Sex is everywhere. We turn the mildest of topics into full-blown innuendo with the slightest change of voice. When you finally walk in the door and we are together, neither of us can wait.

You push me against the wall, reach under my skirt and pull my panties down just far enough so that you can plunge your hand deep into my wet, waiting and wanting cunt. Two fingers, two strokes, only just enough to know I am open and hot for you. I beg you—"Fill me with your hand. Now. All the way." I can take it. I want it.

Your thumb is on my clit, pressing hard. Nothing is gentle about this. We are both too overwhelmed with desire to be slow right now. Deeper. More. I spread my legs farther, tilt my hips toward you and beg with my voice as well as my body. "Please, take me." Every thrust of your hand rushes me toward that peak I need so much. I grip both hands around your strong, powerful arm, feeling the muscles flex and contract.

I shudder once, twice with orgasms so encompassing that I can't even give voice to them, the sound of desire frozen in my throat. My clit is on fire with the rough handing, but even so I feel a third hot hard peak of coming crest, flooding my cunt and womb and hips and body.

I think I'm done and I start to relax, but no, you won't let me. Your hand, deep inside me, is still moving. I can't imagine how I can take it, but I also can't dream of you pulling out, leaving me empty and gaping without you. Thrusting, pumping, you demand more of me. In a voice of pure desire, you tell me I have to come again. You need me to come again. Just one more. And somehow, because you ask for it, because you need it, another orgasm roars to the surface, peaks—I can feel it throughout my entire body, every fiber of my being caught up in this overwhelming, crashing sensation of pleasure. My hands convulse and lock around your arm. You thrust into me once more, twice more, saying, "Yes, yes, baby, that's it. Come for me." Unbelievable that I have endured it this long; the peak finally crests and I collapse. There is no strength left in my body. I start to crumple and you catch me in your arms. We sink to the floor together, desperately clutching, unable to comprehend any reality but the touch of each other.

IGNITION SWITCH

Delilah Devlin

I have a hypersensitive clit. Touch it with a calloused finger or the scrape of a nail, and I come out of my skin.

Men don't get it. I can demonstrate how I like it touched, but most think arousal dulls the nerves, because the more aroused *they* get, the harder they rub and press—like my clit's a damn ignition switch and all they have to do is push it more insistently to get me revved.

I explained my problem to my best friend, Morgan, one night over drinks. She studied me with her smoky gray eyes. "Do you mind my asking why the hell you go for dick?"

The question shocked me. The answer was on the tip of my tongue, but I held it there. *Why indeed?* It isn't as though I truly craved a man.

Her lips curved—just the corners. "I bet if you showed me, I'd get it right."

The suggestion tantalized. I raised my bellini and took a quick sip, stalling before I replied. Morgan was attractive. I liked her full curves. I'd had the usual feminine curiosity about what she looked like nude, but never allowed myself to go *there*.

I swallowed, bubbles tickling the back of my throat, then forced a smile. "Are you teasing me?" I asked, surprised by the huskiness of my voice.

Her eyes narrowed, and she sat back in her chair. The glide of a toe up the inside of one calf made my breath catch. "Does it feel like I'm teasing?"

The underside of the table was in shadow. No one could see what she did. I didn't want to deflect that wicked toe. Arching a brow, I eased open my knees.

She glided along my thigh, dipping beneath the hem of my short skirt until she found my silky panties. "You're wet." She pressed into the fabric to trace my slit. Her toe wiggled, burrowing.

Moisture seeped. Not something I could hide. Her teeth flashed and she continued to prod. I ground against the toe digging into the silk.

She stiffened her toe for me to ride. "Let me come home with you. Show me."

I wanted to. *Badly.* But would sex change things? "I don't want this to become awkward, Morgan. I like you."

She grinned. "My toe's up your cunt. I like you too."
She pulled away, tracing a slick trail down the inside of
my thigh. She reached to swipe her handbag from the
floor. "Come on. It'll be fun."

I opened my apartment door and strode inside. Morgan
followed, dropping her purse and jacket on the couch.
Then she turned, crooked a finger and walked backward toward my bedroom door, her hands already busy
unbuttoning her blouse.

I followed, dragging my feet, but feasting on the
sight of her tawny skin, revealed one item of discarded
clothing at a time. When she reached the doorway, she
stood in her bra and panties. Her hands disappeared
behind her back. Her bra loosened, and she shimmied
it down her arms.

I couldn't help but stare. Her breasts were large and
heavy, the skin a pretty honey color. The brown tips
were hard and distended. Morgan cupped them both
and gave a throaty laugh. "I'll let you play. No need to
drool."

"I'm not drooling. Just curious. I'm a little short-
changed in that department."

"You worried I'll be disappointed?"

I opened my mouth to deny it, but caught myself and
shrugged. "Maybe."

Her thumbs hooked in the bands on each side of her
hips and she stripped off her panties. "Your turn."

When I hesitated, she came after me. Inside a minute,

my blouse and skirt were consigned to the floor. Her palms kneaded my breasts through my padded bra then peeled down the cups. She opened the fastening between my breasts and drew off my bra, standing so close her breasts rubbed mine.

My nipples puckered and tightened. Arousal shot straight to my pussy. I gasped, but didn't step back. Instead, while she looked at me from between her slitted eyelids, I cupped my breasts, nipples exposed to scrape the tips over hers.

"Not so hard, is it? Doing what feels right?"

I met her gaze, straight on. "So, are you going to watch me?"

"I learn best by doing."

"Of course you do," I murmured.

We lay down side by side on the bed.

"Don't do anything," she said. "Don't touch me unless it's to move me where you need me." She gave me a push.

I rolled to my back, one knee folded inward to conceal my sex.

Morgan leaned over me. Her mouth glided over my cheek to my lips. Mine parted, inviting her inside. The tip of her tongue touched mine. Air whisked from my lungs. Blood rushed south to plump my pussy.

She bit my lip, then snuggled into the corner of my neck. "I love the scent you're wearing. I wanna spray it on my panties and wear you there all day." She nipped my collarbone and scooted lower, a knee pushing mine aside. Her lips drew on each nipple until my heart fluttered and my flesh prickled with goose bumps. Then she was moving again, her tongue tracing a straight line toward my mound.

Hot palms widened my thighs. She rested on her elbows as she bent and licked my folds. More moisture seeped from inside me. My clit hardened, painfully engorged. When her tongue stroked over the hood, I hissed air between my teeth.

"Too much?"

"I didn't expect it to feel that good. I usually tense up when anyone gets close. I wasn't ready."

She laughed. "Don't forget to breathe." Two fingers forked at the top of my folds and pulled up, exposing my clit without touching it. Morgan blew a stream of warm air over the hard knot.

When she bent again, I watched, enraptured, as she slicked the flat of her tongue over my clit, coating it with moisture. One finger pushed inside her mouth, pulling free with a wet strand attached that broke when she touched me again. "Tell me if it's too much."

It was. But I didn't want her to stop. It was like having my own finger work my clit, but not. The strokes were light, but she surprised me, toggling and rubbing, then leaning down to lick me again. The sensations she built, layer by layer, were sublime.

My heartbeats pounded in my temples. My thighs and abdomen quivered. Moans crept up the back of my throat and leaked between my lips as she continued to minister to my swollen clit.

Her lips enclosed it, and my back arched. The first gentle tug sent me screaming through the stratosphere.

When I fell back, her mouth still suctioned. I thrust my hands into her hair and pulled.

She released my clit and kissed my inner thighs before glancing up. Hunger smoldered in her glance, as well as more than a little pride. She crawled up my body and slanted a thigh over mine before snuggling into my side. "I get it right?"

I grunted softly and pulled her close. "Morgan, you tripped my switch."

DRESSING DOWN

Heather Towne

I'm a real fashionista. I *love* clothes—shopping for clothes, buying clothes, wearing clothes. I even have my own blog, Fashungirl, where I model my latest purchases.

That's how I met Katie. She emailed me after I posted a video of myself parading around and discussing my latest outfit—a hot-pink minidress with a ruffled skirt and a pair of white vinyl go-go boots. She loved the outfit, said I looked "cute" in it and asked if she could come over sometime and show me some of her clothes. Since she lived in the same city, I said, "Sure!"

We shook hands, giggling, kind of nervous. Then she kissed me on both cheeks, and I told Mom we were going upstairs to my bedroom. Mom was sooo relieved that Katie wasn't actually some dirty old man.

Fact was, Katie was eighteen years old, like me, and looked a lot like me—blonde hair, blue eyes, girly body and bubbly personality. We could've been twins.

"Here's my latest fab find!" the girl gushed, pulling a dress out of the bangled leather bag she'd brought along.

I plucked the silky red slip-dress out of her hands and pasted it to my body, rubbing the super-slick fabric. "Awesome!" I yelped.

"Go ahead and try it on. We're about the same size."

I instantly stripped off my sparkly purple tee and white skinny jeans, dropped the slinky dress over my head and let it slide down my bare body. Katie zipped me up at the back, as we stared at my reflection in the full-length mirror in my bedroom.

"You look way sexy!" she breathed in my ear.

I grinned, tingling all over. The dress fit me like a glove, and really showed off my smooth, tanned arms and legs, my feminine curves. Katie reached around to adjust the plunging neckline, and her fingers brushed over my nipples.

I jumped, zapped with sensation. All the excitement of meeting a fellow fashungirl, trying on her stuff, had really gotten to me. My nipples were super-hard, brimming with feeling, poking the dress out on my quivering body so that Katie couldn't help but notice.

"*Nice,*" she murmured, pulling down on the material so that my boobs just about popped out. Then she smoothed it down, her hands running up to cup under my breasts.

I full-body shivered, gasping for breath. Katie clasped my boobs and squeezed them, breathing soft and hot against the nape of my neck, staring into my gaping eyes in the mirror. And then her fingers fluttered out and pinched my throbbing buds, rolling them in the silken fabric.

"Ooooh!" I moaned.

I couldn't control myself. It felt so warm and wonderful, my nipples buzzing between Katie's fingers, her body burning into mine, my cunny welling with wetness.

"I think you'd look even hotter *without* the clothing," Katie whispered, before kissing my neck. Her hands slid right into the dress, grasping my bare boobs skin-on-skin.

I absolutely shimmered, every hair on my body standing on end. "I...I...d-don't know, Katie," I babbled, staring at the girl licking my neck and fondling my boobs, feeling it all with a wicked intensity. "I've n-never done anything like..."

"You don't have to do a thing," she said. "This time."

She turned me around and slipped the spaghetti straps off my shoulders, so that the sexy garment slid down me to the floor. Then she looked at my totally naked bod, running her eyes all over me.

I just about burst out crying, I was so full of emotion. When Katie cupped my boobs, bent her head down and sucked a vibrating nipple into her mouth, I did cry out—with joy.

Katie tugged on and tongued one jutting bud, then the other, bobbing her blonde head back and forth. I clutched her smooth, rounded shoulders while her warm, wet tongue and mouth made me dizzy with delight. She knew just how to tease my tits for maximum pleasure, sucking the tips with her glossy lips until I almost floated right off my feet with feeling. My cunny totally flooded.

Katie headed lower, going down on me. She dragged her shiny pink tongue down my heaving tummy and into the blonde fur of my pussy. I just about exploded with passion, when she flicked my clit and licked my slit.

"Ohmigod! Yes, Katie!" I wailed. I was sooo into what the girl was doing to me—what no girl, or boy, had ever done before.

She was down on her knees, gripping my trembling thighs, licking my supersensitive cunny. She stroked long and hard with her wide, outstretched tongue, covering every inch of my dripping, dazzled slit.

Then she spread my puffed-up lips with her fingers and plunged her tongue right inside my cun. I grabbed on to her head, shocked to the core. Her tongue drove deep into me, stuffing me full of wild sensation. She pulled her head back and then pushed forward, pumping my pussy with her long, stiffened tongue.

"Oooh, Katie!" I shrieked, bursting with bliss. I clawed her blonde hair, shaking, absolutely gushing sweet release right into her mouth.

She helped me lie down on my bed afterward, and we cuddled and kissed, all tender and glowing. I'm supposed to do to her what she did to me, next week, when she comes over again to dress up—and then dress down.

SIGNATURE

Jean Roberta

A auuggh!" Carli had never made a sound like this before.

My own sounds were more staccato: "Uh! Uh! Uh!" I reminded myself of an old-fashioned train chugging uphill.

"'We—almost—there?" she huffed.

"Yep." I couldn't say more.

Oh, the joys of a man-free lesbian life: we get to move our own furniture from room to room. The carved oak chest Carli inherited from her late grandmother definitely belonged in our bedroom, even if getting it there killed us both.

"O-kay," she said. "I have to stop for a while. We can maneuver it into place later."

"Sure."

I'm old enough to be her mother, but I seem to have more endurance. She, on the other hand, has impressive bursts of energy.

Like the chest, Carli has a smooth finish that invites the viewer to touch it. Now she was covered in a damp sheen of summer sweat, her sandy-blonde braid sticking to her neck and one freckled shoulder. She threw herself on our high queen-size bed and closed her eyes.

Her brave little breasts looked almost flat beneath her halter top. Her tight thighs spread themselves apart, covered only in denim shorts over ridiculous bikini panties with a design of pink and blue teddy bears.

I'm a dirty old woman, I'll admit it. I won't admit to being a predator.

Carli "came out" at fourteen, when her bff showed her some new tricks. At twenty-two, she had a repertoire of tastes and skills. I outed myself at thirty, as a divorcée with two kids and a job I was terrified of losing. I was still making up for lost time.

I crawled up and straddled her. I couldn't resist an exhaled, "Ha!" She giggled without opening her eyes. So that's how she wanted to play.

I carefully reached under her neck to untie her top. That was easy. I pulled the fabric down until her two pale breasts were naked under me, their large pink nipples soft and unaware. That changed as soon as I breathed on them.

I nuzzled her neck, and my hot mess of dark brown hair fell onto her skin. I licked the salt from under her chin and over a pulsing vein. No wonder animals show their necks to signal vulnerability and surrender.

I had other goals, however. I stroked her firm upper arm before lifting it out of the way. Then I plunged my nose into the soft skin and pungent hair of her armpit. Ahh.

She opened her eyes. "What are you doing?"

She sounded like Red Riding Hood, puzzled by the appetites of a bitch wolf. "Smelling you," I explained, moving my head so she could hear me. "No one else smells like you."

She squirmed, not with delight. "I don't have any deodorant on. Nothing."

"I hope not," I warned her. "I asked you not to."

"But I'm really sweaty. I can smell myself."

I showed her a toothy grin. "Good." I stretched out my tongue to savor her taste. "An excellent bouquet, earthy but delicate. Completely organic, with no chemical aftertaste. It's your signature scent."

"Oh, Donna." She was clearly embarrassed and learning to enjoy it. She seemed to know this was my way of claiming her. Not that I hadn't already, but intimacy is a process that requires repetition.

There is old furniture, and then there is the well-loved chest that Carli inherited, complete with family memories. There are a lot of cute young women, but only one Carli.

I hoped she could sense the weight of my womanly breasts hanging over her, even with her eyes closed. I hoped she felt protected by the pressure of my thighs and the shelter of my hips.

I moved my nose around in the hollow where her springy hair grew like wild grass in a valley. She jerked from the tickling.

I cupped both her breasts, sliding my hands over the now-red nipples, as insistent as the beaks of baby birds. There was only one thing to do next: suck them hard.

"Uh." I loved the soft grunt that seemed to flow directly from her lungs as she steadily lost control.

I pulled my mouth away to tell her something I thought she needed to hear. "Mm, honey. Your smell, your taste. It's what I want."

I straightened up to peel her shorts down over her lean hips, exposing her adorable oak-blonde bush, pulling her silly panties down to her knees, her ankles and completely off.

There she was: a nymph of a girl who could have posed for a painter in the Renaissance, and who could have been identified by the shape of her rib cage, the constellation of her freckles, the slight bikini-line crease in her belly. Her legs were spread so far apart that she looked ready to give herself some attention, if I didn't do it soon.

I wedged my hands under her thighs to hold her in place and ran my snuffling nose from the top of her bush to that part of her slit where the scent was strongest.

"Oh!" she sighed, letting me know I was getting somewhere.

"Mm," I hummed into her wet opening. I took a lungful of her aroma, then ran a pointed tongue inward, searching out her clit like a bloodhound on the trail of a fugitive.

I noted the differences in taste and temperature between her outer lips and her hot inner channel.

Her swollen clit was ready for me. I licked, prodded and wiggled it, tasting her. Her hips and thighs moved, gradually finding their rhythm. I wouldn't let her dislodge me.

"Donna!"

I knew what that meant. I let go of one thigh so I could slide two fingers into her, downward and inward below the trembling flower of her clit. I explored her slick inner walls while pulling her flesh into my mouth. I ran my tongue back and forth across a bursting nub.

"Ohhhh!" She threw her arms around my back as she raised herself halfway off the bed. Her cunt clutched my fingers, inviting me to stay. I could feel her heartbeat.

"You, baby," I told her. She knew what I meant. I had exes and so did she, but at that moment, no one else counted.

It's a paradox: we're all the same, and we're all different. "Lesbian" means something different in each relationship. Whatever might happen between us, I hoped I would never forget what it was like to take in the essence of Carli. And offer her mine.

THE AIRPLANE STORY

Victoria Janssen

Drusha twisted restlessly in her seat before burrowing beneath the airplane blanket and squeezing Kelli's hand.

"There yet?" Kelli mumbled. She was wearing orange earplugs to defend against engine noise and had tied back her scruffy curls with a faded purple bandanna. Her eyes blinked wider and focused on the Bollywood film flashing across tiny screens throughout the darkened cabin. She glared blearily. She looked cute when she was irritable.

Drusha unscrewed an earplug. "When we get there," she said, "we'll be sleeping in a dormitory."

Kelli leaned into Drusha and said, "Duh."

"Three weeks!" Drusha said. "No..." She made the descriptive American Sign Language gesture that meant *fucking*.

"We're not going on vacation."

"But…" Then, "Don't tell me to grow up."

"You said it for me," Kelli said, grinning. The corners of her eyes creased, as did the lines bracketing her mouth. She murmured, "Look, I'm not totally happy about what we won't be doing in Malaysia, but maybe we can get a hotel room for the last night, or something."

Drusha grabbed Kelli's hand again and squeezed. She murmured back, "Or you could follow me into the bathroom back there."

Kelli grinned again. "Naughty girl."

"I'm serious." She leaned closer and spoke more softly. "I'll leave the door unlocked, and stand on the toilet lid. Wait a few minutes and follow me in."

Drusha couldn't tell what Kelli was thinking. Did she think this was a stupid idea? Childish? Disrespectful to the dispossessed people they were traveling to help?

Finally Kelli looked at her. "You're too tall," she said. "I'll go first."

Drusha stared at her watch as the seconds ticked away. Despite it being two o'clock in the morning, more than one person was up and wandering the aisles of the jumbo jet: a bleary man with a baby; a fidgety boy; a young woman wearing headphones. Drusha wondered if any of them had ever had sex in an airplane bathroom. She imagined them watching; well, not the baby. Or the boy. That was too weird. Two minutes, thirty seconds.

Four minutes. Their flight wasn't even close to over,

and she already felt as if she'd rolled down a hill covered with rocks. A good orgasm would squeeze out some of those kinks, she thought. And maybe give her a new one, all about jumbo jets.

She smiled apologetically at the man with the baby as she squeezed past him. She just barely made it to the door of the bathroom ahead of a skinny teenager, who looked disgusted.

Kelli crouched on the toilet lid, wearing a dubious expression. Drusha didn't give her the chance to change her mind. She leaned forward and kissed her, tugging at her sweater with both hands.

Kelli dragged her mouth free. "There's no damned room in here!"

Drusha's butt was crammed against the door. She was glad she'd locked it; she'd look pretty stupid if they tumbled out into the aisle. "Keep quiet!"

"So now you're the cautious one?" Kelli yanked up Drusha's T-shirt. Her words puffed against Drusha's ear and made her shiver.

Drusha grabbed the waistband of Kelli's sweats and yanked her forward. The door held, and she got hot, awkward weight pinning her. She fumbled to open Kelli's bra.

"Forget that," Kelli said. "Get your hand down my pants."

Drusha shoved the bra up with the sweater and popped the button on her own jeans. She yanked down her zipper then slid both hands into Kelli's sweatpants.

Kelli wasn't wearing any underwear.

"You bitch!" Drusha gasped. "You wanted to fuck the whole time!"

"Handy now, huh?" Kelli whispered, and licked her ear. "Get your fingers in there, I want to come."

"Like I'm going to tell you *no*." Drusha hooked her fingers into Kelli's pussy. It felt steaming hot, thick and slippery and just the way she liked it. She wondered if Kelli had gotten herself started while she was in the bathroom alone.

Kelli knelt on the toilet seat, one hand down the back of Drusha's jeans and the other underneath her T-shirt, scraping lines with her short nails.

Drusha had three fingers in now and was using her thumb to massage Kelli's clit with its own hood. She rubbed faster, panting against Kelli's chest. "I wish I had a dildo!"

"Try getting one of those through customs," Kelli said, between gasps. She was close, Drusha could tell. If it hadn't been for the sink, she would have sunk to her knees and licked Kelli until she came. She made do with pressing the heel of her other hand into Kelli's mound. Kelli writhed until she came with soundless puffs of air. Drusha was pretty sure it had all taken about three minutes.

"Fuck," Drusha said, holding her. "My underpants are all wet."

"Should've gone without," Kelli said. "How the hell am I going to get you off?"

"If you need *me* to tell you that…"

"Brat." Kelli squeezed her ass, hard, then tugged on her belly ring. "Push your pants down."

Drusha peeled her jeans off. Her underpants went with them. Suddenly she could smell herself more than she could smell Kelli.

Kelli looked down at her pubes like they were art. "Put your fingers in your pussy," she said. "Shove them in with my come all over them."

Liquid gushed out of Drusha's cunt, already sopping as a wet sponge. She braced herself against the door. She formed her three longest fingers into an arrow and pushed inside herself.

Kelli shoved her T-shirt up and squeezed her tits, rubbing the heels of her hands against Drusha's nipple bars. "Fuck yourself," she growled. "I want to hear it."

Drusha let her head fall against Kelli and jerked her arm, thrusting as fast as she could. She couldn't help but bump Kelli with each stroke. Kelli didn't seem to care. She kept working Drusha's nipples; Drusha had come from that alone, before.

She hunched her shoulder, trying to reach farther inside. Just then, Kelli began flicking her clit. Drusha sucked air against an inner twisting that all at once sprung free, whirling her into loose-limbed, shaking aftermath.

Drusha hadn't noticed before, but she could feel the plane's vibration in the door at her back, an extra stimulation that now helped soothe her down from her frantic peak.

Kelli said, close to her ear, "I came again after you did. You are so fucking hot. I really thought you were going to scream and the flight attendant would catch us and I'd end up losing my tenure."

"If you did, I'd keep you as my love slave," Drusha said. "Rich kid, remember? Trust fund?"

"Does a trust fund cover love slaves?" Kelli kissed her. "We'd better get out of here. You go first."

"Like nobody's going to be able to smell me."

"I have baby wipes."

"The fuck?"

"Good for trips like this. I stuck them in my sock. Hold on—there." She kissed Drusha again. "Now go, before I ravish you again. That'll have to wait until the hotel."

"I'll make plans for that hotel. *And* for the plane ride home."

BACKSTAGE NERVES

Heather Day

Paige's concentration was lost the moment Lydia strode into the dressing room in a skintight belly-dance dress that matched the long, red hair flowing dramatically behind her.

"Right, solo done. Just our big finale to go!"

Paige rolled her eyes. She'd been practicing for the finale when Lydia burst in and had now lost her place completely.

"Do you think we've got time for one more run-through?" Paige's eyes flirted with the clock above the door.

"Darling," said Lydia, placing her hands on Paige's shoulders, "we've practiced it a million times. If you don't know it by now, you never will."

Lydia was right, Paige knew, and yet she still

couldn't help feeling nervous. It was the same every time she performed; she loved choreographing a routine, rehearsing and planning the costumes, but when she was finally backstage at a show, surrounded by exuberant performers, colorful veils and the mingling scents of perfume and hairspray, she'd start to feel sick and would vow never to put herself through the ordeal again.

Feeling suddenly ridiculous in her skimpy blue bra and skirt costume, Paige crossed her arms protectively across her stomach, sending the rows of gold coins around her waist into a jingling frenzy.

"Oh, Paige, chill out," said Lydia, "or do I have to come over there and make you relax?"

Paige's reply was interrupted by a knock at the door.

"Five minutes, guys!" called a runner from outside.

"Perfect, just enough time." Lydia grinned mischievously and Paige knew without a shadow of a doubt what her girlfriend was thinking.

"Whoa, we can't. Not here, not now." Paige gestured around at the dressing room, trying to appeal to Lydia's sensible side, even though that had never been the most successful strategy in the past.

"You know your trouble?" said Lydia, sauntering over and planting a kiss on Paige's forehead.

"Falling for my dance rival?"

"No, you think too much. Now let me relax those shoulders. How can you dance sensually if you're all tense?"

Paige closed her eyes and enjoyed the feeling of

Lydia's soft hands working the knots out of her shoulders. Just as she felt the tension start to leave her body, however, she felt those hands ease down toward her cleavage and the tension flooded straight back.

"Lydia!"

"Okay, Okay." Lydia held up her hands in mock defeat. "I can see you're not up for it. Guess I'll just change into my costume, then."

Lydia stood before Paige, slowly peeling off the slinky dress she'd worn for her solo. Paige watched as the body she knew so well was revealed; the full breasts she loved to caress, the hips that mesmerized when she danced, the creamy legs that seemed to go on forever. Beads of sweat still clung to Lydia's skin from the exertion of her solo and Paige found herself wanting to reach out and kiss them away.

Lydia stood before Paige completely naked, the dress pooled around her feet. Her hand was placed cockily on one hip and her long hair just covered her nipples.

"Still think we haven't got time?"

Paige realized she'd been snared; the warmth growing between her legs didn't care how little time there was and demanded further attention.

Lydia saw the shift in Paige's expression and grinned. The two girls came at each other in a whirlwind of passion and excitement, kisses and caresses landing wherever they happened to fall. Paige's hands roamed Lydia's back, squeezed her arse and scratched down her shoulder blades as their mouths met violently. They

pressed together, hot and fierce. Lydia's voluminous
breasts smothered Paige's, constrained as they were in
their sequined bra. Lydia reached for the clasp.

"No, wait; no time," breathed Paige, her voice
hoarse.

"Okay." Lydia shrugged, lowered her head to the
double mound of Paige's cleavage and began to kiss and
nibble at the exposed skin. Paige moaned and curled her
fingers in her lover's hair but couldn't resist a glance at
the clock.

As if reading her mind, Lydia started to move more
quickly. She pushed aside layer after layer of Paige's
flowing skirt until she reached the treasured prize
beneath.

"Oh, Paige honey, you're so wet!"

Paige couldn't have replied even if she'd wanted to.
Lydia knew her too well and manipulated her desperate
clit with practiced ease, running teasing fingers around
and then lightly across the tiny, wet bud while her tongue
dived between into the cleft between her breasts.

"Oh...oh!"

Paige tipped her head back and moaned with desire,
pushing her hips forward in her desperation for a firmer
touch. After a minute more of teasing Lydia relented
and with strong fingers switched to the quick, circular
motion that she knew would be an instant hit. Sure
enough, an uncharacteristic list of expletives issued
from Paige's lips and she wailed like a person who really
didn't care whether anyone heard her or not.

"Oh...fuck!" Paige panted out at the height of her orgasm, juddering and shuddering as Lydia held her tightly between the legs and placed a gentle kiss on her lips. Her body felt limp, peaceful and completely relaxed.

"Mmm, that sounded nice!" Lydia grinned.

Snapping back into the moment like a pro, Paige glanced at the clock. A minute to go.

As Lydia rushed to pin up her hair up and clip on her bra, Paige froze.

"Oh, my god, scratch marks!" Two bright red streaks marked their passion across Lydia's shoulder blades, clearly visible above the skimpy bra. Lydia examined them in the mirror. Her amused expression suggested she wasn't terribly concerned.

Paige was just about to reach for the concealer when the door burst open.

"You're on, guys!"

Lydia yanked up her skirt just in time to avoid showing the runner more than she'd bargained for.

"Come on, gorgeous." She laughed, grabbed Paige's hand and sprinted to the door. "Let's give them a show to remember!"

IN THE BUSH

Debra Anderson

On the drive up to the campsite, I start to worry whether I had turned off the stove before we left.

"Babe, did you check the oven?"

"Try to stop worrying." Sasha's calm voice always makes everything go quieter, like she's turning down a dial somewhere inside me.

Sasha lays her hand on my leg. Little sparks shoot out from where her fingers curl around my inner thigh. For the last five years, this is what she does when I drive—a way to remind me that she's right there, beside me, when she knows I'm probably going a million miles in my head, agonizing about something.

"I checked everything before we left. We're going to have a good time with Mindy and Tara."

I make myself unclench my teeth. Mindy and Tara

are the types of laid back people who never worry about mosquitoes or running out of drinking water or getting poisoned from food left out in the sun. A rabid raccoon could bite Mindy in the face and she'd still be smiling and saying, *Hey, what's everyone stressing out about? Just let me finish my beer before we go to the hospital.*

"It's going to be great," I tell Sasha and concentrate on making sure none of the other cars crash into us.

People drive so badly when it's a long weekend.

"What a night," Sasha calls to Mindy and Tara before slipping into our tent.

"Come on, quick, the bugs are getting in," I hiss.

"Okay, I didn't realize I was sleeping with the Bug Police," Sasha jokes and seals the tent.

It makes a loud noise like something tearing.

"Good night!" Mindy calls.

"Don't make too much noise," Tara yells.

I listen to hear them zip up, but there's only quiet, punctuated by rustling and giggling. I lean over to tell Sasha, because they'll be covered with bug bites tomorrow, but she covers my mouth with hers and pushes me down. Our sleeping bag slips underneath me and the air mattress bounces up and down, pressing us against each other. Everything feels different here than in our bedroom at home where I always need everything in its place and Sasha lets me have free rein. It's shaky and unsteady inside the tent—this space where nothing is the same. Maybe I don't have to be, either.

Sasha pulls off my skirt and panties with one hand and yanks up my tank top with the other, undoes my bra and stares into my eyes. The air is cool against me. I feel bare under her, like suddenly I have miles of skin I never had before. Sasha looks beautiful, but strange in the moonlight, like someone I don't know. My hand slides on her stomach, moving across her chest, pulling there, tighter. I draw her down closer. Something catches in me.

"Do you think they put out the fire?"

"Yes, yes, the fire is out," Sasha whispers into my neck.

Her breath so close stirs me. It's like there's a bunch of dry autumn leaves rattling around me in crazy circles that I can't control, and she's the windstorm. When Sasha brushes her mouth over my neck my legs spill open and I let her take me, unlike at home where I always have trouble staying in my skin and it feels better to be the one touching someone. She's sucking hard there and it's as though all the tightness in me bleeds out from that one spot. My legs fall open wider and I can feel how wet I am. It's seeped down onto the sleeping bag underneath us; this throbbing between my legs erases every other thought. I pull Sasha's hand there and she pauses for a moment, checking with me. We don't usually do this.

"Please," I whisper, clenching her tighter around the wrist.

She runs her finger over the swollen split of me and I buck up against her, eager.

"Not so fast," she teases.

I can tell she enjoys being the one to make me beg. Usually it's me who strings her painfully along, forces her to ask if she can come.

But I don't want to wait.

"We're not playing that game," I bark.

"Shh," she says. "Mindy and Tara will hear."

"I don't care. You need to fuck me and you need to fuck me now."

I push Sasha against me again, kissing her roughly and pulling her tongue into my mouth, holding her face close.

Her finger pushes into me and nothing else matters but this. For once, I don't feel like I have to hold on to everything so rigidly. It's like climbing outside of a closed, hard little shell that's been pressing into me only to find that outside, there is so much more space than I ever realized.

"More," I say in a low growl, panting.

Sasha comes back at me with three fingers and I'm full with her, twisting against her as she fucks into me, slow at first and then fast. I let everything else go except the shape of her above me, the feel of her inside of me. I'm rooted to the ground by Sasha's fingers pumping into me, my cunt clutching at her.

She pushes her tongue deep inside my mouth. It's so full I feel like I can't take any more of her and I struggle to breathe and then relax into her. She pushes deeper into my mouth and I suck at her, desperate. Sasha pulls hard at one of my nipples, and it's like she's ripping out a bright string of light that surges from my chest. I come spread-eagled underneath Sasha, my legs straining against the air mattress, this pulse in my cunt ebbing through me like someone's dropped a huge, heavy rock in a lake and a million circles are pushing outward in the water, each one almost pulling me under, insistent. She pulls her hand out slowly and wraps her arm around me. I curl up against her, drifting off to the sharp smell of bug spray, the faint coconut scent of her sunscreen and the campfire's smokiness deep in the roots of her hair.

I wake up to the sound of Mindy and Tara banging pots and pans.

"Are you guys ever coming out?" Tara hollers.

I stretch against Sasha and realize I've slept without any of the protective pj's I usually wear when camping. Sasha's body feels nice against mine, the flannel of the sleeping bag rubbing softly against us.

"Morning." She smiles.

"I wish it was last night again," I say, kissing her.

"There's always tonight," she says, dipping briefly between my legs.

At the picnic table, Tara makes omelets on her camping stove. She wipes the raw egg from her hands on her thighs and then pours the OJ, but I'm so thirsty I figure it won't kill us. Sasha looks at me and waits for me to say something. It tastes good—clean and cold, and the acid snaps at my tongue.

"We checked the weather today and a bad storm is coming so we're going to pack up early—"

"I think we're going to stay." I look at Sasha and then back at our tent.

"You're not worried?" Tara looks confused.

"For once, I think everything is going to be okay," I say.

When I look down, Sasha's hand is curled around my thigh. I can feel the warmth and weight of her on me like I've never felt it before—five fingers steady, wrapped around me, ready for anything. For once, I'm right here beside her, and nowhere else, no matter what storms may be coming.

WHAT NEXT?

MJ Williamz

The harder I strained, the tighter the scarves got around my wrists and ankles. The more she tickled me, the harder I strained. She was a cruel woman. Fun, but cruel.

I'm an exhibitionist, so being tied naked and spread-eagled to the bed had me growing more aroused by the minute. My clit swelled, thinking of her sea-blue eyes focused on it. I wanted to pull my lips back, to show her off, but was unable. So I lay there blindfolded and bound to her four-poster bed, nipples and clitoris at attention as I waited for whatever games she had planned.

The tickling finally stopped. I relaxed against my restraints. I felt cold metal against my nipples and then the pinch of clamps. She draped the chain across my mouth, and I knew that it was within my ability to keep the tension as it was or tighten it. I told myself I'd lie still, for the pressure was perfect.

I heard the buzzing and tried to brace myself for it, but when she placed the vibrator against my clit, I jumped, causing the clamps to bite harder into my tender nipples. I cried out in pleasure and pain and tried to focus on the sensations between my legs.

She plunged the toy deep inside me, and I arched my hips as much as I could. I threw my head back, and the clamps closed tighter.

"Please rub my clit," I begged.

"What?"

"Please. My clit. Please."

She pulled the vibrator out of me and knelt next to my ear. I heard the vibrator loud and clear and then it was muffled. Then loud again, then muffled. I listened as her cunt sucked it in deep over and over again until I thought I would burst. I strained again against my constraints, only to have them tighten around me.

I heard the toy buzzing loudly again and smelled the powerful scent of my lover's arousal. Something hard traced my lips; then I tasted my partner as she shoved the coated vibrator into my mouth.

Before I could fully enjoy it, it was gone, and I lay there wondering what she had in store for me. Anticipation was growing as intensely as my clit. She took the chain out of my mouth just before I heard the bed creak and felt the moist warmth radiating from her pussy as she straddled my face, then lowered herself onto me.

I lapped greedily at her hot cunt, savoring every drop of juice that poured forth. She moved her clit between my lips, and I sucked and nibbled and tugged on it. Then her pussy was on me again, and I felt her rubbing her clit. Her thighs quivered and her cunt clenched my tongue as she climaxed again and again.

She climbed off of me, and I heard her fighting to catch her breath as I struggled with my own. Finally, she pried my thighs apart, causing the scarves to cut into my ankles. I felt the cool drip of the lube on my cunt and heard the distinctive snap of a latex glove. I felt her fingertips against my opening, then fullness as she drove her fingers inside me. The sensation of them twisting inside me made my pussy twitch. And then I was empty again.

I lay there in silence wondering what she was doing when suddenly my cunt was pummeled again, this time with more fingers. Once again, she pulled them out then quickly filled me again. I felt myself stretching to take her, and I knew more was on its way.

Finally, I was filled completely and felt her hand close inside of me as her knuckles pressed into my sensitive walls. She twisted and turned while pressing deeper and deeper with each thrust. I bucked against her as best I could, my head thrashing on the pillow as she fucked me harder and faster.

It seemed as if my clit must surely be the size of a golf ball by then, but it went untouched. I knew better than to plead for attention there. I didn't want her stopping again. I was so close, but she knew I could only come when she rubbed my clit.

Still the hammering continued. I was bouncing on the bed. To hell with the pain of the constraints. I needed to come, and she was deliberately ignoring the throbbing mass of nerves that so desperately needed her.

Finally, when I thought my clit would burst open, I felt her mouth close on me. She sucked my clit between her teeth and flicked the tip of it with her tongue. My world went black before the bright colors burst behind my eyelids as, one after another, the orgasms ripped through my body.

I lay there exhausted and tender as she slipped her hand out. She left the room without a word, and I could only ask myself, *What next?*

THE VIRTUES
OF BEING
FORWARD

Veronica Wilde

T he Phoenix summer morning was already hot when
Elle got out of bed. It was just after seven A.M. as
she padded into the living room and peered through the
blinds. The Rainiers' yard was still empty. She sighed
and went into the kitchen.

She was still drowsy as she cut her grapefruit. She
could have slept in today; her kids were in San Diego
visiting their other mother, her ex-partner, Stephanie.
These two weeks had been circled on the calendar for
months with *KIDS IN CA* written across them. But
in Elle's mind the weeks were noted with a different
command: *GET LAID*.

It had been a long time since she'd had sex. Embar-
rassingly long. But everyone over thirty seemed to already
be coupled up around here and having kids made meeting

women hard. Sometimes she made vague plans to hit up a bar—but the truth was, she was painfully shy. Her greatest fear was being too forward and getting rejected.

Then Muscles had shown up across the street doing the Rainiers' yard work every morning.

Now Elle gladly skipped sleeping in each morning. Muscles, as she'd named her, was a tall, strapping girl with short, ruffled, honey-blonde hair, a deep tan and a seriously athletic physique. Elle never tired of watching her lateral muscles move as she washed the Rainiers' car or her biceps and deltoids flex as she cleaned up the eucalyptus leaves that scattered across the courtyard. From watching her through the blinds, Elle couldn't tell how old she was exactly, but guessed her college jock days weren't far behind her. But where had she come from? The Rainiers didn't have any kids. Yet there she'd been for the last four days, disappearing into their house when the Arizona summer sun rose too high in the sky.

Every night Elle vowed to bring her a glass of iced tea and say hi. Every morning she chickened out.

She checked again—Muscles had yet to appear in the Rainiers' yard—and headed off to take a quick shower. After drying off and putting on a white tank top and shorts, she looked again.

Her stomach dropped. Muscles was bringing a suitcase out of the house.

No. She couldn't let another fantasy die, couldn't let such a mouthwatering specimen of a butch woman drive out of her life without even speaking to her. If she didn't act fast, she knew she'd regret her cowardice for months.

Elle quickly poured a glass of iced tea and ran outside, the ice cubes sloshing onto the road.

Muscles straightened up with a surprised look. Elle cleared her throat. "Hi." Her heart was hammering with nervousness. "I'm Elle. I live across the street and I noticed you've been, uh, helping out the Rainiers."

The girl's green eyes traveled over her to settle on her breasts. Elle flushed as she realized she'd forgotten to put on a bra.

"Nice to meet you. I'm C.J. I've been visiting my aunt and uncle." She gestured at the house. "But I'm headed back to Texas today."

Dammit. She was too late. Elle tried to think of something clever or seductive to say. But her usual shyness closed her throat.

C.J. drank the iced tea in one long swallow. Elle watched her throat muscles move.

"Wouldn't mind another glass of that," C.J. said. Her eyes glinted significantly in the sun.

Elle's stomach filled with butterflies. "Follow me," she managed.

As she led the way across the street, she was conscious of being at least ten years older than C.J. Not to mention that C.J. was young, brawny and gorgeous, and probably seduced women all the time. *Be cool*, Elle told herself. But her hands were shaking as she opened her front door.

"Nice place," C.J. said, walking into the cool dimness of the house. "Wish I'd met you earlier."

"That's two of us," Elle said. She reached for the empty glass to refill it. C.J. placed it on the kitchen table instead and backed her against the granite countertop.

Elle's heart raced. It had been so long since a strong butch woman had loomed over her with this kind of magnetism and swagger.

"On the other hand," C.J. said, pushing up Elle's tank top, "if I'd had these perfect tits distracting me every day, I wouldn't have gotten anything done."

She pulled off Elle's top, then lifted her up and sat her on the counter. The air-conditioned chill quickly stiffened Elle's nipples into sensitive pink points. She'd never been topless in her kitchen but before she could react, C.J. lowered her head and sucked Elle's right nipple into her mouth. Elle gasped from the jolt of her warm tongue. Pushing her breasts together, C.J. licked her nipples until they were stiff and aching. Elle groaned and leaned back, succumbing to the divine sensation of a skilled butch tongue on her tits.

Abruptly C.J. stepped back. With a dirty grin, she pulled off her shirt and shorts.

Elle felt almost light-headed at the magnificent sight of C.J. naked. At long last, those bronzed muscles were fully exposed, from her broad shoulders to her wash-board stomach and rock-hard quads. "You are spectacular," she said quietly.

C.J. merely grinned again and undid Elle's shorts,

sliding them off until Elle was completely nude on the countertop. The polished granite was cool under her hot skin; too excited to be self-conscious, she leaned back and spread her legs in a wordless plea for attention.

C.J. unleashed her tongue over her pussy, licking and stroking Elle until she cried out. The sensation of a new mouth was electrifying, like a skilled, intelligent storm that knew just how to suck her clit and play with her pussy lips. Elle squirmed with delight as C.J.'s strong tongue pushed inside her, probing her inner walls. Almost mindless with pleasure, she spread her thighs as wide as she could.

C.J.'s tongue withdrew and traveled up to her clit, circling her tender bud with agile pressure. Elle moaned helplessly, running her hands over the beautiful firmness of C.J.'s butch young body. "Make me come," she begged. "Please."

C.J. laughed dirtily and slid two fingers inside her, stroking Elle inside and out at the same time. Elle rubbed her own nipples, a white-hot tension rising inside her. That tension turned into a hot whirlpool of pure bliss as C.J.'s tongue washed over her clit, and her orgasm broke in a wet, creamy gush of euphoric throbs.

"Oh, my god," Elle gasped. C.J. gently lifted her off the counter, holding her as if she understood her legs were shaking too hard to stand.

C.J. grinned. "Normally I take more time than that… but, uh, I really do have to hit the road." She began to dress. "So can I stop by for another iced tea next time I visit my aunt and uncle?"

Elle merely nodded, still too breathless to speak.

C.J. kissed her for the first time. Then she was out the door, leaving Elle to stare after her and contemplate the virtues of being forward.

PIERCED

Maxine Marsh

We hadn't made it ten minutes from the tattoo shop before I pulled the car into a parking lot and made Cass pull up her skirt and show me her pussy. She smiled triumphantly then leaned back against the passenger-side door, put one leg up on the dash and the other up on the shoulder of the driver's seat, giving me a spectacular view of her newly pierced clit.

"You were so quiet at the shop," she said. "Do you like it?" She knew damned well I liked it. The desperation in my voice a moment ago when I'd told her to spread her legs made that pretty clear.

I had been more nervous than she was—I mean, holy shit, my clit is so sensitive it hurts if I touch it the wrong way—but she'd been dead set, so I'd gone with her to hold her hand for the proceeding. Actually, I think she'd been holding mine. Anyway, to my relief, it was over. We had been on our way home, Cass sitting next to me in the passenger seat, her pelvis kind of dipped upward to avoid jarring her newest addition. A clitoral hood piercing would have been one thing, but no, she had to go all the way with it. That was Cass, all or nothing, and pulling me right into the fray alongside her.

I leaned to get a better look, approaching cautiously, as if at any moment it might spring to life and strike at me like some protective sentinel. Close up I could see the pale shine of light reflecting off the stainless steel. My eyes followed the tiny ring as it disappeared into her red, swollen clit.

I must have looked concerned, because she said, "I'm okay, Amy. Really." Amusement rode her voice.

I continued studying it. "He was totally hitting on you." I meant the piercer who'd done the honors.

"Yeah, well, maybe it had something to do with my pussy being right in his face."

I laughed. "That was kind of hot. Watching him touch you."

Cass put her hands up in mock-defense. "Hey, I told you that you could be the one to tease my clit out if you wanted."

"I was too nervous."

"You just wanted to watch him do it. You are such a voyeur."

I saw her pussy clench. Mine clenched along with it. I reached and tentatively ran a fingertip over her labia, and was rewarded with a heavy sigh.

"It's starting to throb." Her voice was heavier than just a few seconds ago.

"You know you love it." It was true, Cass was a total pain slut, but she knew I got off on her being one. I ran a fingertip along her soft pussy lips again. Her slit was glistening and I could smell the arousal that had been on her since she'd got the piercing. "Tell me what it felt like." I continued gently massaging the folds of her poor, wounded pussy.

"At first, when he was touching me, trying to pick the right spot, it was clinical. Those gloves and the swab were cold. But then I looked up at you and saw your nipples were hard. You were obviously turned on."

I wasn't going to deny it. Watching her clit come out from its hiding spot as the piercer had prodded it really got my heart thumping. "And then?" The smell of her was flooding my senses. I had to touch her. I pushed a finger into my mouth, which had begun watering the moment she'd spread for me, and covered it with saliva.

"You being turned on must have turned me on because that's when he said my clit was definitely big enough to pierce. He rubbed it a few times and then pulled the hood back. It tickled when he marked the dot on the side of it."

I slipped a finger inside her. She gasped. I worked it into her warmth at a slow pace, trying not to jar her clit. Mine was already pulsing hard between my legs.

"Then he grabbed the needle and you grabbed my

hand. I was so excited that you were with me. I wanted you to experience it with me."

My finger found a good rhythm, stroking her silky insides as she whimpered under her breath. I kissed her thigh.

She enjoyed my thrusting for a minute before continuing. "And then just like that, he pushed it through."

"What did it feel like?" My free hand had found its way into my panties, and I pushed two fingers into my pussy, while my palm rubbed delicious pressure over my own sensitive clit. I fucked us both in unison.

Cass breathed hard between her words. "It was like my clit got struck by lightning. And I..." Her voice trailed off and her head fell back against the window.

"You totally came," I said. It was true. I'd watched her eyes roll back and her whole body shake on that little table. My pussy had gushed at the sight of her familiar convulsing. The piercer had chuckled a little before slipping the ring in place.

"Fuck, that feels so good. I've been dying for you to touch me since we left the shop." Cass pushed her hips forward, that *fuck-me-harder* look on her face, jarring be damned.

My cunt was tensing around my own fingers, ready to join her in her first post-piercing climax.

"Amy, please," she begged.

I stalled. "I probably shouldn't until it heals. You know, germs and all that." I loved teasing her.

"Just a little. Please, please, please." She could have reached down and finished herself off, but she didn't. She wanted me to do it, wanted to share it with me.

"I love it when you beg." I nibbled on her inner thigh a few times before moving my kisses up the short distance to her engorged little nub. Her smooth skin smelled so delicious that I could barely keep myself from putting my mouth wide over her whole pussy and ravaging her, but I could feel her muscles flexing around my fingers, and knew she wouldn't need much to finish.

My own clit was tweaking and hot bolts of delicious pre-orgasmic convulsions wracked my pelvis. Cass was practically sobbing, grinding against my fingers, her cream dripping down my hand and onto the seat. And there, directly in my vision, was that beautiful steel ring passing through her swollen, delicate clitoris. I smiled, and with a single flick of my tongue over her piercing, she came. At the feeling of her legs trembling around my head, I pushed my palm against my clit and I came, too.

I lay my head against her thigh, panting hot breath over her damp pussy, examining her reddened clit. "I am going to have so much fun with this." I couldn't help but reach up and tap it lightly. Cass yelped, reached down and put a protective hand over herself. With her free hand, she pulled me up her body and drowned me in a kiss.

FINAL EXAM

DD Symms

Knock, knock." Kylie stood at the door, hoping Tanisha was in the room. She crossed her fingers and danced back and forth while her blonde hair swayed over her shoulders. The dormitory was practically empty at two o'clock in the afternoon. She held her knuckles high to knock again when the door swung open.

"Hey, what did I do?" Tanisha laughed and put her arms in front of her face. She was wearing blue panties and a tank top without a bra.

"It's what I need you to do," said Kylie. She rushed in, shut the door behind her and grabbed Tanisha around the waist. She kissed her friend on the lips and squeezed hard. "Take a shower with me."

"What?"

"Please, baby." Kylie guided her friend to the twin

bed and pushed her onto the mattress. She straddled
Tanisha and kissed over her face and neck and then lifted
off her tank top and fondled her tits. "C'mon, shower
with me. I need it. I want it badly." She kissed Tanisha's
dark curls, circled her tongue around an earlobe and
then fondled Tanisha's tits before flicking her tongue
against her nipples.

Tanisha put a hand between Kylie's legs. "You mean
that?"

"Yeah." Kylie squeezed her thighs tightly and
panted. "Yeah, do it. Right there." She moved like she
was humping her friend's arm.

"What the hell? We've got the weekend." Tanisha
laughed.

"No, now. I've got an econ final, and I can't relax."
Kylie grabbed Tanisha's tits and squeezed. "I need to let
off steam."

Tanisha tossed her head back. "Ow, girl. Cool it,
now."

Kylie lay on top of Tanisha and rubbed noses. "It'd
help me. I've been poring over the material." She pleaded
like she was bargaining for her last breath of oxygen. "I
need a release, babe, please."

"Okay, okay." Tanisha looked to the door and then
back at her friend. "I must be crazy. Sarah's coming
back soon."

Kylie stood, grabbed Tanisha's hand and pulled her
up. "Thank you. Thank you."

Tanisha found a towel and hid her breasts right

before Kylie hauled her out of the room and down the hallway to the showers. "You owe me."

"Any time. Oh, I've been so wound up." Kylie pushed the swinging door back and stepped onto the cool tile. She entered the first stall.

"You got fingers, use them."

Kylie stripped off her tank top and shorts. She hugged her friend and gave her a kiss so passionate her tongue easily swept over Tanisha's lips and along her teeth. "I did. Last night. This morning. But I need you." Kylie fumbled with the faucets and turned the water on full spray. "My cunt needs you. So badly. I love how you kiss me—there."

Tanisha stripped off her panties and stepped under the water flow. "Brrr. I'm glad it's almost summer."

Kylie's nipples stiffened. She adjusted the water warmer. "C'mon, suck." She held her tits and Tanisha took one in her mouth, licking and sucking deeply. Kylie ran her hand over Tanisha's neck and pressed on her shoulders.

"Just get to it, huh?" Tanisha slid down Kylie's wet body.

"Yeah." Kylie moaned and leaned against the tile wall while the water cascaded over her face, down her neck, over her tits and along her tummy. Tanisha squatted on the floor, moving her tongue to Kylie's cunt, licking forcefully inside the folds moist from the shower and Kylie's own insatiable pleasure. Tanisha pursed her lips and sucked and rubbed her tongue furiously over her friend's clit.

"Wow, I need this." Kylie pinched her own nipples. "And my ass, please. I lubed it. Finger me." Tanisha obliged, and the sensation of her anus being probed with a finger was so delightful that Kylie grabbed Tanisha's hair and pulled her close. She moved her hips forward and the force of the contact shook Kylie's body with an orgasm, forcing a cry from her that echoed off the walls. She braced herself, trying not to slip. She thrust her hips forward a second time and then released her grip on Tanisha, who stood, kissing Kylie's breasts on the way up and leaning against her friend.

"Better?" Tanisha laughed.

"Yeah. Much." Kylie's breathing relaxed and she reached around Tanisha and turned off the faucet. "Yep. I do owe you. Big time." She wrapped her arms around Tanisha's soaked body. "That was so fucking good." She stepped out.

Tanisha grabbed the towel and ran it over her shoulders, down her back and between her legs and then handed it to her friend. "So you're completely satisfied?"

"Yeah." Kylie grinned. She rubbed the towel over her face and then rubbed her thighs.

"For now, huh?" Tanisha put her panties back on. "How are you going to feel after the exam?"

Kylie laughed. "You know me well." She wiggled into her shirt and shorts.

Tanisha placed a finger under her friend's chin. "Too well." She gave Kylie a kiss.

"And I'm glad."

"Me, too." Kylie tiptoed to the door, peeked down the hallway, and led Tanisha in a mad dash back to the room.

STIFF PEAKS

Rose William

"Have I ever told you that I love your old-fashioned housewifey ways?" Cam came up behind Belinda and hugged her as she beat egg whites with a whisk.

"No, I don't think you have. Usually you complain that things could go so much faster if I just used a food processor to shred things or a dough hook to make bread dough."

Belinda was wearing a dress with a full skirt, an organza half-apron tied around her waist. She looked like June Cleaver. She didn't dress like this every day; sometimes she wore jeans, and she wore a lot of contemporary dresses and skirts. But Cam loved when she was in entertaining mode, putting her hair up, wearing a fluffy dress and making absolutely delicious things in their tiny apartment kitchen. Right now there was a roast resting on the stove, potatoes dauphinoise in the oven and the promise of little meringue nests for fresh fruit. That's what all the egg white whipping was for.

"You know, I really do think that food means more to people when it's done with love and time and patience. But Jen and Nancy are going to be here like, now, and I kind of wish this was just *done*."

"Honey, it'll get done, and lots of times they're late. Just keep whipping." Cam looked down at Belinda as she continued to beat the egg whites. Her nails were painted a pale opalescent pink, and her arm was both delicate and strong. Cam could see the muscles flexing as she worked to get stiff peaks as soon as possible.

Her dress was modest, not showing any skin, but formfitting. Belinda's breasts moved slightly up and down as her arm moved in quick circles. Cam felt her blood rush to her clit; it was getting stiff much faster than the egg whites were.

Cam slid her hands up from Belinda's waist and cupped her breasts.

"Hey! What are you doing? That is *not* helping." Belinda paused and started to turn around to face Cam.

"No, keep whipping. I will be *right* back. You know you're going to be totally worn out by the time they leave tonight. Let's have some fun right now."

"Oh, honey. We don't have time for that. Why don't you just finish setting the table?"

"Nope! We totally have time, and we only need wine-glasses on the table. It'll take about five seconds." At this point, Cam was calling out from the bedroom. She emerged a moment later with a prominent bulge in her pants.

"Sweetie, I really don't think there's time." But Belinda couldn't help but look at the bulge. She loved the way Cam fucked her. In their four years together, Cam had explored each and every nerve, every crevice and curve of Belinda's body, and knew how to touch each spot in endless combinations to make her come.

Cam pressed herself up against Belinda. She was whipping the egg whites more slowly than before, and they were still pretty egg-whitey.

"Keep going. You'll kill me if you get too distracted and don't get that finished. So you have to keep going, or I won't be able to fuck you."

"Okay, but I still can't believe that we have enough time."

"Just trust me."

Cam reached under Belinda's skirt and ran her fingers up to her inner thighs. As her hand worked its way up, Cam realized that Belinda wasn't wearing any underwear. June Cleaver probably didn't do that at dinner parties. Belinda leaned back as Cam started rubbing her clit. She was already getting wet. Cam was working her magic.

Belinda kept beating the meringue. Cam unzipped her pants and pulled out her cock, still rubbing Belinda. She dipped her fingers into Belinda's pussy, feeling how slick she was. Although she'd fucked her hundreds of times, every time Cam felt how wet Belinda was, it still made her knees weak.

Her fingers slid in quickly, going in even deeper and faster than she had intended. Belinda was so wet and ready that her pussy practically swallowed them. She moaned and put both hands on the counter.

"No, no, don't stop. This will only work if you can keep getting everything ready. I'm going to fuck you hard, just the way you like. I'm going to slip my dick into you, and rub your clit, and make you come, hard, but I don't want to keep you from finishing dinner. So just keep doing what you're doing."

"Oh, fuck, Cam. I'll try. Just do it, now. They're going to be here soon."

"Yeah, baby, I'll fuck you now." Cam slid her cock suddenly into Belinda, and both of them moaned. Both of them loved that first moment when Cam's cock slipped into Belinda's pussy. Belinda loved suddenly feeling all filled up. Cam loved that feeling of pushing into her for the first time, feeling the head of her cock pop into Belinda.

She started to slowly slide in and out. Belinda moaned but continued whisking the egg whites, which by this time were starting to look like maybe they would be done by the time Jen and Nancy arrived.

"Oh, Cam, faster. Fuck me faster." Cam wrapped her arms around Belinda, holding her up as the cock started sliding in and out faster, Belinda's tits bouncing. Cam was surprised to feel her own orgasm building already. Usually it took her a while to catch up to Belinda. But this time, she could feel the base of the cock pressing into her clit with every thrust and feel the particular inner warmth of a strong orgasm starting to roar up from her depths.

"Oh, Bea, I'm going to come. Soon. I want you to come with me. Don't worry about the damn eggs, just focus on my cock. Come with me, baby."

Belinda gasped and pressed back into her, shoving the bowl away from her and bracing herself against the counter. Now that Belinda could hold herself up, Cam moved her hands—one up to Bea's breasts, and one down to her clit. She fucked fiercely, feeling each stroke hard against her clit. Belinda's moans were getting louder and the pauses between them were narrowing. Belinda was about to come, too.

Cam let go, fucking fucking fucking as an orgasm tore through her, rising from deep within her belly, fiery heat spreading through her chest and rocketing out of her in a long, low moan. Belinda grabbed Cam's hand and clamped down with her fingers and her cunt, and she came inwardly, with a quiet gasp.

They took a few moments to catch their breath. Cam eased slowly out and kissed her neck. Belinda was the first to get back on track, looking up at the clock.

"One minute. We have *one* minute. Go, go!"

But before either of them could do anything, the doorbell rang. Cam glanced at Belinda, braced for a panicked-hostess outburst. But Belinda just smiled and adjusted her apron. No doubt about it; Cam definitely loved her housewifey ways.

BIRTHDAY DANCE

M. Marie

An explosive chorus of drunken, hyperaroused catcalls startled the crowd as I followed Madison into the private rooms. A quick glance back at the rowdy celebrants thronged around our table made me flush hotly, and their vulgar suggestions increased. I quickened my steps. Madison had already reached the doorway and held the curtain aside for me. With an amused smile, she nodded me through before pulling it closed behind us.

Inside the private rooms, the lights were much dimmer. I could make out bodies moving near the doorway, and they caught my interest, but Madison's light touch on the small of my back snapped my focus back to her.

Madison took the lead and guided me to a secluded

love seat in a small alcove. She sat down and patted the cushion next to her.

"Have a seat." Her throaty voice made my pulse skip. "We have a few minutes 'til the next song starts."

I nodded and dropped down onto the worn fabric. The loud music that thundered in the main room didn't carry fully into this private area. In our small hideaway, only the steady beats of the bass found us. My nerves hummed a loud chorus in my ears.

As Madison leaned forward to adjust her sheer thigh-high stockings, my eyes were drawn instantly into the deep valley between her large breasts. My heartbeat surged in nervous anticipation, and, despite my inhibitions, I couldn't look away.

The pulsing baseline was beginning to fade out—but my pulse was still pounding fiercely—when Madison, satisfied at last with the high cut of her hosiery and the low cut of her blouse, turned her full attention on me.

"Big group you're here with. Any special occasion?" she asked with a smile, her tone coaxing out my confidence while her hands slowly began to coax open the buttons of her blouse.

I welcomed the conversation eagerly. It gave me something to focus my thoughts on besides her swift fingers.

"A birthday. Two actually—mine and another coworker's. He thought it'd be fun to celebrate here for a bit before going to a club," I explained.

"Oh?" Her fingers paused and her smile brightened

in the dark alcove. "And when he left to get a dance, I'm guessing someone thought it would be fun to buy one for you too, right?"

My reluctant smile answered hers. "Does that happen a lot?"

"You'd be surprised. Most of the female customers that come here do get roped into it like that, though. It turns guys on to think of their sisters and wives getting it on with strippers, I guess." The corners of her glossy lips twitched upward, teasing me.

Flustered, I dropped my gaze to my lap while I tried to think of a response. As my silence stretched out, Madison lowered her hands onto the couch, slid her body closer across the seat, and asked in a hot-breathed whisper, "Does it turn *you* on?"

I stared at my clenched hands while my face flushed. My white knuckles were probably the only part of my body that wasn't burning bright red. Feeling overexposed, I avoided her curious gaze as I admitted in a hoarse whisper, "I-I've always been curious."

She rose to her feet and moved her lips, but her reply was drowned out by a crescendo of heavy beats as the current song climaxed.

The next song slid in with long, drawn-out notes. In front of me, Madison's hips caught the rhythm and began to sway slowly. Her hands returned to her blouse. I watched as, with each steady beat, another button was pulled free. My breath caught when she released the final one and pulled the garment off. Under the white blouse, her breasts were round and firm. She rubbed her nipples between her thumbs and index fingers until the nubs hardened into rosy peaks, then, sliding her palms under the heavy breasts, she then lifted them up and pressed them together with an inviting look in her eyes.

The provocative display aroused me more and more. I licked my lips slowly and shifted in my seat as the music's tempo increased. Madison's hands were on the waist of her pleated skirt now. An approving gasp escaped my parted lips as she sensuously rolled her hips and let the garment fall to the floor.

She was naked underneath. Her smooth, firm body wearing only sheer knee-high nylons made me ache with a desire I rarely allowed myself to indulge. My gaze followed the roundness of her breasts and the curve of her hips down to the nude swell of her privates. Unconsciously, I moved my right hand to my crotch as I felt my own pussy grow wet at the sight.

Madison noticed the gesture immediately. Slapping my hand aside, she straddled my legs and pressed her hot body flush against mine.

"You're here to touch me, not yourself," she admonished with a sharp thrust of her pelvis. I gasped in surprised pleasure at the hard friction. Encouraged, she leaned back in my lap, jutting her pelvis forward and tilting it up to give me a titillating peek between the swollen lips of her vagina.

My hands tightened around her waist, then her

thighs. They itched to slide inward, but I hesitated. "I'm not sure how to touch you," I admitted apologetically.

"Is this your first time?" She gave another hard thrust of her hips. Her tone was casual, in keeping with the club, but her serious eyes suggested something much more intimate.

I nodded.

She responded by reaching up to slip the straps of my dress over my shoulders. My lace bra was pushed down to my waist next, and then—with my small breasts exposed and the nipples stiffly aroused—she cupped my left breast with one hand and used her other to catch my wrist and raise my hand to gently cup her right breast as well. Pausing a moment to catch my eye, she released my wrist and began to trail her free hand down my soft stomach while her left hand gently massaged my breast.

After a moment's hesitation, I followed her example, mirroring her moves. Together, we gently penetrated one another. I tensed up as she slipped two fingers past my panties and between the lips of my pussy, but when I shyly breached her privates in exchange, the silky wetness that surrounded my fingertip immediately made me grow moist and receptive to Madison's explorations.

I didn't last long. Under the experienced thrusts and strokes of her fingers, my pussy swelled and my body shuddered with new sensations. Madison was breathing heavily and I hoped my own unsure reciprocations had pleased her, but I couldn't catch enough breath to ask.

As the song faded out, giving way to the next, I sagged back into the love seat, both exhausted and exhilarated. Madison dropped down beside me.

"One more song?" she coaxed in a breathless whisper.

"At least…"

DESPERATE MEASURES

Geneva King

Mina was up to no good.

Mischief radiated from every pore in her body as she sauntered into the room. Our eyes met, hers determined and mine terrified. Then she smirked.

When Mina smirked, I was in trouble.

Just to cement my foreboding, she lifted the hem of her dress until I could see her cunt.

Before my eyes could focus on anything other than her hairless lips, she winked and walked away.

I started after her, determined to stop whatever hare-brained scheme she had cooked up, but my supervisor, Tom, stepped squarely in my path.

"Any problems, Gibson?"

"No." Unless you count the Wandering Flasher walking around. "All well on this front." I tried to peer around his body, but the man was built like a tank. A big, hulking, girlfriend-blocking tank.

"The boys downstairs expected some trouble for the opening, but as I told them, we didn't have issues with last month's exhibit and this one isn't nearly as popular." He chuckled as he bounced on his feet. "Still, a little overtime never hurt anyone."

"No, not at all." I pushed past him, but Mina was gone. Dammit. "Excuse me, I need to find someone."

I ran through the foyer, causing the artist to look up in disapproval. Thanks to Mina, my job was flashing before my eyes: watching the exhibits, writing reports, joking with the guys on break—okay, fine, it wasn't perfect, but it was steady and paid well and...dammit where was Mina?

Maybe she got bored and went home.

If you believe that, I've got a bridge in Brooklyn to sell you.

I skidded to a stop as I caught sight of her. It was no wonder I'd missed her; she was almost hidden in the corner staring up at one of the sculptures.

All right, Therese. Keep calm. Take her firmly by the arm and escort her out. And whatever you do, don't look at her ass as she sashays away.

Mina turned as I scuttled down the row of chairs. She watched me, and, almost dreamily, her arm swung out and hit the exhibit behind her.

It seemed to take forever for the pieces to fall, but finally they landed with a clatter that hurt my ears.

Everyone went silent, and then the artist ran over, wailing with rage.

Several guards quickly surrounded Mina, but she looked unfazed and merely batted her large brown eyes at Tom. "Sorry, officer, I don't know what happened."

Tom grunted, unmoved. "Ma'am, you need to come with me."

"Are you going to arrest me, officer?"

"That remains to be seen." His eyes swept over her, but his tone was as curt as hers was flirtatious. "Step this way.

"Wait," I piped up. "I'll handle it. I saw everything."

"You sure?"

I nodded and he relinquished his grip on Mina's arm. "She's all yours, Gibson."

"But we were having so much fun—ouch! Not so rough." She yelped as I dragged her away to the office, knowing she was enjoying every moment.

I slammed the door and rounded on her. "Dammit, Mina! What have I told you about coming to my job? I could get fired."

"I missed you."

"Next time, send a text."

She pouted, her full lips poking out deliciously. "That's not very personal." She leaned into me. "And you aren't being very nice. I went through a lot of trouble for you."

"I. Am. At. Work." I said it through clenched teeth, although the truth was that I was having trouble focusing on anything except her luscious mouth and the soft breasts pressing so firmly against my chest.

"I just wanted to kiss my girl." She leaned over until her mouth was a mere inch from mine. "But if you want me to go…"

Yes. Sort of. Not at all. "Now you're getting it."

"Fine." She sighed dramatically as she stepped back. "Go on and book me so I can go home. Alone."

"Oh, hell, come here." I grabbed Mina's face and kissed her.

"Again," she breathed in my ear.

Sadly, that was all it took. I pulled her close, my tongue exploring her eager mouth. Our bodies melted together as my hands ran down her back and squeezed her ass.

"God, you're packing, aren't you?" When I didn't answer, she brushed her pelvis gently against mine. "I can feel your cock between my thighs."

If she kept that up, I was going to come on the spot. "Cute." Reluctantly, I released her. "You got your kiss. Now get going."

"Feel this." Mina guided my hand under her skirt and rubbed it against her bare lips.

"Mina—somebody might come."

Mina gave me her best sex siren look. "They think you're hauling me off to Sing Sing. We've got time." She pulled my fingers back. "I want you to fuck me," she whispered. "It's all I can think about."

"Then go masturbate," I said as sternly as I could,

even as my fingers betrayed me and started to explore on their own accord. "You shaved."

"Yep." Mina inched her skirt up, giving me a fabulous view of her handiwork. "Took me all morning."

My hand was full of her warm cunt and as I ran my thumb over her clit, her eyelids flickered. Decision time. "Wait here."

Before good sense could intervene, I locked the door. The click was ominously loud...and a little satisfying.

"On your knees, prisoner."

She sank down on the cold floor, every inch a queen on her knees. I practically ripped my zipper open, never taking my eyes off her face, and pulled out my cock. It was my pride and joy, six inches of thick, brown silicone; I sometimes wore it for confidence as well as utility.

"Suck my cock."

She raised her eyebrow. "What?"

"You heard me. Suck my cock."

With a loud sniff, she parted her lips and wrapped them firmly around the shaft. I loved getting head just for the visual and the sounds she made as the spit-covered dildo slid in and out of her mouth until I was creaming and couldn't wait another minute.

"Stand up."

As she scrambled to her feet, I pushed her against the desk and kicked her legs open. I rubbed the cock against her slippery lips and thrust into her with one movement. She cried out, but bent until she was flat against the desktop, giving me full access to her dripping hole.

I wasn't gentle, pulling at her hips as I pounded into her, but she pushed back against me, her muffled grunts propelling me closer and closer to orgasm.

"Come for me, baby." I reached for her clit with one hand, the other sliding under her shirt until I found a nipple. "Come on."

I brushed my lips against the back of her neck, feeling her tremble beneath me, trying to keep my own orgasm at bay. Then finally, she stiffened and came against me, her release triggering mine.

When we could stand, we adjusted our now-rumpled clothes. "So, officer, what's my sentence?"

"Looked like an accident to me."

She winked before leaving. I waited a beat before rejoining the party. Mina probably thought she'd won, but she was getting a hell of a surprise Monday at work.

AN EXPLANATION

Sharon Wachsler

I wake up in pain, of course—but wet. Do I ask Geena, my personal care assistant, to bring me an oxycodone, or attempt to access nature's painkiller instead? My joints unlock just enough for me to slide a hand under the covers and stroke my clit. Endorphins it is.

There's a knock at the door. Shit! I yank my hand away, groaning as fire bursts in my shoulder. Where's a tissue? I need to wipe my fingers before Geena... Too late. The door opens—to Holly.

"Hi, cuteness," she says.

I hiss, "Come in. And shut the door!"

She does, sitting on the chair next to my bed, her eyebrows raised.

"I was diddling," I say. "I thought you were Geena."

"No, she just left for the post office. She'll be back

in fifteen minutes. She asked me to check on you if you woke."

I grin. "So you're here to see to my needs?"

"I'm not on duty long," Holly teases.

"Do we need 'long'?"

"I don't know. Do we?" Holly hops onto the bed. I wince at the mattress's movement jarring my bones. Holly ignores my grimace. I'm grateful. I want to have fun, not be Sick Girl.

Super quick, she whips back the covers and slides her hand under my panties, her middle finger parting my lips.

I moan. I'd forgotten how good that feels. We almost never touch because of my pain.

"Wow," Holly murmurs. "You *did* start without me."

I can't manage actual words after that, just sounds: A gasp when she dips her index finger into my cunt, a moan when she pulls it right back out. A melting sigh as she brings my juice to my clit and makes small circles.

Back and forth she moves from cunt to clit, dipping and circling. I'm lost in pleasure. She slides closer so she can reach my breast with her other hand, jostling me. I flinch.

"Oh, I'm sorry." Holly pulls her hand away. "I didn't mean to—"

"Shut up," I mumble. "Keep going."

Holly chuckles and fumbles under my T-shirt, finding my nipple and gently squeezing it. The heat zings right down to my clit. "Oh, fuck, yeah," I murmur. Holly's hands go still.

"Hey!" I whine. Does she want me to beg?

Holly is frowning at my bedside clock. "Geena's gonna be back soon."

"Fuck me now!" I say.

She doesn't need telling twice.

She slides her already-wet index and middle fingers into my cunt, and pumps in and out, using her thumb to ride my clit. It's exquisite, and I just hang in that bliss for as long as I can, until the waves become too strong. My cunt starts to flutter, and Holly squeezes my nipple, hard.

I give way, screaming and squirting, shoving away the thoughts about how I'll handle the aftermath with Geena. I buck against Holly's hand, dimly aware that normally such gymnastics would require massive pharmaceutical intervention. I know I'll pay for this later, but I don't care. I feel so damn good, so happy—for once—to be in *this* body.

Holly is still going, trying for a second round, but I can feel the spasms starting—the unfun kind elsewhere in my body. The immobilizing pain is coming.

"Stop, stop," I say weakly. I crab-walk a hand to cover hers on my breast. I beam at her. "That was great, but I need to stop."

"How about a cuddle—for afters?" She gives me puppy-dog eyes because we both know what my answer has to be.

"My afters is going to be a couple of Percocet." I try to offer some hope. "I might be up for cuddling later."

"Okay," she says, still looking sad.

"C'mere," I say.

She moves closer.

"No, closer!" If I had the strength, I'd pull her right against me.

When our noses are an inch apart, I take her chin and guide her in for a kiss. A long kiss.

"My goodness," she says, when we draw breath. "How forward of you!" She bats her eyelashes.

"I thought I owed you that much, considering."

"Considering I just gave you a screaming, ejaculating orgasm?"

"Yes, that."

"Okay." Holly stands up, looking out my window. "Here's Geena. I'll go tell her you just woke up in pain and to bring you your pills."

"Wait!"

Holly pauses at the door, staring bemusedly at the big, wet cum stains on my underwear and sheets. She lifts her nose and sniffs like a rabbit. "Gosh," she says, wide-eyed. "Did you know it *reeks* of sex in here? I'll ask Geena to turn on the air filter."

"No, please!" Can she really be so vengeful? "Tell her to bring me a towel because, um..." I look wildly around the room.

Holly picks the water bottle off my nightstand and dumps it on my lap.

"Hey!" I shriek.

"Oh, dear," she says, and slaps her cheek. "You knocked your water bottle over when you woke up! Should I tell her you need help changing and making the bed?"

"Ye-es," my teeth chatter. "Th-thank you *s-s-s-so* much."

"No problem," she says sweetly, her hand on the doorknob.

"Holly?"

"Yeah?"

"You'll have to earn your 'afters'—again—after that little stunt."

"I'm counting on it." She steps out the door, calling, "Geena, you're back!"

FLOATING
IN SPACE

Dena Hankins

The airlock hatch bumps my shoulder, trying to close. I swallow at the sight of Cyfal's asscheeks, bisected by the safety harness's straps.

She is naked and I already want her so badly that my breathing hitches.

The harness holds each thigh, her hips, ribs and shoulders. The single side of a Y-strap attaches to the bulkhead and the double side is clipped to her shoulder rings.

Cyfal started without me. Her hand is between her legs; her elbow moves in jagged circles. Perhaps she thought I'd chicken out. She is brash, volatile. Her come-on made my pulse pound in my cunt. I may be quiet and steady, but I want to see her explode when I fuck her.

I push into the airlock and float to her attachment point. The air lock auto-seals behind me and Cyfal jolts at the clang. When she turns, I unzip my jumpsuit from neck to crotch, exposing the safety harness against my skin, as instructed. The slick webbing slides against me, warm, when I reach for a tether.

Before I can clip in, Cyfal tugs her tether and shoots toward me. I catch her and absorb most of the impact. She settles into me, arms around my shoulders and one leg between mine, while the rest of her energy rebounds us toward the middle of the air lock. I restrain the impulse to grab for the attachment handle.

The girl is good in zero gee. We end up floating near the end of her tether. With her face above mine, I can tuck my lips into the hollow of her collarbone and inhale her smell, unmasked by perfume. It glows from her heated pores and floats, concentrated, from her cunt.

Cyfal says, "You came." Her voice carries excitement and vibrates my lips as I kiss my way across her throat.

"Of course. I want you."

"Have you ever been naked in vacuum?"

I lift her breast into my mouth and scrape her areola with my teeth, then suck. Scrape, then suck. Cyfal hums and stretches her arms above her head. My hand slides down the floating curve of her breast to her ribs and waist while I create a slow rhythm, pulling on her nipples. When she shivers and contracts, her hands shove at the shoulders of my jumpsuit.

I release her to pull my arms out of the suit. Cyfal

scrapes her nails across my back and I purr against her sternum. At the sound, she turns them edge-on and scratches me hard. I grunt at the sudden pain and bite the side of her breast.

Cyfal turns wild in my arms. She runs her hands and nails over my shoulders, around my waist, across my belly. She clamps her legs around my thigh so I can't drift off, thrusts one hand into my jumpsuit, and digs through my pubic hair to seek out my clit. The other hand pinches and twists my nipples. I twitch and moan. Too much, too hard, too quickly.

Cyfal squeezes my clit between two fingers and makes small, fast circles. An unexpected rush convulses me, a quick and dirty orgasm that flattens me with amazement. I push Cyfal down on my thigh, hard, both hands on her waist, and she lowers her head for a deep, sudden kiss. Our first.

We get to know each other's mouths until my back bumps gently against the air lock bulkhead. Cyfal pulls a double tether from an attachment point and clips it to her hip rings. "So. Are you a vacuum virgin?"

I had forgotten the question. "Naked?"

Cyfal's lips curl. "That's a yes."

She clips the other ends to my shoulder rings and takes up most of the slack. I hold her to me by the strap around her hips and we press our lips together again. Breaking the soft suction, Cyfal raises her head. She rocks her clit against my thigh muscle, writhing in slow motion. I can smell my cunt on the hand she grips my

shoulder with. It mixes with her cunt's smell soaking the
nubby fabric of my suit. The blend makes me breathe
deeply, intoxicated.

"I'm going to start the purge cycle."

Vacuum can be survived for about ninety seconds,
but consciousness only lasts about ten. The biggest
danger is bursting a lung trying to hold my breath, but
that's a rookie move. I won't make that mistake.

I don't know this woman, really. We've worked
on this ship together for six weeks and been dancing
around the sexual tension since we met. Adrenaline
rushes through my body. I'm alive and alert, brilliantly
lit inside, and I want to do this with Cyfal. She could
need an hour of stimulation to reach orgasm, but I have
a feeling that she's actually very close.

She stares at me, intent on my reaction, and I say,
"Set a five-minute delay."

Cyfal punches the command buttons. I massage her
breasts while sucking on her nipples. Her moans change
to cries and I move down her body, biting and sucking
as I go, panting with excitement I don't try to hide.

When I reach her pubic bone, Cyfal sighs and lets
her legs flow up and part in front of my face. I move
in and draw my tongue up her cunt lips from back to
front. Licking and sucking, I gnaw on her thick outer
lips and spread them. Her smell is salt water, but her
texture is cream and I moan against her cunt. I want to
exhibit some finesse, but Cyfal responds strongly when I
burrow in, when I suck her clit into my mouth and move

my head in tight circles, nearly out of control.

The air lock opens.

Air rushes out, pulling us hard against the tethers, making my jumpsuit slide down my legs. It is replaced by silence and a pressure inside as we realize that we are full, stuffed with blood and guts, tight with need and desire. I release my breath and Cyfal makes one last gasp, but my mouth is still full of her taste and I do not stop.

Cyfal shivers, shakes. Her legs tense and she drums my back with her heels. I plunge two fingers into Cyfal's cunt, searching for the spot. When her belly jumps, I know I've found it. I pull down and press up against her clit with my tongue, as though licking my fingers. As my body begins to shake with its need for oxygen, I pull more and more desperately until, deep in fear and burning with arousal, I feel Cyfal freeze, then push.

Holding tightly against her muscle's spasms, I know only her cunt, her clit, her orgasm. It devours me and I feed on it.

The air lock closes.

Sweet air blows and we both gasp and cough. The spasms force us apart. I pull myself back to her by the tether and hold her close, thigh to thigh, cheek to cheek, our hearts pounding together. When I pull away, Cyfal is smiling. "Where is your jumpsuit?"

I look out the air-lock window and, sure enough, there it is: floating in space.

FREEWAY FALLING

Cal Gimpelevich

Late night on the freeway, headed home, tightening my thighs. I'm checking to see if my clit's still sore from last night. Yeah. Definitely feeling it. The sensation is closer to raw than painful. Nerve endings feel exposed so just the friction from my jeans makes me wet.

Or maybe that's the woman sitting next to me whose body I'm getting to know. She's got long, curly hair tied back, loose strands framing her face and one hand traveling lazily from my knee up toward my crotch. She is a little older, a little taller and a little more optimistic than I am. An ethnic mutt who looks black Irish. Yesterday she met my parents. Does that make us a couple? Two months ago I didn't know her name.

She stares ahead at the long stretch of road, her other hand draped casually over the steering wheel. The whole posture screams nonchalance, slouched back in her seat, looking like another zoned-out driver. Which I might believe except for the creeping fingers unbuttoning my fly and sliding under the elastic band to my briefs. With a Cheshire cat grin, those fingers pry me open and jump inside.

I spread my legs wide and push against her, wanting to get fucked and knowing this is nowhere near the right position. She circles my clit, teasing me where I'm tender. Little shots of pain mix with the pleasure, mingled enough that I can't separate sensations into good and bad. Either way, I'm feeling something strong and my body's response is to drench the whole area with lube, along with my clothes and possibly the seat. She manages to get a good angle and slips farther inside my cunt, fingers curled to hit my G-spot. I lose my cool and start to gasp, interrupting the conversation we've kept up throughout, pretending I'm not getting fucked.

She left her license at home, so we're doubly screwed if we get pulled over. *Hello, officer. Nice evening, isn't it? What's this? Well, you see I lost something in there and needed help getting it out. Nothing to worry about, a couple quarters is all. We need them for the toll.* More likely she'd pull out real quick and we'd do our best to hold straight faces in a car reeking of lesbian sex.

She sneaks a glance from the highway and plants a kiss on my throat. Her eyes are hazel, playful. Sometimes they look black. Lashes dark like natural mascara. My hips are bucking against her touch, sparks from my cunt making me jump. She settles back into her relaxed pose, this time looking cocky, getting as butch as she ever does. The smile says: *Yeah. I can fuck my girl in the car and outside the park and all over your house, if I want. Got a problem with it?*

We're talking about her job but I'm having trouble concentrating because the pressure's building inside, getting faster and stronger along with her strokes. I really want to come. It won't happen in this position, but I don't care. I want her. I want last night again with one of her hands pumping me from behind and the other one playing steadily rougher with my clit. I want her naked with my hands running over every piece of flesh, tracing the tattoo stretched along her side, showing what's inside. I want us filling each other at once and getting off on the reactions. These images stream through my mind: a mix of memory, hope and porn. She's bitching about her manager when I lose those last shreds of focus and all thought gives way to the action in my cunt. With final jolting, beautiful motions, she's done. I'm not, but that's okay.

She pulls out and wipes the excess lube against my thigh, squeezes. I shudder. It's a sweet gesture, but I'm so turned on that every touch feels electric, pushing toward one end. Orgasm, for me, is rare, but I feel myself getting closer. Reaching the edges, even starting to come, but unable to finish. Getting this near, even, is strange.

Blue and yellow patches of light play across her face, illuminating pieces before passing back into shadow.

Nose, eyes, chin, chest. I run the tips of my fingers along her skin, so light they barely touch. Gentle teasing drives her wild. I cup her pubis and travel east, unbuckling the seat belt for a better hold. She puts it back on—"This part's harder"—but straps it over my hand so I can touch her. Her vulva's soaked and it's easy for me to slide into a sweet spot.

The car's gotten slow and careful. "The faster we get home the faster we can do this for real," she says.

"I'm having fun now." She feels hot against me, hot and smooth. Easy to get lost in.

She switches lanes so we're barely pushing sixty behind a big rig. "Besides, it's illegal to drive without a seat belt. They're a vital part of any car."

"Is that so?" Subtle spasms erupt around my hand, the tremors growing steady into a full-blown quake. She's trying hard to tell me why seat belts are important, but her voice cracks and the monologue fades into deep-throated noise.

"What was that again?" I ask.

"They're important because—because, I, um, mmmm." I go faster, vibrating one finger over her clit. "Okay," she says. "Yeah." Her hips buck against me, jerky. Straining against the car's built-in bondage. "See, I can feel that in my feet, and one of my feet is on the accelerator."

"Should I come out?"

"Probably."

I do, reluctant to let her go. I run along her labia,

exiting so she moans and shudders one last time.

"Cigarette?" she asks.

I light one up and hand it to her. She rolls down her window. The smoke curls out and gets sucked behind us into freeway. There's something sexy about that cigarette clamped between her hand and the steering wheel. About her distracted puffs. She looks like a woman contrasted against my perpetual adolescent boy. My stick takes longer to light, but I get it and inhale. In a funny way, smoking in the car feels more forbidden than screwing did. I lean over and let my head rest on her shoulder. Kiss the tender skin connecting neck to head. She ruffles my hair. The scents of tobacco and sex linger all around.

Outside, other cars zip past. Moonlight bounces off their hoods, blending with the stars and taillights. Everything glows. It's late at night and we're driving toward bed in her dark, persistent little Honda. Soon we'll be naked, pressed into heated curves, bodies debating between sleep and play.

THE FLIGHT HOME

Nicole Wolfe

Ella put her thumb between two pages of *In Cold Blood* and looked across the aisle at her mother. The mother-daughter Vegas vacation had been the most fun they'd had since Ella came out to her on New Year's Eve; so much so that her mother had fallen asleep within minutes of them reaching cruising altitude. So, apparently, had most passengers of the dimly lit late flight, including the cute Japanese girl to Ella's left. Ella had been seated on the two-seat side of the plane and figured being next to this Asian cutie the whole way home was a nice cap to a nice getaway. Ella tried to flirt with her as they both curled up under blankets and exchanged pleasantries, but the Japanese girl snuggled into sleep before the first beverage service.

Something brushed Ella's foot. She looked down to

see if her bag had shifted out from under the seat in front of her. It had not. It was the Japanese girl's foot. She had kicked off her shoes and turned in her seat to rest the left half of her back against the window. She appeared sound asleep, except for the fact that her cotton-socked foot was rubbing Ella's.

Perhaps she's dreaming, Ella thought, but then the girl's eyes opened and locked with hers. She smiled.

A rush of heat walloped Ella's body as the girl's hand slithered from under her blanket to hers. Ella gasped as fingertips brushed her hip. She noticed she was shaking hard enough to rattle the pages of her book, so she put it into the pocket on the seat in front of her to keep the fragile quiet around them. The girl reached up and turned off Ella's reading light, and then pushed up the armrest between their seats. Ella didn't stop her.

The girl took Ella's left hand and pulled it under her own blanket. Ella's thighs clenched at the first touch of her knee. She looked across the aisle to her mother. She was still asleep. The woman to her mother's right was asleep. The man to her mother's left was absorbed with sitcoms playing on his laptop computer. The two people in front of Ella and the girl were watching "Today Show" highlights.

Ella was shocked and delighted to find the girl's sweatpants pushed down to her thighs. The girl had a soft, small patch and held herself open for her. She was soaked, and Ella wondered how long she'd been fucking herself before she decided to invite her neighbor to the party.

She was hot, and her muscles seemed to pull Ella's fingers into her. She smiled and squirmed. She rubbed her clit and spread her knees as best she could in the small space. She slid one finger in with Ella's, the two of them sliding back and forth and filling up her sweet cunt. She pulled her finger out, and Ella put in another to take its place. She grinned and put her slippery finger in Ella's mouth. A small orgasm rushed through Ella, but she caught herself before she made too much noise. The girl was sweet, almost like fruit juice, and Ella hoped her own wet pussy would taste just as good for her.

The girl pulled Ella's hand to her mouth. Her tongue darted between Ella's sticky fingers, cleaning her sweetness from them. She put Ella's hand between her breasts so she could rub them through her sweatshirt. She leaned over a bit to look across the aisle. Ella shot a quick look, wondering if they'd been caught.

Everyone was still asleep or engaged with sitcom DVDs. The girl smiled again and lifted her sweatshirt to her neck, exposing her little tits. Ella's hand was all over them. She wanted them in her mouth, rubbing against hers, and slippery with her come. The girl's eyelids fluttered, and she pushed Ella's hand back to her pussy.

Ella rocked two fingers inside her while the girl pinched her nipples and bit her lip. She washed Ella's hand with come and then sat up, surprising Ella with her speed. She got shoulder-to-shoulder with her and yanked her shirt back down. The girl's right hand rubbed Ella's pussy through her wet pants. Ella fumbled open the button and pulled down the zipper. The girl's hand scurried inside. Ella's thighs clenched as the girl rubbed her clit. Ella wanted to slip her fingers inside too, but the girl held Ella's left hand to her spread cunt. Ella didn't want to risk using her right hand and having someone on the aisle realize what they were doing.

They sat back, arms crossed and fingers playing with each other's pussies under the blankets. Being against the window gave the girl an advantage. No one could see her left hand playing with her breasts under her shirt or rubbing her clit under her blanket.

She leaned over, sticking out her tongue. Ella leaned in, snaking out hers. The tips touched, shooting lightning through their bodies and making their hands wetter than they already were. The girl pawed at Ella's left breast with her free hand, pinching her nipple through her shirt and making her squirm. She put her fingers in Ella's mouth, getting them wet so she could rub her spit on her nipples. Ella clenched on the girl's fingers once, twice, and then shifted in her seat as she came. She slid forward a bit so the girl's fingers could push all the way into her. Ella bit down on her fist to keep from screaming.

They had to stop when the flight attendants started preparing for the landing. They licked their fingers clean and managed to straighten up their pants before the attendant passed their seats. The sound of the attendant checking on the overhead bin woke up Ella's mother.

Ella's mother looked over to see her daughter reading

In Cold Blood. Her Japanese neighbor appeared to be sleeping. It looked like Ella hadn't read much since she'd fallen asleep, but she was happy. Ella's mother couldn't figure out why, because she knew that book was damn depressing.

PATIENCE

Jennifer Baker

Sit on my face." Amelia's already unzipping her jeans.

I look up from the folder for my next appointment. A part of me is surprised, but shouldn't be. After our last meeting it was the next step to further blurring the lines.

My phone rings. On the other end Jack asks if I'm ready for my 4:00 o'clock. I tell him to give me five minutes.

Amelia holds up ten digits.

"Make that ten," I say.

Amelia comes around the couch in my office with her lips curled in her mischievous way. I had stopped saying this wasn't professional, wasn't right, and ceased mentioning my pseudo-girlfriend—a withdrawn "artist" on perpetual retreat in Europe.

* * *

The first time Amelia and I met she said she wasn't sure who she could talk to. Only twenty, she admitted as she bit her lip ring that she had a lot of feelings she didn't discuss with anyone. When I mentioned my girlfriend in casual conversation a brightness to her face revealed her interest, and after that she kept staring at me. I felt her eyes lingering all over my body. She always turned back to look at me before leaving, saying with a smirk more than a smile that she looked forward to seeing me again.

Amelia became more open, and talked about how much she liked the beach; how she often went there before coming to see me, swam, and watched the couples walking around. She admitted she wanted something like that with another woman. Thought about someone all the time, but wouldn't say who. She licked her lips as she spoke, revealing a tongue ring.

When I asked her to discuss this woman, she grinned at me for a while, making me uncomfortable. She stared at my legs as I crossed and uncrossed them. With her fingers lingering near her crotch, she pushed her head back as she bit her lip ring again.

I knew she was testing me, teasing me to see if I'd react. I kept still, held her gaze and refused to look away as she described taking a vibrator and pushing it against herself until the pulsation made her scream this lady's name so loud she couldn't deny her feelings anymore.

It took a few weeks for her to reveal that her dreams

were about me, and constant. She couldn't focus in classes, always got wet at the beach in anticipation. She thought about fucking me, sucking every orifice of my body. She wanted to bend me over the couch and plunge her fingers inside me, hear me cry her name. She always touched herself when she had these dreams, and said she came so hard she went dizzy afterward.

When she told me this I believe I held back, gulped down the arousal surging through me and tried not to fan myself with my shirt to combat the rising heat in my body. I attempted to not think of the girlfriend I hadn't heard from in two months—probably fucking someone else—as I listened to a girl fifteen years my junior tell me how sexy she found me.

"You have a schoolteacher look," she said. "The wire frames and pencil skirts and all that. You look so put together all the time. I can't help it. Makes me wanna ruffle you up."

I cleared my throat, trying to get back on track. "It seems that you're more comfortable with yourself now than you were when we first met."

"I was never *uncomfortable*. Just lonely. At school everyone is childish. Immature. I need someone on my level, older."

"Perhaps you should seek out someone closer to your age?"

"Uh-huh. So, how's your *girlfriend*?" The way she asked was mocking. It made the heat of my excitement fizzle slightly.

"We're not here to talk about me. We're here to talk about you."

She rolled her eyes and mumbled, "Fine. Doesn't change that I wanna fuck you."

Before we parted I told her we'd have to discuss boundaries next time.

After that I suggested breathing exercises for relaxation, more for myself than her. I couldn't take another hour of her staring, arousing me with her stories, crossing a line I didn't need crossed, but I wanted to cross it the more I thought about her tongue ring. I shook my head and reminded myself that it was unprofessional.

As she closed her eyes I did the same. Exhale. Inhale. *Deeply.* As we kept breathing I felt my mind drift somewhere else while my legs were spread, my skirt lifted and my panties lowered. Amelia's breath was warm on my thigh as she pushed my skirt up to my hip. I became so wet I couldn't help but scoot down toward her face.

Had my door been open anyone in the office passing by would've seen the back of my head rolling right and left as she tasted me. But she didn't want me to come. Amelia stood up when the clock hit 3:55 and said she'd see me next week.

"Next time, we should discuss desire," she said playfully.

After she left I cursed her and made myself come before my next appointment.

* * *

Now Amelia lies flat on the couch, naked except for pink ankle socks reminding me how young she is.

Any line that had been drawn was eradicated when her tongue was inside me, so I strip down to nothing but my bra and crouch over her, reverse cowgirl, so I can taste her. Her nails dig into my ass, pull me down so she can bury her lips in mine. I lurch up, sighing as I shift forward to suck on her clit, smooth in my mouth, hardening as she groans into me. Her breath makes me hotter. It's tit for tat as I lick her, she licks me. We're a cunnilingus seesaw. She pulls me down, then I move forward to delve between her legs.

Her tongue licks me like a lollipop, flicking, flicking, flicking. I push my fingers inside her, and they come out slick. I rub her clit then glide my fingers around the red hairs leading to her pulsing cunt.

"Please," she says. I like being on the teasing side this time, back in the seat of power.

Her tongue goes faster and I feel myself throb, clench, buckle and explode. She kisses me, sending shivers through my body as I hover over her. I gather my focus and lean forward. My tongue hits her folds, tasting of salt from the sea she swims in; I hum against her clit and feel her legs tremble in my grip. Once I start to nibble she shakes harder.

"Fuck, right there," she whispers.

The phone rings again and I decide we're done for the day. I climb off her, grab for my clothes on the floor and toss a few items her way. She gapes at me.

I button my shirt, smooth it down and point to the door, to my next patient beyond the walls. "Next week, we'll have to practice patience."

TRAIN WHORE

Gemma Parkes

Monday evening, a crowded tube. Always the same at this time of night. Bad day at work, clients arguing over suggested proposals, too hot; sweaty bodies standing alongside my own, reaching upward to hold on as the train twists and turns its noisy way down a cold metal track. My mind is full of office problems, the proposal foremost, causing tension in my weary shoulders. A station approaches, a screech of brakes—passengers surge forward—a hot tender hand on my ass…?

Tuesday evening, a better day. Proposals altered, better understanding all round. Another hot day, another sweaty train ride, familiar faces, familiar smells. Arms reaching up, holding on, spreading musk. Nudging me. Redundant umbrellas intruding on space, fooled by the forecast of rain. Suits, skirts, white shirts. Tired bored faces. Humming and rattling, gentle swaying as a station approaches, the one before mine. A surge of people brush past. A soft hand sweeps along the curve of my asscheek. I turn but blank faces give nothing away.

Wednesday, proposals accepted. A long happy lunch, a celebration of difficult negotiations. Relieved smiling faces all round, a little giddy. An earlier ride home. No standing, very little sweat. Read a magazine, listen to gentle rattles, sway with the engine taking me home. Lonely ride. Uninterrupted departure. Feels strange. Something missing.

Thursday. Easy day, calm office, slight hangover. Quiet mood. Usual leaving time. Head for platform. Anticipation. Heart fluttering. Observing passengers around me. All female. Tall, short, beautiful. Eye contact made! Surely not? Long, jet-black hair, blood-red lips, knowing smile, knowing…

She moves closer, buried in the surrounding bodies, hand reaching beneath my skirt. She strokes my ass with gentle open fingers, both cheeks, slowly, her lips breathing heat against my neck. It's her stop. She gets off the train. Couldn't sleep.

Friday. Can't concentrate at work. Long, slow day. Idle chatter about weekend events. Clock-watching. Five P.M. train. Saw her! Heart thumps. Standing closer, wry smile. Sharp business suit. Black skirt, white blouse, straining, straining. Feel nervous, look away. Dry mouth. Look back. Her stop. She comes close, breathes deeply. She links my willing arm and we get off the train.

No conversation. Her BMW. Her drive. Follow meekly, heart pounding now, feel wired. Damp. Incredibly excited.

She unlocks her front door and pulls me inside. Against the wall, her blood-red lips claiming mine, tongue against tongue, hands deep in my hair. Gasping. She unbuttons my blouse, unhooks my bra, squeezes my nipples. Her mouth slides down and she nips them hard. I yelp and tug her black, glossy mane. She swirls her hands around my breasts, making circles. I'm yielding to her passionate touch. Her knee presses against my sex. She pulls up my skirt, urgently. Greedy painted fingernails scratching. Pulling down damp panties. Stroking eager fingers along my slippery entrance. Two enter me, and I feverishly push against them. Twisting, frigging, curling toward my G-spot. I want her, I need her. My hands find her breasts, freeing them from her tight white blouse. Small, pert, horny. I squeeze, she groans, I pull her close. Our breasts press together, rubbing, urging, willing. Four erect nipples, protruding, tingling. I take off her blouse, her bra, her skirt, and look down to admire pure white lace covering shiny black pubic hair. She slides lower along me, dropping to her knees. Her warm wet tongue finds me, slides up; flat lapping, pointed probing. Teeth nipping. Thumbs open me wide, tonguing fast. My voice is a whimper. A deep, panting whimper. Nails scratch my ass, digging in, pulling me onto her hot tongue pushing deeply, upward, in and out, in and out. I cry out, grip her beautiful whore's hair, and pull her deeper, my legs wide; wet. Her fingers slide against my ass bud and squeeze inside against tight resistance. Her tongue deep, she fucks with long wet strokes, claiming me, taking me. I cry louder, pull her to me, and ride her face, grinding against those blood-red lips covered in my juices. My legs begin to shake and tremble, my clit throbs furiously, building and building. I jerk as the heat rips through my body, disabling me, making my legs tremble violently. I twitch, I writhe, I give myself up to the orgasm climbing and spreading itself throughout me and eventually spewing forth from my mouth as a shrill cry cutting sharply through the humid air.

She kisses the last gasp from my mouth and holds me close, warm, wet...spent.

We slide to the floor. A contented human puddle.

IN THE CLOSET

Emily Moreton

Lucy's in back of the stationery closet, giving it one last chance to give up the red paper she needs for the director's latest memo, when the door creaks open and bangs closed. She hears shuffling feet and opens her mouth to shout a hello, since she's tucked round behind a rack of lab equipment and doesn't want to give their elderly receptionist a heart attack.

Before she can make a sound, there's a metallic thump, like someone walked into one of the filing cabinets. She abandons the endless yellow paper, ducks around the units to check on whoever it is—and halts abruptly.

No one walked into the cabinet—she was pushed into it, or backed into it, maybe, because that's Jill, the junior chemist in lab three, being pinned against the cabinet by

Sam, the new lab tech. Lucy's got a perfect view of both their profiles. Neither of them looks like they're in need of any assistance she could provide. They're too wrapped up in each other, kissing frantically, clutching at each other's clothes, and Lucy can hear their harsh breathing.

She should leave before this goes any further toward its obvious conclusion. She could clear her throat, apologize, even though it's not her fault they didn't check to see whether the closet was empty before going at each other....

Then Jill spreads her legs, tugs Sam closer with a hand on her ass and Sam jerks her hips into it with a low moan that's really criminally hot. Like something out of really good porn, and in the fight between the director's memo and the live-action porn in front of her, Lucy's not rooting for the memos.

She really needs to start going out again. Then she could be the one getting shoved into walls and groped by attractive women.

"Fuck, come on," Jill says, pulling her mouth away from Sam, who takes advantage by relocating to Jill's neck, her short hair pale against the flush of Jill's skin. Lucy tucks herself a little farther behind the storage units, just in case, but Jill doesn't look her way, just says, "Seriously, if Mellows notices I'm gone—"

"Didn't anyone ever teach you patience?" Sam asks. "Christ."

Jill snakes her hand between their bodies, does something that makes Sam jerk and moan again. That moan—Lucy's going to be hearing it in her fantasies for weeks, if the way she's getting wet is any indication.

"You were saying?" Jill asks.

"I forgot," Sam says. She grabs Jill's face in both hands, kisses her again, sloppy and fast.

When Jill hitches up Sam's skirt, Lucy bites her lip not to groan, and then Sam yanks open Jill's pants, pushing them down with her underwear. Jill pulls Sam closer, between her spread legs, and Lucy has to press a hand to her own crotch, fingers tight against the seam of her suit pants.

She's not going to get off on two of her coworkers having fast, hard, needy, hot sex; to their hands on each other's arms, their mouths crushed together, their hips rocking into each other, the flashes of skin...

She blinks, comes back to herself just enough to realize that she's rocking her own hips in time with their thrusts, fucking herself through her pants with her own hand. She forces herself to stop, clutches at the side of the shelving unit instead.

"Wish I could fuck you," Sam says. Her voice is hoarse. "Push you up against the wall and just stick my cock into your hot, sweet pussy."

"Not here," Jill gasps. She sounds totally breathless and tips her head to rest her forehead on Sam's shoulder. "Fuck, don't stop."

"Not gonna," Sam says. "You close? I want you to come on my fingers."

Lucy closes her eyes for a moment, but that doesn't

help, because the image has been burned on the backs of her eyelids, and all she can hear is the slide of skin against skin, their panting breaths, and she wants to come so bad it hurts. She presses against the shelving unit, but can't quite stop the tiny jerks of her hips.

"God, I need…" Jill shoves one hand between them, wraps it around Sam's wrist and angles Sam's fingers, her other hand clutching at Sam's shoulder. "Oh, fuck…"

"I got you," Sam says, and Jill moans, hips jerking frantically, obviously coming. "That's it," Sam says. "That's it, God, you're so hot."

"Fuck," Jill says succinctly, her body melting back against the cabinet like all her bones have gone liquid.

Sam stills, and Lucy thinks she's going to get herself off. Instead, she manhandles Jill around to face the cabinet, takes her hands and positions them against the edges, then drapes herself up against Jill and… For a crazy moment, Lucy thinks she's actually wearing a strap-on and is going to fuck Jill; then Sam angles her body slightly differently, and Lucy can see that she's rubbing herself off against Jill's hip.

Lucy bites her lip so hard it's painful and even then barely manages to choke off the moan that wants to make itself heard. Her fingers are white-knuckled on the shelving, keeping her from just giving in and getting herself off. Then Sam clutches at Jill's bare hips, ruts against her frantically for a few moments and stiffens, obviously coming, even though Lucy can't see.

The noises are more than enough.

The two of them stand unmoving for a long moment, their breathing quieting. Then Jill, sounding amused, says, "I can't believe I let you talk me into that."

"Yeah, I can see how much you hated it," Sam says. She steps away, pulls an honest-to-god handkerchief from her shirt pocket and wipes them both down, then helps Jill refasten her pants and straightens her own skirt.

Lucy's pretty much reduced to chanting, *Leave, leave, leave*, in her head, but the next moment stops her. Sam cups Jill's cheek gently, then leans in and kisses her softly. The obvious affection makes Lucy feel kind of guilty for watching them, for getting off on it.

Though not guilty enough that, when they finally leave, looking mostly put together, she feels too bad about shoving her suit pants open and, oh, god, yes, getting her hand to her own aching cunt.

She closes her eyes, pictures Sam fucking Jill and Jill taking it, moaning with it, and it only takes a handful of strokes before Lucy's coming on her own hand, clutching at the shelving to keep herself upright when her knees turn to water with the best orgasm she's had in months.

She's been back at her desk for an hour, trying to ignore the discomfort of her sticky underwear, when her email alert pings.

It's from Sam: *Hope you found what you were looking for earlier. Give me a call if you didn't—maybe we can give you a hand.*

BORN TO RIDE

Piper Trace

Tess had a response to her ad in less than five minutes. Perfect, because her soon-to-be-ex-husband would be there soon to pick up the last of his belongings. The ad she'd posted had been eye catching, and she figured that was likely to happen when you posted your cheating husband's favorite possession on Craigslist in a fit of rage:

$500 and it's YOURS! Ex-husband's motorcycle. Runs. Loud. Stupid. Will not make you cool. Will not make your penis bigger. Is not a 500-pound vibrator that will make up for the fact that you can't give your wife an orgasm. Want it anyway?

BikerBroad's response read: *Best ad ever! Address? I've got no interest in a bigger penis anyway.* Tess's mouth crooked up; whoever BikerBroad was, she'd made Tess smile. Tess couldn't remember the last time that'd happened.

Twenty-five minutes later BikerBroad knelt in Tess's garage examining the bike. Thank god she didn't live far. Tess's husband was coming to finalize the dividing of their lives, and she wanted the bike gone before he got there. No matter how mad his face would look when he found out what she'd done, it wouldn't nearly be enough.

Tess gazed down at BikerBroad's strong, tan shoulders; the tank top looked good on her. The woman looked up, eyes narrowed. Her tousled and cropped dark hair created a strong contrast to her piercing blue eyes. Her jawline was strong for a woman.

Very sexy.

Tess had been attracted to women before but never acted on it. Married at eighteen, she'd only ever had sex with her husband. He hadn't honored the same vows.

"D'ya know what this is?" the woman asked, and Tess shrugged. "It's a Harley Softail." BikerBroad gave Tess a quizzical look, then added, "It's worth a lot more than five hundred dollars."

"You want it?" Tess didn't give a shit if it were made of gold, as long as it was off her property in—she checked her watch—twenty-nine minutes.

The biker stood up, searching Tess's eyes. She asked softly, "Did he ever take you riding?"

Tess shook her head. "He said I wouldn't like it."

BikerBroad held out her hand. "I'm Carly, and I'm

going to show you what you've been missing." Five minutes later Tess's arms were wrapped tightly around Carly, her thighs pressing against the woman's hips as she drove the bike up the long gravel drive. She wondered if Carly could feel her heart pounding as she pulled herself tightly against her.

It was exhilarating! To have the open air licking against your face felt like flying. Tess closed her eyes and her mind expanded into the wide-open space all around her.

By the time Carly parked the bike and Tess hopped off, she was blushing. The combination of the fast ride, the powerful engine between her legs, and her closeness to Carly's hard body had worked magic on Tess. The flesh between her legs had blossomed into an arousal she hadn't felt in years. She checked her watch: seventeen minutes.

"I can't believe I never did that!" Tess shook out her long chestnut hair, her heart pounding. Carly was still straddling the now-idling bike. Tess watched Carly's eyes travel to her chest, and looked down, following them.

Her nipples strained against her thin bra and thinner T-shirt. Carly was staring at her nipples. An unfamiliar pleasure coursed through her at the woman's attention.

Carly raised her eyes to Tess's. "You know, your ad was wrong."

"It was?"

"The bike is, in fact, a five-hundred pound vibrator."

Carly raised her eyebrows over her bright eyes, tele-graphing a challenge to Tess. Tess's breath caught at Carly's provocative words. "When's the last time you had a 'fuck-yeah' orgasm?"

Tess didn't recognize her own voice. "A long time."

"Let me show you." Carly patted the empty leather in front of her.

Tess looked at her watch: fifteen minutes. She didn't want her ex to catch her screwing around on the bike with Carly.

But why?

She thought of her wasted loyalty to him and the years she'd waited for it to feel right. It never had.

But this did.

Fourteen minutes. She quickly straddled the bike to face Carly, "We've got less than fifteen minutes."

"I won't even need ten." Carly's voice was husky, and a spasm of desire crashed over Tess.

"Lean back." Carly lifted Tess's legs over her own so that Tess was spread wide in front of her. Her short-shorts were loose at the legs, and Tess was sure her panties were visible...and wet.

Carly reached over her and revved the bike. The rumble vibrated through Tess and her pussy began a slow throb. "Good?"

"Not enough," Tess panted, her eyes pleading. Tess wanted to come; she needed it. "We don't have much time." Thirteen minutes.

"I'll get you there," Carly assured her and lifted Tess's

shirt. She pushed up her bra and cupped her breasts, pinching her taut nipples. Tess gasped and arched toward Carly, who seized the invitation and sucked one pink nipple into her mouth. She teased it with her teeth while her other hand expertly worked Tess's other one.

Tess slitted her eyes and checked her watch. "Ten minutes," she panted.

"Nearly there, pretty girl," Carly's voice came breathily. She unfastened Tess's shorts and opened the zipper wide. Sliding her fingers under the band of Tess's panties, she angled her body so that she could bury her hand in Tess's shorts, cupping the woman's slick pussy. With the other hand, she revved the engine again. Tess yelped in delight at the sensations.

"That's it," Carly coaxed. "Come for me, pretty girl."

Carly found Tess's firm clit and pressed it with her thumb, plunging two other fingers into Tess's throbbing pussy. She hammered the throttle, causing a thundering vibration that traveled through Carly's fingers, pulsing them against Tess's clit and that perfect spot deep in her pussy.

Carly's tongue burned across the sensitive flesh at the base of Tess's neck. She revved the engine rhythmically, driving Tess to the edge.

Tess opened her eyes for only a moment, seeing the digital numbers on her watch read the exact time of her husband's promised arrival. She was out of time, but she didn't care. She was two seconds from what promised to be the most powerful orgasm she'd ever had.

Carly growled right in her ear, "Come on my fingers, pretty girl."

Tess did.

The orgasm crashed through her, boosted by the bike's vibrations, just as Carly had said. Tess cried out, overcome by the intense pleasure the woman gave her. She let her head fall back on the handlebars.

There was barely time to turn, stow the bike, and straighten Tess's clothes before they heard the sound of another vehicle crunching down the gravel drive. Carly grabbed Tess and pulled her close. "He's not divorcing you; he's setting you free." She kissed Tess lightly on the cheek and added, "Let him have the bike, but leave the wet spot." She winked, and Tess laughed out loud.

THE REAL THING

Anna Watson

Delores staggered to the kitchen to get herself a post-cock Coke.

"You want anything?" she called back to the butch in her bed, a real cowboy, this one; a real catch. Her words came out so hoarse and soft, though, she was sure he couldn't hear. She cleared her throat and ran a tongue over her teeth. Damn, it was hot. Sweat slithered down her back, under her breasts, off her forehead into her eyes. The can of Coke, the last one, was pushed way to the back of the fridge, just this side of frozen. She pulled it out and smeared it across her face—oh, that felt good.

"Baby?" she heard from the bedroom and her cunt jumped. Holding the Coke by the rim she got back there quick, not even stopping to pee.

"What you got there, sweet thing?" The cowboy lolled against Delores's pillows, legs spread to the blow of the fan. Delores ran her eyes up and down the cowboy's long body, stopping between his legs, where the cock she'd been so busy with earlier still stood up and ready. She didn't answer, just started rolling the Coke over her breasts, making her nipples perk right up. The cowboy grinned a lazy grin and moved a hand down. Delores hugged the can between her breasts and licked around the rim. She closed her eyes and could hear the cowboy taking in a breath. Still hugging the can in her cleavage, she ran her nail lightly over one nipple. She dipped her finger into the condensation on the can and rubbed her nipple a little harder, pinching it, then wetting it some more. The bed creaked as the cowboy shifted position.

"Show it to me, baby," came the cowboy's voice, tough and growly, "work those big titties."

Opening her eyes, Delores watched him watch her as she moved the can over one breast, then the other. It was so cold it gave her goose bumps, and her nipples got harder and tighter. The cowboy groaned and muttered, "That's good, baby."

She watched as he handled his cock, the casual way he treated it, just wrapping his fist around it and taking what he wanted. She started to pant, dropping the can lower and lower until she was straddling it, feeling like she could swallow it whole with her wet, open pussy. The can was still cold as hell and she jerked as it touched her clit. The cowboy's hand moved faster on his dick.

Delores began to rock on the can, lost in the crazy feeling of ice down there, imagining it smooth and red, the aluminum tang. The cowboy laughed low.

"You look so good, baby, you look so good humping that ol' can of Coke like it was my dick up there next to your pussy; you go on, darlin', you go on."

Delores ran the can back as far as she could reach, and then up, back and forth, using both hands as the cowboy yanked his hard cock. Just about then her legs gave out and she fell onto the bed on her knees, thighs locked around the rapidly warming can, breathing fast.

"Uh-huh," murmured the cowboy. "Don't stop, baby, you do what you gotta do."

Delores pulled out the can and pushed it to his lips, smiling as he kissed and licked it. He made little grunts of satisfaction as he tongued the can. She took it back from him and started to shake it, shimmying her tits the way he liked, moving her whole body. She could hear him working his dick faster, his breath coming from his belly like it did when he was almost there.

"C'mere," he rasped, running his arm up under her pussy, pushing the lips apart, fingers gentle and hard, filling her hole, coming out and roaming around, back inside; thumb on her clit, finding a rhythm and settling. Delores kept shaking; the can was body temperature now. She could hardly think with the cowboy's hand in control of her pussy, and he was still tending his own business, too, but right then, right then when it counted, Delores had enough of what it took to get right over that cock as the cowboy started his final thrusting pump. She popped the top. The cowboy hollered and let go, and Delores was there, coming hard, mouth full of cock and Coke, swallowing and swallowing just as fast as she could.

FEMME'S
THE BREAKS

Allison Wonderland

Do I have to beat the pants off you?"

Dominique has accessorized her threat with a suggestive smile and wanton wink. But I'm no fool. That receptive look is really a deceptive hook.

"You and your feminine gills," I mutter, slouching on the padded bench of her vanity table.

"Frills," she is quick to correct me. "And what do you think you're doing? Slouching towards Bethlehem? Sit up straight."

I consider making some sort of clichéd remark about that, but like I said, I'm no fool. Instead, I reach for the button on my jeans and pop it open.

As soon as I get out of these clothes, I've got to get into some others. Dominique and I are performing in *Hit the Switch*, this reversal revue at the nightclub we frequent. Femmes go butch, butches go femme. Dom's the femme, I'm the...well, I prefer the term *tomboi,* but my girl's a bit of a traditionalist.

Except when it comes to sex. In the bedroom, my little Femme Dom takes over. "Isn't that right, Dom?"

"What?"

"Sorry. I thought I was thinking out loud."

Dom answers with a scoff, an eye roll and a smile—in that order. She separates the dress from its satin hanger, preparing to imprison me in the leprechaun-colored frock she's picked out for the performance.

"What was wrong with the yellow one?"

"It bunched up in all the wrong places and made you look like scrambled eggs."

"I like scrambled eggs."

"Stop sniveling. The dress won't kill you. I'm not Medea."

Dom makes out like I've never worn a dress before. I have. But I prefer to dress down and not up. Dominique, on the other hand, is the girliest girl I know. Even the suit she's wearing for the show is fitted and feminine. I'm sure the judges will deduct some serious points for that. Then again, maybe they won't. Maybe they'll appreciate the way it suits her curves.

"You're staring," Dominique says. "I may have to hose you down." She plucks a pair of nylons from her dresser drawer. I've mutilated most of the tights she's bought. Not...maliciously. They're just too complicated. The only stockings I like are the kind you hang over the fireplace at Christmas.

Dom kneels at my feet, a rare treat. She rolls the panty hose over my toes, draws them up my calves, stretches them between my thighs. The tights make me itch and twitch and bitch. Ah, the trappings of femininity.

"Get in here," Dom orders, and I maneuver my feet into the gaping mouth of the dress.

Now the skirt is crawling up my legs and the bodice is creeping along my torso and Dominique is zipping it up like a sleeping bag. I take a moment to adjust to the sensations. The dress is close fitting and sticky and I feel like a papier-mâché project. But I also feel kind of... subversive, like I'm shaking up the system. More than shaking it up—sabotaging it. If I walked outside right now, most people wouldn't suspect for a second that I'm as gay as a dildo is long. That's got to be so fun for Dom, putting one over on people all the time.

Dom's arms form a belt around my waist. "*Freaky Friday*, meet *Some Like It Hot*," she remarks. "And I'm thinking of the Marilyn Monroe character, FYI."

"I can see the resemblance," I quip, stooping to pick up a pair of dismembered stockings. I head toward the wastebasket but never make it that far. "Remember on our first date, when you told me you didn't want to be tied down?" I query, twisting the hosiery between my hands.

Dominique blushes. "Why are you bringing that up?"

"I thought you meant that you didn't want to be

tied down *to* anyone, but clearly that's not the case. So maybe you meant that you didn't want to be tied down *by* anyone?" The blush brightens until it looks like a sunburn. "Oh, you didn't mean that, either?"

"I..."

I snatch her up and kiss her, the deep sweep of my tongue making Dom shudder.

"We need to leave," she murmurs. But she doesn't protest when I whip down her slacks, nor does she struggle when I wrap the lacerated lace around her wrists. And she accuses me of not being able to exercise restraint where she's concerned. Shows what she knows.

"Don't worry." I bend Dom over the vanity table. "It'll be touch and go." I give her backside a couple of caresses, followed by a few rough rubs. This can't be that hard, unless I do it correctly.

Dominique watches herself in the mirror. Naturally—it's a vanity table. It's quite a sight, actually: me dressed up, her trussed up.

She flexes her wrist. "They're tight."

I flex mine. "They're tights." Little Miss Do-as-I-Say-Knot-as-I-Do never cuts *me* any slack when she ties me up.

Wham, bam!

"Thank you, ma'am."

I grin, my hand hot on her tail. It bounces off her ass, causing the flesh to fidget.

I continue to lash out until Dominique's rump is princess-pink and glowing like a firefly. Why give a spanking if you're going to do it half-assed?

I peer under her posterior. Her pussy is shiny with desire. I fondle her with my nondominant hand because the other one is sore from all that spanking.

Dom moans.

"Don't come." I clutch her arm. "Get off."

Dom groans. "Do you want me to climax or not?"

I help her off the vanity, then out of the restraints. "You aren't the only one who needs a good licking," I inform her, perching on the tabletop, feet on the bench, heels squishing the seat cushion. Dominique shoves her hands up my dress. My tights get ripped. I can't get blamed this time.

Dom's on the floor now, trapped between my pussy and the panty hose, which, along with my underwear, are stretched tight across my knees.

Dominique's head moves beneath my skirt. Her tongue swirls along my folds, unfurls inside my cunt, twirls around my clit. Her movements are graceful and skillful, and it isn't long before I'm arching like the bow of an arrow, shoving my snatch into her mouth.

"Get off." Dominique's head emerges. She rams her hand between her legs. "Your knees," I clarify, and she sighs but complies.

I pack my digits into her pussy, stuffing her like a cannoli. My fingers slip and slide through her sex until she comes, crushing my digits.

I pull my hand free, spread my middle and index fingers into a *V*-shape, and we lick the lust from them.

"Let's hit it," I suggest. "The road, this time."

Dominique answers with a scoff, an eye roll and a smile—in that order. I hoist the hosiery to my waist. Now that they're disfigured, they're almost comfy.

"Just so you know," Dom says, her tone tart and her smile suddenly sinister, "you didn't take control." She strokes my face, her nails chafing my cheek. "I gave it to you."

IN THE SCULPTURE GARDEN

Cha Cha White

"Yo Cath, check out the hooters on this one." Todd stopped in front of a female nude sculpted in flawless white marble.

Inside the museum it hadn't been so bad, but once outside in the sculpture garden Catherine was finding Todd intolerable. The brilliant sunshine seemed to increase his ugliness, exposing his unsuitability for this place. Amid the graceful rows of marble nudes and neat gravel paths lined with olive trees, he stood out, garish and discolored, like a livid bruise on a lovely face.

Catherine crossed a cool arcade to stand beside him in front of the "hooters" in question, feeling offended in spite of herself.

"You're so one-dimensional, Todd," she said, hating herself for taking the bait. "You can calculate the forward volatility on a group of foreign currencies in your head, but you can't appreciate art to save your life."

"Nobody ever got rich appreciating art, babe."

Belatedly recalling that the only wise course was to ignore her obnoxious friend—and reminding herself never to drag him to a museum again—Catherine bent forward to read the tiny engraved brass plaque that identified the nude. The statue's breasts were indeed beautiful. Todd was right about that, she had to admit.

VENUS said the plaque, and then in smaller letters underneath, GODDESS OF LOVE.

With protective tenderness, as though to shield the goddess from Todd's uncomprehending eyes, Catherine reached out and cupped her hand around the exposed marble breast, not quite touching it. Venus's form was sculpted so skillfully Catherine felt that if she hefted the perfect roundness in her palm she'd sense the weight of flesh, not stone.

The afternoon sun must have warmed the marble, for it reflected a calming, comforting heat.

"Hey," said Todd, sounding uncertain. "You're not supposed to touch the art."

Rebellious, and triumphant at having shocked him, Catherine closed the slight distance between her hand and Venus's breast. The polished surface glittered, scattering tiny flecks of brilliant light that dazzled Catherine's eyes. The white marble nipple stood erect. Had it been that way before? Had the stone responded to her caress?

Catherine thought of taking the perfect nipple in

her mouth. She leaned closer, taking sensuous joy in measuring the form beneath her fingers, marveling at the beauty of Venus's hips; her narrow, supple waist; her white, sculpted hands with their tiny oblong nails.

"Don't tease me," breathed a voice in her ear. Catherine glanced up, startled.

"Please," the nude Venus whispered. White marble lips moved, the only possible source of the words. The voice was urgent, passionate, but regal rather than pleading—the voice of a goddess who expected to be obeyed. "Touch me, kiss me, put your mouth on me, now! Quickly...before anyone comes."

Catherine stared into the beautiful marble eyes, then lowered her head obediently. Who was she to question the Goddess of Love? White marble eyelids fluttered as Catherine's mouth drew closer, but a sudden thought stopped her.

"What about him?" She inclined her head toward Todd, who stood behind them, his mouth open, looking slightly ridiculous.

Venus raised her glance to scan the ranks of white sculptures on the opposite side of the path. She gave an imperious nod. Silently, two muscular male nudes—their brass plaques identified them as ROMAN SLAVES—stepped forward and grabbed Todd by the wrists and elbows.

"Hey!" said Todd. "What the..."

"He can watch," said Venus, and laughed, a lovely clear sound that rang out like a bell.

Catherine glanced from one end of the garden to the

other. There was no one there, but the space was big and open. At any moment someone might wander out of one of the colonnades that encircled the garden. She felt giddy, intoxicated. They would just have to hurry, that was all.

She smiled at Venus's long, shuddering gasp when her lips met white flesh, white stone, at last. She teased the nipples gently, flicking the point of her tongue from one to the other with soft, insistent pressure. Venus's breasts were warm and yielding; they might have been flesh rather than stone; but when she drew her head back to look, Catherine still saw the dazzling white perfection of sculpted marble.

"Hurry," whispered Venus again. "It's been so long since anyone touched me. Oh, you *smell* good!" She buried her nose in Catherine's hair.

"So do you," murmured Catherine in surprise. Venus's scent was like water from a well, mineral and clean, seasoned with resin and the tang of copper. Her taste held the faintest hint of fresh rain, the salt of the sea, an empty seashell scoured with sand and sun.

"Kiss me here," Venus demanded, and her perfect white hands dropped, trembling, to her sex.

Still obedient, Catherine parted the sparkling white thighs, teasing and tasting the Goddess of Love with her lips and tongue until the marble back arched and the marble toes curled. Catherine wanted to stop and look, to appreciate the beauty of her Goddess in the moment of climax. She imagined the lovely face contorted with pleasure, the abundant hair tumbling loose over marble shoulders.

But she didn't dare stop now. Venus's cries of pleasure rang through the colonnades. Footsteps echoed in the hall with the fountain, but Catherine no longer cared if they were caught. She pursued the Goddess's pleasure with the steady, maddening pressure of her tongue until Venus gave one final delirious cry and cradled Catherine's head in languid arms, satisfied.

"Your turn," said Venus, white shoulders rising and falling as she caught her breath. "But first... Escort him out," she said to the Roman slaves.

Catherine twiddled her fingers at Todd. "Buh-bye," she said, and turned her attention to her Venus.

"Last customer of the day ran outta here screaming his head off," said one museum security guard to another as they made their rounds at closing time. "Real nut job."

"I can top that one," said the other guard. "Something's different in the sculpture garden. Know the Goddess of Love?"

"Sure, the one with the gorgeous tits."

"She's got a friend. Come on, I'll show you." They walked out to the gravel path, where two marble nudes now stood, entwined, on Venus's pedestal.

"Now where the hell did she come from?"

"Damned if I know." The first guard shrugged. "Nice cans though."

"Nice boobs on both of 'em," the second agreed. "Man, I sure do appreciate art."

WHEN LIFE IS INTERESTING

Leigh Wilder

When it came to Shel, Robin had learned to always expect the unexpected, so, though she got a little shock when she opened the door and Shel rushed in with a gun, she quickly recovered, slamming the door shut behind them. "I haven't seen you in forever," she accused. "What the hell are you doing?"

"You know how it is," Shel said, crossing the living room at a sprint, jumping over the coffee table. "Life has been way too interesting for your tastes. And I respect you too much to get you in the middle of it all." She threw open the bedroom door. The bedroom, to Robin's displeasure, hadn't seen much action lately due to Shel's disappearance. She followed Shel and found her fighting with the window leading to the old fire escape. The window was next to impossible to open and Robin always kept a cast iron paperweight on the dresser nearby, just in case there was ever an actual fire.

"This looks like the middle of something to me," Robin said, not caring about "interesting" at the moment.

"Yeah, sorry about that." Shel reached for the paper-weight.

"Wait!" Robin cried, and managed to wrench it out of her hand. "You can't come barging in here after not calling for weeks—*with a gun*—and expect me to just let you break my window and run off again."

Shel danced on the balls of her feet and bit her bottom lip. "I'm kinda in a hurry here." As she bounced Robin could hear the pockets of Shel's heavy long coat rattle and clink.

"I locked the door," Robin offered, pulling Shel away from the window by her pockets. Robin's finger-tips brushed cold metal. "No one knows you're here, and I haven't seen you in such a long time. Don't you remember what happened the last time we were together?" Robin remembered it extremely well. Those memories, paired with her deft fingers, were the only things that made life bearable while waiting for Shel. Now that she had Shel in her bedroom again, she wasn't going to let her go without a fight.

Robin leaned forward, pressing her large breasts against Shel's small ones, and slid her hand down Shel's arm until she touched the metal of the gun still in Shel's hand. She grasped it and eased it carefully from Shel's fingers, and she let her. Robin set the gun gently on the dresser and as soon as it was out of Shel's hand she grabbed Robin and pulled her into a kiss so fast and so hard that Robin had a brief fear of whiplash.

Robin felt a flash of heat between her legs—it didn't take much for Shel to set fire to her. She pushed the coat off of Shel's slim shoulders and the weight of the pockets made it slide off her arms into a clinking pile on the floor. Shel pushed Robin backward so they fell in a tangle of limbs onto the bed. "I don't really have time for this," Shel said against Robin's neck.

Robin pulled Shel's head by the hair so she could speak into her ear. "Make time," she hissed, and bit down hard on Shel's earlobe, certain to get her point across.

Shel yelled out but didn't pull away. Instead she pushed up Robin's shirt and bra to free her round, perfect breasts, but didn't take the time she usually did to admire before she took a nipple into her mouth, sucking hard. This time it was Robin's turn to cry out as Shel flicked over the hard bud with her tongue while squeezing the other breast tightly, then moved her hand down to the button of Robin's jeans.

Robin lifted her hips to help Shel yank the pants and underwear down her legs, but didn't bother trying to kick them off her ankles. With only vital parts exposed and her clothes bunched up at either end of her body, Robin tried to reach for Shel's T-shirt. Shel pulled away. "I only got time for one of us," she explained, voice brisk.

Robin wanted to protest, but it was a little hard to

do as Shel shoved her tongue into her mouth while at the same time pushing two fingers up inside her, meeting no resistance since Robin was so wet. Shel slid down Robin's body, lips touching every part of her as she moved, until her mouth joined her fingers and she began to give Robin's clit the same treatment as she had given her nipple.

Shel pushed a third finger inside, knowing exactly what it would take to send Robin over the edge in a hurry. She picked up speed with her tongue, teasing Robin into a hip-bucking frenzy, and her orgasm slammed into her as fast as Shel had thrown herself into the apartment. Robin clutched at Shel's head as she licked on, curving her fingers up against Robin's G-spot until she came again, still shaking from the first orgasm.

She whimpered when Shel slid her fingers gently out of her, giving her a few last laps to send a few after-shocks through her limbs.

Shel was on her feet in a flash and pulling her coat back on. She retrieved her gun, checked the safety and slipped it into one of her crowded pockets. "Sorry about the window," she said before picking up the paperweight and smashing through the glass.

Robin stumbled over to her, jeans hanging off of one ankle. Cold air blew in from the broken window as Shel slipped her hand into her sleeve and broke away the sharp edges of glass. "Call me when you can," Robin said, knowing Shel would be out the window any second. "Promise me you will this time."

"Of course." Shel took something glittering out of a pocket and pressed it into Robin's hand. "I'll see you when life isn't as interesting," she promised, kissing Robin on the cheek before throwing a leg over the windowsill. Robin opened her hand—Shel had given her a diamond tennis bracelet. She looked up to thank her, but Shel was gone, and someone was knocking on her apartment door.

Robin clutched the bracelet tight in her hand as she struggled into her clothes and hurried to the door. A cop was standing there. "Um, hello, officer."

"Sorry to bother you, ma'am, but a suspect was seen entering your building—female, about five foot five, short dark hair, wearing a long coat?"

Robin shook her head, holding the bracelet behind her back. "I haven't seen anyone like that. What did she do?"

"Armed robbery—jewelry store. Thank you for your time, ma'am. Call us if you see anything."

"Of course," she said.

Once the door was closed she leaned against it and let out a nervous laugh. Maybe Shel would call her when life was less interesting. Or when she needed bail.

COWBOY
DIRTY

Roxy Jones

The long, slick shaft leans toward me,
obscene in purple flecked with gold,
grunting low
and mean,
Baby, please. Do it again. Take me. Own me.

We've ripped the sticky sheets
and knocked the pictures from the wall
with condoms stolen from your daddy's drawer
and an old pair of 501s buttoned up tight to hold it
  in place.

Lick me, baby.
It's giving me that look, stiff and pointed like a dirty
  compass,

begging me for more.
I want that
soft
pink
flesh
one more time, baby.
Baby, baby...
Slide open for me, tight and wet,
Take it, darlin,
be my girl.

I giggle
as I lean down against your chest,
listening to your breathing,
the way your heartbeat slows
from the machine-gun rhythm of fucking like porn
  stars
to a slow *thump thump* as you fall into dreaming.
(Backs arching, thighs rubbing, lips tasting salty
  sweet sweat and more...)

My heart swells with pride, remembering how
my body invited you in,
loving so strong as you slid it in deep,
no prisoners,
no mercy,
riding my hips bareback,
'cuz *baby don't need no saddle.*
How you looked, gazing down,

eyes wild with a woman's desire,
but flashing that mischievous little-boy grin.
The way you spread my knees and slid your hands
down along my shuddering
inner
thighs

made me gasp

like the world had just. Stopped.

The way your hips pressed into me,
rough
and
sweet,
(Baby, baby, baby...my baby...god, yes, baby...)
as your eyes rolled back and your fingers raked my
   sides,
signing me like a work of art.

I watched your chest rise and fall awhile
and then slid my leg back across your still-sleeping
   form,
kissed your breasts
and spread my body over yours
saying,
"Yes, I belong to you,
my fierce, dirty cowboy,
and you—

my sexy,
amazing,
dangerous
creature"
 *(the fire in her eyes was hotter than Hell, and twice
  as hungry)*
—"are Mine."

SAUCY CHEEKS

Giselle Renarde

S orry I'm late!" Marigold looked for the blaze in
Donna's eyes, but found amusement instead. "Some
snooty bitch wouldn't leave my department at closing
time, then I wait forty minutes for the damn bus and, of
course, three came at once…"

Donna cocked her head in the direction of two look-
alike dykes. That was the whole point of this dinner,
actually—the friends getting to know the girlfriend.
Great first impression she'd made, but the women
seemed amenable. They introduced themselves, and
Marigold immediately forgot who was who. They were
strikingly similar in appearance: heavy-set; short, sandy
hair; dark clothes; lots of piercings.

"Nice to finally meet you." Marigold's chest tightened as she slouched into the empty chair. "Sorry again

for being…" She glanced at her phone. "Oh, god, I'm over an hour late!"

"We had to start without you." Donna smiled as though tardiness were no big deal. "In fact, dessert's on its way."

"I'm really sorry," Marigold repeated, seeking some recognizable response.

Donna set a hand on hers. "You're off the hook."

The other women laughed, and one said, "Until you get home!"

Marigold felt a blush burn across her cheeks. *How did they know?* Did Donna discuss their private life with other people? The thought made her uneasy, and she squirmed in her chair.

Donna's friends started talking about some new movie, and Marigold was glad the focus shifted. Was nothing sacred? When she shivered, Donna noticed and wrapped a white pashmina around her shoulders. Marigold shot her a look that asked, *Are you sure? You know I'm messy.*

When Donna nodded, Marigold absorbed the warmth of her woman through the fabric. Coffee and cake came, urging Marigold to sit taller. That chocolate mousse slice drizzled with raspberry coulis made her mouth water.

"Dig in, honey." Donna handed her a fork.

"Thanks." Marigold smiled as Donna's friends kissed, and jumped when she felt Donna's lips on her cheek. They'd never kissed in public before. This was…

new. Wonderful. She felt all warm and fuzzy, sipping coffee, her girlfriend's pashmina draped around her body.

And then it happened: Marigold took a forkful of mousse cake, lifted it to her mouth, and watched in slow motion as a drip of red coulis slipped through the prongs of her fork, beading against soft white fabric. *It'll be okay*, Marigold told herself, but as she wiped up the droplet, the cake itself tumbled down. It broke into three layers: cake, mousse and deep chocolate icing. Oh, god, it would never come out....

"I'm sorry," Marigold said for the fourth time in as many minutes. "I am such a klutz. I'll wash it."

"Maybe ask the server for some soda water?" one of Donna's friends suggested. Marigold's head was buzzing. She stood, flicking the cake to the table and removing the pashmina.

"I'll come with you." Donna pushed her chair back and rose. "I'm sure we can get it out."

Marigold never felt so small as when she'd done something wrong. She walked to the washroom in a daze, feeling the hot press of Donna's front against her back.

"I'm sorry," she said again when they'd passed through the bathroom door.

Before she knew it, Donna's mouth was slanted across hers, their lips a tight seal, tongues wrestling. This never happened. *Never*. But it was happening now—Donna was kissing her in a public bathroom, and kissing her hard! Marigold couldn't get over the heat coming off her girl's body. She felt consumed by it.

"I thought I'd be in trouble," Marigold whispered, panting.

Donna tossed the pashmina in the sink. "Who says you're not?" The growl in her voice made Marigold loopy, and she couldn't believe it when Donna yanked her into the end stall. "Pull down those pants," Donna instructed, even before the door was closed.

Marigold did as she was told, dropping slacks and cotton underpants to the floor.

Sitting fully clothed on the toilet seat, Donna patted her lap and Marigold fell onto it. At home, this was standard practice, but they were in public...well, in a public washroom. When the top of Marigold's head met the toilet paper dispenser, she turned around to watch. "I'm sorry I was so late."

"You're off the hook, remember?" Donna's eyes were kind. "The pashmina? That's another story."

"Sorry." Marigold's pussy clenched as she awaited sweet punishment. "If I can't get the stain out, I'll buy you a new one."

Donna seemed to time her "Thank you," exactly with the first smack against Marigold's ass. Marigold let out a yelp, hoping there were no other patrons in here. They hadn't even checked.

"How many?" Marigold asked as the second slap fell.

Another one—three so soon, and all in the same

spot. That cheek was already red. "How many do you think?"

"Ten," Marigold said without reflection. She knew she'd want more.

Four came down hard in that same tender spot, and Marigold couldn't contain her squeal. Lower for five—that one came down around her thigh. Six did, too—other cheek, other thigh. Marigold shifted in Donna's lap, clenching her muscles tight. "Harder," she begged. It was good, but it wasn't nearly enough.

"Harder?" Donna asked, surprise in her voice.

"Please?"

Harder is exactly what Marigold got for seven, eight, nine. They fell in quick succession, and they were solid spanks every one of them. Marigold hissed, but she wanted more, oh so much more!

Ten was a disappointment: off the mark, falling in the middle of her asscrack without connecting properly. "Bonus round?"

"Saucy cheeks!" Donna teased.

The next one was much more precise. It caught the burn of her right cheek, and she felt her flesh ripple. Switch for the next one. It came down hard on her left cheek and sounded like a cracking whip. Marigold was squealing now, her pussy dripping wet and her feet running in place along the floor in anticipation.

The next few alternated in rapid fire: one, two, one, two, back and forth across her burning bottom. The pleasure-pain crossed the threshold to pain-pain, and

Marigold couldn't stop herself from crying, "Ow...it hurts," as those precious blows fell one after another.

Marigold's skin sizzled red-hot with friction when Donna determined the punishment was complete. Her bum burned so badly she couldn't put her panties back on right away.

Donna left the stall for a moment, and came back with her pashmina, wetted in cold water. Again, she folded Marigold over her lap. This time she soothed the burn, tracing soft, cool wetness across Marigold's poor searing bottom. It was an act of such love and compassion Marigold almost wanted to cry.

After a time, they left the stall and stood together at the sink, trying to rinse the chocolate and raspberry stain from that beautiful white scarf. Marigold jumped when one of their dinner companions poked her head in the door and handed them a glass of soda water. "Hope this does the trick," she said, and promptly scuttled away.

Marigold met her girl's gaze in the mirror and smiled. "Your friends are nice."

LAST MINUTE

Catherine Paulssen

With a cappuccino in each of my hands, I watched Felice fooling around at the gift shop. She held a huge smiling balloon in front of her face and entertained some random kid, whose little body wriggled with laughter. His mother eventually dragged him away, and Felice straightened up again.

"Wasn't that the cutest little fella?" she asked. "I might buy you this balloon to cheer your...Jen?" Her playful face crinkled into a frown. She took a few steps toward me through the buzz of the airport's check-in area.

"Miss! You haven't paid for that balloon!" a shop assistant snapped.

Felice ignored her. "Hey, what's the matter? We'll see each other again in two months, and—"

"I love you," I blurted out, and watched her expression change.

Fear gripped me. I had ruined it, hadn't I? You're not supposed to tell a coworker who's been at your branch only half a year on office exchange that you love her. Not even if she's become your best friend in those six months, not even if the sound of her laughter makes your heart beat faster every time.

I gulped. "I'm sorry, I shouldn't have. It's just—"

"Why didn't you tell me earlier?" She lifted my chin. "Why the hell did you wait until the last minute?"

My stomach made a little flip. Her voice was calm. Not at all upset. And her frozen-lake eyes looked at me as though I had just articulated the long-sought-after explanation of some scientific marvel, not something that would ruin our whole friendship. "You...do you mean you—"

She laughed. "I've been in love with you ever since your cute rendition of 'You Are My Sunshine' at the karaoke bar!"

This time, the flip was stronger. Before I could process what she'd just said, her lips pressed against mine, and I could hear her giggle under our kiss. The moment before I closed my eyes, I saw the smiling balloon fly away, floating up toward the airport's glass ceiling.

"I was drunk," I pouted, clumsily trying to disguise how giddy I felt inside.

"You were so adorable." She bit her lips, and for some moments, we remained lost in each other's grins.

"Come!" she said, putting down her coffee and taking my hand.

"You have to pay for that balloon!" an annoyed voice called after us.

Felice rolled her eyes and hurried back to throw a bill on the counter. I watched her blonde hair flying along with a floaty top that didn't do nearly enough justice to her curves.

I didn't want to talk. I didn't want to discuss what all of this meant. I didn't want to think up ways to make it work over a distance of a thousand miles.

I wanted to taste her lips again.

"There!" She pointed to an empty black bubble chair somewhat hidden in a corner. We fell into the chair and snuggled against each other, her fingers brushing my fringe out of my eyes. At the mere touch of her fingers, I could feel happiness rush to my face and color my cheeks pink.

But that was nothing compared to the tingles she evoked when she ran two fingers over my lips, creating sizzles that shot right through to my belly button.

"We can talk all night over the phone, huh?" She grinned.

I cupped her face with both hands and kissed her again. This time, it was all different. I savored it. Her body pressing against mine. Our knees touching. Her fingers fondling the nape of my neck. And those lips… I made them mine, and it was like discovering a whole new world. So gentle. So demanding.

So desperate.

"You…" She shook her head at me, but there was an impish twinkle in her eyes. "Telling me *today*." Again her fingers stroked my face. "Lean against me," she whispered. I did and then watched her arrange her jacket over my thighs. My breath hitched in my throat as her fingers crawled underneath my skirt and touched my naked skin.

"You're so much braver than me," she continued in a loving whisper as her hand tugged my panties away. "I thought it was better to have you as a best friend than not at all." Her finger crawled underneath the mesh, and I opened my legs as far as the limited space allowed. "When all I could think about was undressing you piece by piece…" She kissed my eyes, my nose, my mouth. "…and running my lips over your naked skin."

I nestled my head against her shoulder and relished watching the small patch of black bra that came in and out of view every time she moved. Taking a shy glance around, I let my finger explore the smooth skin of her neck down to the rim of the lace.

I liked how her breath quickened.

Felice took my hand and kissed my fingertips. "They'll be all yours, baby." She didn't give me any time to pout, just parted my pussy lips with subtle fingers. "You like that?" she softly rubbed the length of them.

I wished I could scream out how much. Impatiently, I poked my pussy closer to her touch. The tip of her finger met my clit, and I jumped as liquid heat shot through me.

"Shh," she soothed, making sure we appeared to passersby as mere innocent snugglers, when in fact, she was working me up in the most tantalizing way beneath the jacket's cover. Nuzzling at my ear, she continued to whisper about how she could feel me pulsating underneath her thumb, how she imagined it was her tongue instead, what we would do once we were in each other's arms again.

"You're so creamy," she sighed and dipped deeper into my pussy to massage me so eagerly I had to bury my face in her neck to keep from crying out. The peach and almond scent of her conditioner will forever smell like the sweetest caress to me.

"Oh, please…" I pressed my mouth against her skin, damp from my breath, and prayed it would muffle my moans. Torn between obeying my body's urge to spasm around her fingers and remaining as still as I possibly could, I dug my nails into her arm to find some outlet for the sensations overwhelming me as she circled my soaking clit and cradled my writhing body.

Huddled against her, safe in her embrace, I came down from heights so intense I wanted to kiss her senseless for raising me to them.

"I wish we had more time," I whispered as I regained my breath.

"I will never regret a single moment. This was…" She shook her head, and a tender smile grew on her face. "…the best first date I've ever had."

I hugged her, laughing, crying and soaking up as

much of her peachy scent as I could.

I kept my eyes shut as we kissed good-bye, and for what seemed like hours, I remained curled up in the curve of the chair—numbed, happy, sad, bewildered, shaken—while the last traces of her lips evaporated from my skin.

BREATHLESS

Ariel Graham

I ran into her. Knocked her flat. Came round the corner of the pool building on the running trail and didn't expect anyone else on the path because it was a cold, gray April day in Northern Nevada, spitting rain. Anyone with any sense was inside at 5:30 P.M.

I've never had any sense.

So I ran into her. Full-body contact.

It wasn't pretty. I wasn't pretty. The end of a long run and my Swedish ancestry not only means keep moving or get fat in my midthirties, it also means running makes me turn beet red and appear minutes away from a coronary event.

She cushioned my fall.

I apologized before I even got her out of the juniper bush. She might have been upset if she hadn't been laughing so hard.

So when I asked, "Are you all right?" it was partly regarding mental processes. Maybe she'd hit her head?

She let me help her up and we both stood in the early, cloud-induced twilight. My sweat started to chill on my legs.

My breathing relaxed enough for me to ask again, "Are you all right?"

"I'm not hurt." She took that shuddery half breath that comes at the end of sobbing or laughing. "You startled me." Obviously, but before I could be stupid and snide—"Y'think?"—she put a hand on my arm and said, "Sorry. It's just so silly. Bad movie pratfall silly."

The sun came out, just a little. Raindrops glittered in her hair. She was about my height, five six, with dark brown hair, some red highlights that looked natural, and tilted green eyes. She grinned.

I went on blushing, but since I was still red from running, she wouldn't be able to tell. She looked at me, though, as we stood under the trees beside the river that runs through downtown Reno. Rain still pattered down, mostly missing us. The air smelled thickly of clean wet sage and a little of wet dirt.

"I'm really sorry," I said, because I hadn't so far, and I *had* fallen on her. "Did I hurt you?"

She shook her head. "Few juniper berries maybe in unexpected places. What about you?" she asked, just as I realized we hadn't both made it out of the bush unscathed.

My right ankle had started to send up signals of alarm. It seemed very seriously irritated about some-

thing and the pain was like having a hot railroad spike
driven up through the outside of that ankle.

"Um." I didn't want to admit it. I hate being hurt
even more when other people know about it.

"You're listing to the left," she said, and took my
arm to steady me. "Can you stand on that leg?"

"My car's right over there in the lot." I'd planned to
finish the trail where it ended on a city street, then cool
down by walking back to my car before figuring out
what to have for dinner and what to do with the long,
empty night in front of me.

"Mine's closer." She pointed to a minivan near the now-
closed-for-the-evening pool building. "And I have ice."

"Ice?" I wondered idiotically if she wanted to sell me
drugs. I couldn't remember what ice was.

"Ice. Cold stuff? I had a soda. There's ice left. And
I'm sure I have a plastic bag. We can put it on your ankle
and I'll drive you back to your car."

"Listen, no, I'm fine, I'll just…"

"Please? I came around the corner without looking.
I'm at least equally responsible. I'm Alyson. I don't bite.
Unless you like that."

I teetered and the world revolved once, too fast.
Really?

The night was looking up. "I'm Emma."

Alyson's minivan was warm, which made me realize
how cold I'd become. My teeth started to chatter the
minute the heat came on, which seemed contrary of my

body (big surprise).

"You're freezing," Alyson said. "I've got a zipper sweatshirt back here. Let's get you out of those wet clothes."

We'd pulled over next to my car but neither of us made a move to get out. I met her eyes and couldn't look away. It didn't seem possible. This wasn't my style.

Do you even *have* a style anymore? I asked myself. Because it had been a damn long time since Elise left, breaking up the E-girls because a graphic design job in L.A. sounded better than anything she could find—or had—in Reno.

I was probably quiet too long, but this time my body came to my rescue. Wracked with a wave of new chills, I shivered, my hands moving up and down my icy arms. Very slowly I pulled my T-shirt over my head, then started ungracefully freeing myself from a damp jog bra. Alyson held the sweatshirt ready for me to turn and slide into as we sat facing each other in the minivan bucket seats. I got the thing rolled up and off my shoulders, then over my head, and heard her take a small breath. She moved forward, draping the sweatshirt around me like a cloak, both hands on my shoulders briefly before she brought them down over my pecs, along my collarbone and down to cup my breasts, her thumbs flicking my nipples as the heat coursed up inside me and the shivering changed to something very different.

She leaned forward, bridging the console between us, lowered her mouth to my right breast, and circled the nipple with her tongue; all of it fast, as if we were suddenly running out of time. I wanted to point out where we were but she sucked my nipple hard into her mouth, still running her tongue over it, and reached one hand down to press insistently between my legs. I didn't care where we were or how much time we had.

It was like making out in high school again, in someone's car, not even taking time to climb into the back. Her fingers moved in hard, fast, long strokes right through my running tights and I shuddered under her hand, stroking her hair, tangling my hands in it. My body tightened, pulsed, and I came, my hips up and forward, everything pulsing with pleasure.

I came down slowly. It was getting dark outside. A couple passed the van, walking hamster-sized dogs on leashes. The rain had stopped and the van fogged up. Trees, sky, couple and dogs were hazy.

"I want to catch my breath and reciprocate." Alyson wore low-rise jeans and a belt over slim hips and a flat stomach. I wanted to see what was under them but the front seat of her minivan was going to be a challenge. I glanced toward the backseat, still cramped, but an improvement. "Want to move somewhere a little more comfortable?" I asked, nodding in that direction.

"Or a lot more comfortable?" She nodded toward the key in the ignition.

Suddenly the evening didn't look so long and empty.

CARAMEL

Louise Blaydon

H er body glides over yours like dark poured caramel, brown sugar sweetness under gold. You drink in all of her: the muscles in her arms, her neat waist under your fingers. The look on her face is teasing, measured, as she slips a hand up between your legs.

"Zoe," you breathe, and she says, "Don't say anything," drawing clever fingers through your slickness. She finds you, presses; leans up to kiss you, and her mouth is warm and wet and tastes of peppermint, as if she made very sure to suck on a breath mint on the drive home. The thought is strangely sexy—she wants you; she wanted it to be perfect for you—and you kiss her back and thrust up against her hand, spreading your legs in a silent request.

She laughs against your mouth like cinnamon,

deep and rich, and slips two fingers up inside you. You cry out, and she laughs more, rubbing her face open-mouthed in the hollow of your throat, working your clit with her thumb. She's strong, very strong; her dancer's muscles stand out in her forearms as she works you, tense against the insides of your thighs. She's hot and wet and slick against your leg where she's straddled it, rubbing just slightly, and the feel of it makes you moan under her fingers, under her mouth.

"*Zoe*," you cry out again, "oh, god, Zoe—*fuck*—" and she says, "Patience," like she knows you're on the edge. And her fingers slow perceptibly, circling you with excruciating, tortuous gentleness, until finally you throw your head back, buck your hips against her and scream in frustration, and she flicks your clit with her thumb and lets you come.

Afterward, when you can breathe again, she shimmies up your body until she's kneeling over your chest, legs astride, her back a graceful curve. You take her by the hips without a word and press your tongue into her musky slickness; and when you make her come, you feel as if you just remade the whole damn world.

CATS AND DOGS

Fran Walker

Renee wrung out her hair. Her service dog, Jake, fetched a towel and dropped it into her lap. She dried off and shifted from the shower seat to the wheelchair, then wheeled herself into the kitchen. The front door banged.

"In here, Cat!"

"Hey, hon." Cat entered the kitchen and dropped her briefcase on a chair. "Christ, students are a disrespectful lot these days. If it weren't for them, my job wouldn't be half bad."

Renee laughed. "Spoken like a true teacher."

"Nice outfit," Cat said, winking.

Renee spun her chair around, pretending to model the faded yellow towel. "Do you want the good news or the bad news?"

Cat groaned. "Go on, give me the bad news and get it over with."

"Your brother Greg called. He broke up with Arnie."

"Again?"

"Apparently Arnie said something unforgivable."

"Like what—'I think you've got your first gray hair'?"

Renee laughed. "Something like that. Anyhow, Greg needs a place to stay."

"Again?"

"Cat, he is your brother."

"And one of life's little testicles. All right. When's he coming?"

"Around six, he said."

Cat slumped into a kitchen chair. "Tonight? Quick, tell me the good news."

"You've got mail." Renee pointed to a large cardboard carton sitting in the corner.

"What the hell?" Cat picked up the box and placed it on the kitchen table. "I ordered two little vibrators."

"I figured you must've ordered some extra stuff."

"Nope." Cat examined the label. "Right name. Right address. Let's open it up."

Renee handed her a craft knife. Cat slit the tape and opened the box, then set it down next to Renee's chair.

"Holy hell."

Two small pink vibrators, neatly packaged in cardboard boxes, nestled atop a pile of leather and lace. Renee reached down and lifted out the objects, setting each one on the table. A dildo harness, a leather bustier, a mask, elbow-length black gloves and a whip. A red and white maid's outfit: mob cap, blouse, skirt, frilly apron, and white ankle socks.

Cat started giggling as she scooped out several silicone dildos shaped, variously, like a dolphin, a can of hair spray, and a Madonna cradling baby Jesus. By the time they got to the red velvet handcuffs, the rhinestone tiara, and a bizarre multicolored object that Cat said looked like a cross between a six-headed dildo and a dog's plush toy, they had both collapsed with laughter.

"Whoever packed our order must've been smoking something mighty good," Cat said.

Jake sniffed at the table, then barked.

"Jake, go lie on your mat." Renee pulled on the long gloves, then waggled her hands at her lover. "What do you think? Are they me?"

"About as much as the maid outfit is me." Cat tied the apron over her suit and donned the cap. She plunked the tiara on Renee's head then curtseyed. "What doth your ladyship desire?"

"Explain to me what that thing is, menial servant girl." Renee pointed to the plush six-headed dildo.

Cat picked up the object. Peeling away Renee's towel, she ran one end of the dildo across Renee's breasts.

"It tickles!"

Cat grinned. "There you go. It's a dildo tickler." She traced its fuzzy end down Renee's belly to her crotch.

"It's too weird. Like having sex with a teddy bear," Renee said.

"Would you prefer the Mary and Jesus dildo?"

"Ew."

"Maybe you can use this for a pincushion, my quilting queen," Cat suggested. She dropped the plush object into Renee's lap.

Renee reached up to touch Cat's face, then grimaced in frustration. She peeled off the gloves, dropped them, and stroked Cat's cheek. "Mmm. Much better. Let's take this silly thing off." Renee untied the maid's apron and tossed it on the table, then unbuttoned Cat's suit jacket. Cat quickly peeled off her clothes and draped them over a kitchen chair along with Renee's towel.

"Come here." Renee pulled Cat closer and nuzzled her breasts. "Yum. I'm so glad you're short." She licked Cat's left nipple.

"Oh, yes!"

Gently she pushed Cat's thighs apart and slid her hand between them. Cat moaned. Renee stroked Cat's pussy lips, using her index finger to slide them apart and trace the insides. Cat sucked in a short, sharp breath.

"Maybe we should try one of the real toys," Cat said, her voice unsteady. She rummaged through the pile on the table until she found one of the pink pearl vibrators then took it out of its box. "Oh, good, it already has a battery in."

Cat turned on the vibrator and pushed aside the plush object to slide the vibrator between Renee's legs.

"A little lower," Renee murmured. Cat adjusted the vibrator's placing. "Oh, yes, just there." The buzzing vibrator tickled and rubbed at the same time.

"Want me to sit on the table?"

"No." Renee locked the wheels of her chair then tugged at Cat's leg. "Put your foot up here."

Cat raised a foot and rested it on the wheel. Renee explored Cat's pussy with both hands, finger-fucking her and rubbing her clit. The vibrator shifted a bit. Renee reached down and moved it, pushing the plush object against the vibrator to hold it in place.

Cat leaned closer. Renee rubbed harder on Cat's swollen bud. The ultrafast vibrations against her own clitoris, combined with the smell and feel of Cat, drove her wild.

"Cat!" she moaned, rubbing faster. She felt her lover's legs grow rigid. Her own flesh pulsated in time with the vibrator. When Cat cried out, Renee came in a rush. Her orgasm felt as if it would shake her out of her chair.

Cat sagged against her.

The front door banged shut. "Hello!"

Cat tossed something at Renee, who held it across her front. Cat grabbed something off the table and used it to shield herself as she spun around.

"Sorry. Sorry." Greg stood frozen in the kitchen doorway.

Renee tried to hide behind the towel, then realized what Cat had tossed her was the maid's apron. The vibrator still buzzed between her legs. Cat was holding the leather bustier. Renee started to giggle.

Greg backed up. "Sorry, sis. Didn't mean to interrupt your..." His eyes widened. "This wasn't just sex, it was an orgy!"

"It's a bunch of stuff we got sent accidentally," Renee said hastily. "We don't use it."

"So you're just accidentally having sex with a dog toy?"

"What?"

"That thing in your lap. I bought one for Arnie's dog just last week." His face puckered. "Oh, god. Arnie!" He ran from the room.

"I hope they make up soon. That is going to get really old really quick," Cat said.

Renee picked up the plush object and squeezed one end. It made a loud squeak. "It really is a dog toy."

Her lover handed her the yellow towel. "What should we do with all this stuff? The packing slip says they don't accept returns."

Renee tossed the squeaky dog toy to Jake. "Here, boy."

"And the rest? The maid outfit, and—"

Renee shrugged. "Give it to Greg. Maybe it'll cheer him up."

"Brilliant." Cat laughed. "If a tiara and a Jesus dildo can't take his mind of Arnie, nothing will."

MINA'S TRAIN RIDE

J. Caladine

Mina was not the type to easily endure a month without sex. That's how long I'd been in New York for work when she decided to join me for a little vacation time. She'd chosen to travel by train to amuse herself while she waited for my negotiations to close. I wasn't there when they met, but I can just imagine how it happened. Mina boarded that train thinking about me and growing more aroused as each mile flew by.

The Woman actually looked quite a bit like me. I suppose I should take that as a compliment. Mina is a dream bottom, and I don't doubt the Woman sniffed her out right away. I'll bet the Woman spent the better part of the day arranging their 'coincidental' crossing of paths with lots of meaningful glances and a little well-placed flattery. I'm sure Mina started thinking the

Woman would do nicely to take the edge off.

What Mina didn't know was that I had finished my negotiations early and boarded the train to surprise her. By the time I spotted her, we were just fifteen minutes from our destination. I was just in time to see her being led by the hand down the narrow aisle ahead of me, and into the Woman's sleeper. The Woman must have been awfully excited because she forgot to lock the door.

I slipped in too, just a minute behind them. The Woman hadn't wasted any time. Mina was on the small bed, bare-assed, pants still around one ankle. The Woman was off to one side, hurriedly harnessing her cock. Both were shocked, but only one was glad to see me. "Baby!" Mina beamed. "I…" said the Woman, caught between outrage at the intrusion and panic at a confrontation with her tryst's lover.

"You," I pointed a finger at her chest, "will sit down and shut up, or I'll have you arrested for trying to fuck a married woman." This was a ridiculous threat but if you'd heard the way I delivered it you'd at least half believe I could do it. In any case, she sank to the floor, frowning in silence.

"And *you*." I turned toward my girl, still lying on her stomach on the bed with her gorgeous ass begging for attention. "I've got a question for *you*." I put my hand to my crotch, silently thankful I'd decided to pack and be ready for anything. "Whose cock do you *really* want?"

"I want yours, baby. Always, yours."

"Then how about we show this amateur what it takes to satisfy a world-class bottom?" In response, she rose onto her knees, lifting her ass and offering me everything. It was a glorious sight. I unbuckled, unbuttoned and unzipped in a flash and pulled out my perfectly curved cock. She let out a little moan of anticipation and wiggled her hips just a little.

I knelt behind her, one arm circling her waist, the other hand guiding my cock into her. She took it right in and I had to smile to myself at how wet she was already. I grasped her firmly by the hips and began to fuck her. I knew I didn't have much time, but I forced myself to start with slow, firm strokes at first, stoking her arousal. Soon enough I was slamming her ass and she had to cry out at the intensity of the pleasure. She was on the brink, but I wanted the most from every minute. I eased my cock back luxuriously before thrusting it deeply into her again. I leaned over her back and moved my hands to her breasts, squeezing hard. "Tell me it feels good," I demanded.

"It feels *really* good."

"And why is that?"

"Because you know how to fuck me."

It was just what I wanted to hear. I turned to look the Woman in the eyes as I began to pump harder and faster. It was time to close *these* negotiations. I placed my thumb on Mina's sweet back door and began to press rhythmically in time with my thrusting. Soon she was desperate to come for me. The Woman gave in and slid

her hand down her own trousers. I turned my full attention back to Mina and moved my hand around to rub
her clit, which was swollen and begging for my touch.
Almost immediately she whispered, "Please, please may
I come for you?"

"Yes, right now," I said, with a note of triumph in
my voice the Woman was sure to catch.

Mina came beautifully. She rocked and moaned and
pushed back onto my cock. I stayed inside her, thrusting
slowly through all the aftershocks, despite the slowing
of the train and the announcements that we'd be disem-
barking in minutes. I gradually withdrew my cock and
moved off the bed. "Time to get dressed, my love,"
I said in a tone that told her we wouldn't be the last
ones off the train. She dressed in a flash. I stared down
the Woman, her lips now a telltale red, while zipping,
buttoning and buckling myself. "Thanks for the bed,"
I offered coolly. "I thought I was going to have to fuck
her crammed in with a toilet." And with that, we made
our escape, unable to keep the smirks off our faces as I
led Mina off the train.

We went directly to my hotel room. I'm sure Mina
expected round two, but I intended to provide an opportunity for a little further reflection on her prior lack of
patience. I took her up to the room, undressed her, and
moved her to lie stomach-down on the bed. I sat beside
her, fully clothed, and slid one bent leg under her hips
to raise her ass. She gave a small moan of anticipation,
knowing what was next. I turned her ass a lovely shade

of pink with the firmest spanking she'd had in some time. Usually this was a prelude to a good hard fuck. "This time," I whispered into her ear, "you're going to wait for it. Get dressed. We're going to dinner."

She wasn't in a position to argue, and she didn't want to. We'd both get hotter still at dinner, sharing the secret of her still-smarting ass, and knowing I'd fuck her the minute we got back in the room. As I recall, it made for a very hot weekend.

SEASON FINALE

Lea Meadows

Olivia Benson is so fucking hot," I said, moving from the couch to straddle Erica's lap as she sat at her desk and banged away at her laptop intently. Sitting this way, I was able to rub up against the hard ridge of her jeans and still watch the season finale of "Law and Order: SVU." Perfection.

"Tara! Can't you see I'm busy here? Go watch your stupid show somewhere else. God, haven't you seen every 'Law and Order' episode ever made?"

She was right. I think I *have* seen every episode. But I was addicted. Great stories ripped from the head-lines, celebrity guest stars, twisted endings and the most important element of any good 'SVU' episode: Olivia Benson.

I know, I know. Every lesbian loves Olivia. What's

not to love? She's beautiful, smart, tough and can fill out a pair of jeans like nobody's business. But I loved Detective Benson for a different reason: she looked just like Erica. Same short, brown hair. Same angular jaw. Same sexy swagger. And the cherry on top—Erica was also a cop. She was my wet dream come true and at the moment that dream was making my nipples harden into painful peaks and my cunt leak onto my thighs.

Erica moved around me to stare at her computer screen and continue typing whatever it was she was typing like I wasn't there. God, she was so sexy, and looking down at her as Benson was interrogating a witness on the TV screen was making me so hot. I smoothed back a lock of Erica's hair from her forehead and planted my lips there, enjoying the smoothness and warmth of her skin. I locked my ankles behind her and slowly shifted forward. The pressure on my clit was intense, and all I wanted to do was ride her like this. My Erica. My detective. It was so delicious to be this close to her, and even though she was trying to cast me aside in favor of her work, my lips made a wet path down the side of her face and locked on to her earlobe.

She paused for a moment, as if she knew where I was going with this, and I giggled as I heard her gasp quietly. And as I bit down, I knew where this was going as well. Though she initially resisted, my detective would ultimately come apart under my interrogation. She'd come apart in waves and I would gladly lap at her skin, at her tits and at her pussy to have her come in my arms.

Better than Olivia, she was my Erica, and as our tongues tangled and our fingers trailed over each other's bodies, I was vaguely aware that I'd just missed the season finale of my favorite show. Oh, well, there'd always be reruns.

AUTOCORRECT

Evan Mora

Hi, Cris, are you coming to the meeting at 4?

I'll be there!

Great. Please meet me in my office in 5 minutes so we can have a brief cunnilingus beforehand.

Excuse me?

I have no words. I typed conference and my phone changed it. I am so sorry.

I'm on my way.

I'm going to be fired. No—first I'm going to be brought up on sexual harassment charges, and then I'm going to be fired. This isn't happening. I close my eyes, trying to keep the panic at bay. I double-check the screen on my phone, but the words are most definitely there. The most epic AutoCorrect fail of all time. How does my phone even *know* the word *cunnilingus*? And since when does "conference" look like "cunnilingus"? Somewhere, an Apple genius is snickering.

And of course, it's Cris. Not one of the dozen straight women who report to me who would've shared a titter and a conspiratorial, *I wish that hunky new VP would send me messages like that.* No—I'm sending lewd text messages to the only one of my subordinates who's openly gay. And perceptive.

There's a knock at my door.

"Lauren?"

Oh, god. I grab a sheaf of papers and look busy just as the door opens and Cris steps inside. And hot—did I mention she's hot? I cross my legs beneath my desk, a figurative *down* command to my unruly libido, which doesn't even marginally succeed. It's just that, well, now that it's out there, the thought of this strong, stylish woman kneeling between my thighs won't go away. And if I'm being completely honest, it's not the first time it's crossed my mind, either.

She closes the door.

My heart is beating far too fast in my chest, fueled by the twin messages of anticipation and need my body is telegraphing to my brain. I clear my throat; opt for professional: "Cris—thanks for meeting with me. I wanted to talk to you about your cost projections for the next campaign before the meeting."

There's a beat of silence, then the audible click of the lock being pressed. She crosses the floor with unmistakable purpose, rolling up her sleeves like she's ready to get down to business. I try another tack.

"Crazy stuff, those iPhones, huh?" I say with a nervous little laugh. But she's around the corner of my desk, spinning my chair so that I'm facing her, effectively trapped by the two strong forearms and very capable looking hands she's got braced on the arms of my chair.

She's going to kiss me, and god help me, I want her to, the heat in her quicksilver gaze turning my insides into a hot, molten mess. And then she does, full sensual lips slanting across mine, tongue stealing into my mouth, laying waste to all my defenses.

"I've been wanting to do that forever." Her voice is a sexy rasp against my lips, and then she kisses me again, nipping my lower lip with her teeth and drinking in the little gasp that escapes.

Her hands move to my knees, warm and solid, fingertips flirting with the hem of my skirt. I lay my hands on hers, but there's no protest; I want this too badly to stop her. The heat in my cheeks rises with each inch of skin that's exposed, but it pales in comparison to what lies below; the seat of my heat, my want and my need, covered by the flimsy barrier of my sodden panties beneath my bunched-up skirt.

She scents my arousal and drops down to her knees, easing my thighs apart and urging me forward. I'm splayed wide on the edge of my chair, and her lips are wending a wet trail up the sensitive skin on the insides of my thighs. She feels so good—I mean *really* so good—that I think I might come before she even reaches my cunt. I'm shivery and restless, fingers tunneling through her hair, winding the short, dark waves around my fingers, trying to get her closer. But she won't be rushed, despite my silent urgings, despite the fact that we have to be in a meeting in less than ten minutes.

"Please…" I say, though it doesn't sound like me, this soft little whimper so full of need. Her mouth brushes against my cotton-covered pussy and I've got to bite my lip to keep from crying out.

"Do you know how often I've imagined this?" she says, teasing me with kisses through the gusset of my panties. "How many times I've stroked myself, imagining you coming undone while I fuck you, right here in this chair?"

I moan, lost in the visual of her stroking off, and then she pulls my panties to one side and her tongue is pressing into my slick folds, seeking and finding my engorged clit and sending me over the edge, almost before she's even begun.

"*Cris!*" I can't stop the breathy cry, and she stands up quickly, covering my mouth with hers, her tongue filling my mouth with the taste of my arousal.

"Shh…" she whispers against my lips, fingers dipping into my still-spasming cunt, "you don't want the whole office to know you're in here getting fucked, do you?" She's thrusting into me, two fingers curling up to hit my G-spot, thumb stroking my clit, sending me right back to the brink.

There's a knock at my door.

"Lauren?" It's Cassie from accounting.

My eyes fly to Cris's. She smiles wickedly and keeps right on fucking me, pressing her other hand over my mouth as she drives me to a second shattering orgasm in as many minutes, my cry of release muffled behind her hand.

"Is everything all right?" It's Cassie again, clearly perplexed by the locked door and strange sounds.

Cris releases me with one last hungry kiss, then makes a show of licking my juices from her fingers. It's hypnotizing, watching her tongue travel their length, her mouth suck them clean. She knows she's got me ready to go all over again, but she just arches an eyebrow and inclines her head toward the door. Right. Cassie.

"Everything's fine, Cassie," I say in a cool, professional tone that completely belies my postorgasmic, disheveled state. "Cris and I just have a couple of things to work out before the meeting."

"Oh. All right. I guess I'll just meet you guys in there." She leaves.

I stand up and try to smooth out my skirt, a process hampered by the proximity of Cris's body and her hands on my ass.

"You know," she says, tongue tracing the sensitive line of my neck, making me shiver, "I don't think we're going to be able to work all these things out today."

"Mmm…" I agree completely, already imagining her naked in my bed. "What do you say to a little late-night planning session, my place?"

"I'll be there."

LURE

Nikki Magennis

She was hovering over the jewelry case when I saw her first, her face a double reflection—two smiles, two sets of teeth. Her fingers tapped the glass, pointing out a silver pheasant studded with paste diamonds.

"How much is the peacock?" Her voice had Irish notes.

I smiled. I didn't correct her. "Let me buy you a drink and I'll call it a gift."

There was a pause, during which I fell over, burst into tears, apologized profusely, tore my clothes off and lay down on the ground and stopped moving.

"Yeah. Sure. Five o'clock?"

I breathed out and released the moon from where I'd stuck it in orbit, let the tides return to normal and the birds sing again.

* * *

I placed the brooch on the table between us. The fake jewels glittered under lights in the bar.

"It's not worth anything much," I said, tasting the froth of the beer on my lips, watching to see if she'd lick hers. Wondering how her smile tasted. Knowing it would be moreish. "Still want it?"

I followed her into the ladies'. Against the full-length mirror, I pushed her flat out, pinned her shoulders, placed her straight and delicate with her back to the glass. I kissed the crook of her neck, the inside of her elbows, the top of her knees. I wanted her splayed across my bed. Spatchcock. How many times had she done this before? Was I counting?

When I gathered my purse from the table and left with her hand tucked into mine, I felt like a shoplifter. Like I'd stolen an exotic specimen from a private aviary.

But: "Come to mine. It's closer," she said, and I followed.

At her building, we ascended in a lift like a gold cage. She had me against the bars, trapped my hands between her lips and bit, gently. I feathered my eyelashes against her cheek, cooed softly. She called my name. A bell rang. We'd arrived.

She offered me a bowl of sunflower seeds, dripped wine into my mouth and let it spill over my lips, run down my throat with a tickle.

Silent, I shed coat, boots, blouse, skirt and socks and let them fall to the floor. I sat there in my underwear, pink and shell colored, shivering. My skin was goose bumped. Her mouth was warm. She drew herself over me like a counterpane. We drifted onto the sofa; I nestled into her corners. The point between her legs was shaved, a little prickly against my cheek. I nuzzled. She smelled of just baked bread and melted butter. I nibbled. Slipped my tongue into a roll, curled it around inside her. I heard her cry out, sing with a full-throated cry.

We hid indoors for two days, pecking inquisitively, opening each other up and looking inside. She gave me a necklace of love bites. I gave her a few secrets, thinly wrapped and not all that shiny once I looked at them in daylight. Mostly, we tried to feed on each other; mouths attached to cunt, breast or mouth; fingers tugging, working, playing; heartbeats rising and falling as we passed orgasms back and forth, dipping into each other like inkwells, writing stories on each other's flesh.

On Tuesday I tried to leave, with my trinkets and my keys wrapped in a silk handkerchief. The floor was wet with her tears. I slipped, turned an ankle. Limped back to bed, where she fed me with pity and promises. I grew fat. We made a chorus of mews like birds imitating cats. Howled all night. Scratched a little. Yes, even the prettiest peahens have claws. And if not beaks, then teeth, always something hard and sharp.

She spat curses at me while I slept. I woke up feverish, tried to wash myself in her future, kissed her until my mouth was numb and my lips were red. I knew, of course, the way home, though the thought made me shake. I had to leave by the window. Naked. Trust my bones not to be brittle, my rubber heart to bounce, my wings to suddenly feather and grow strong. I rocked on the sill. The breeze tugged.

Midair, I called her name, but it came out a strangled crow-squawk. As I tumbled toward the ground, the long, lovesick song fell from my mouth like a skylark's, a hundred invisible silk parachutes, in tatters and rags.

LITTLE MISS GOODY TWO-SHOES

Lucy Felthouse

This garden sure is beautiful. I'd love to live here," said my girlfriend, Izzy, as we walked hand in hand down the gravel path.

"What, out here?" I joked. "You might get a little chilly in the winter!"

"No, silly." She nudged me. "I mean I'd love to live in the house and have this as my back garden."

Izzy turned to face the building we'd recently exited. I turned too. She was absolutely right, of course. An old manor house open to the public, Newberry House was all high ceilings, four-poster beds and creaking floor-boards. A quaint old pile that many people would love to call home.

"It *is* lovely, sweetheart," I said, tucking my arm into Izzy's and steering her round so we could continue our exploration of the grounds. "If I won the lottery, I'd buy you whatever house you wanted."

"Aww, we can but dream, eh?"

"Mmm." I said, nodding and falling into step with her as we continued our stroll in a companionable silence for a while, enjoying the scenery. Every now and again we'd glance back toward the house to see it from different angles. Soon, though, we moved into a part of the grounds where that view was lost.

High hedges lined the path on one side, and a mixture of trees and undergrowth adorned the other. It was a beautiful day. I sighed contentedly, drawing a smile from Izzy and a squeeze of my hand. I squeezed back. Seconds later, I received an entirely spontaneous pressure on my fingers, and Izzy crowded in close to me, her eyes wide and hand covering her mouth.

"Whatever's the matter?" I said, thinking at first she'd seen a spider or something. But she didn't look scared, merely shocked.

She pointed straight ahead. Before us was an alcove set into the hedge. Within it stood a beautiful white statue on a plinth. Judging from Izzy's reaction, though, the beauty of the piece wasn't what had attracted her attention.

"What's up, Izz?" I said, confused now.

"Look at it!" she breathed, her eyes still betraying her surprise. "She's...she's naked!"

I frowned. "Um...yes? What's the problem with that?"

"Well, you can see…everything! And she's touching herself."

Izzy's statement wasn't strictly true. You could see most of the subject's body, including high rounded breasts and curvy stomach and thighs, but the hand crammed between her legs meant that whatever delights lay between them were hidden.

I was reeling with shock that my girlfriend, who'd seen and touched my naked feminine form on countless occasions, was offended by a statue in the grounds of a stately home.

"Izz, what's the problem?"

"Well, it's just that…anyone could see!"

I shook my head, still disbelieving. "Oh, don't be such a Little Miss Goody Two-Shoes. You've seen enough tits, pussy and ass to not be shocked by this, surely!"

She looked at me then, the hurt expression in her eyes enough to make me feel bad. Not bad enough to backtrack—I still thought she was bonkers—but enough for me to want to make her feel better.

I took Izzy's hand and tugged her with me into the alcove, slipping behind the statue. From there, of course, we could see the statue's perfectly molded asscheeks, and the beautiful arch of her back.

"Come on, Izz," I said, indicating what I was admiring, "don't you think she's beautiful?"

Slipping an arm around my girl's waist and pulling her tightly to me, I murmured in her ear, "Wouldn't you like to grip those asscheeks as you kissed her? Feel those tits pressing against yours?"

I drew closer still and flicked my tongue in Izzy's ear, making her squirm in my grasp. "Wouldn't you like to pull her hand away and replace it with yours? Stroke her clit, her pussy? Slip your fingers inside her hot, wet hole and pump her until she came?"

By now, the arm I'd had around her waist had moved, my hand slipping down my girl's back, over her ass and between her legs. I flipped up the hem of her pretty summer dress, cupping her crotch through her panties. I could feel the delicious heat of her pussy through the cotton underwear, and when I rubbed my flattened hand against her vulva, Izzy moaned.

The sound sent an insane shock of want zipping through my body. I tried to tell myself that it wasn't the time or the place to get frisky, but when Izzy rocked her hips, trying to get more friction from my hand, I couldn't help myself.

I grabbed Izzy and pulled her to me, pressing my lips forcefully to hers. She opened her mouth immediately, eager to deepen our kiss. I responded, my tongue exploring my girl's beautiful mouth until she suddenly yanked away, murmuring a single word.

"More..."

I pushed her backward until her body was pressed up against the statue's plinth. Then I dropped to my knees in the gravel, pushing her dress up. I lightly slapped the insides of her calves, indicating she should open her legs.

Obeying, Izzy moved her feet apart a little. I caught the scent of her arousal and immediately had to taste it. There was no time for teasing. I was determined to lick my girl's pussy until she came on my face. I pulled her knickers roughly to one side and pushed my face between her thighs. My mouth went to where she needed it most, the soft skin already slick with juices. I slipped my tongue between her labia, moans and groans issuing from above as I pleasured my girl with my lips, teeth and tongue. I grinned inwardly at the sounds she was making; it appeared she was so lost to lust she'd completely forgotten where she was. I just hoped I could make her come before we got caught.

I alternately flicked and sucked at Izzy's clit, every now and again dipping my tongue down to slurp up the sweet juices that slid from her hot pussy. Before long, the telltale signs of her approaching orgasm became apparent. Her thighs tensed and she bucked against my face, silently urging me to go faster. I obliged, pulling her distended clit into my mouth and sucking it for all I was worth.

Izzy stiffened. Her back arched as she edged toward the precipice, then toppled off, her fall indicated by her wail of ecstasy and the way her hands suddenly gripped my hair and held my face tightly to her cunt. I could do nothing but let her ride it out, my tongue delving in her folds as her pussy twitched and spasmed and her cream ran into my eager mouth.

Soon, Izzy calmed down enough to release me.

I wiped her juices from my face with the back of my hand, looked up at her, and said, "Not such a Little Miss Goody Two-Shoes now, are you?"

SUBMISSION LETTER

Tara Young

I've read your stories about the MILF next door begging her twentysomething mistress for release as she's tied to the bed, a strap-on filling her completely. About the college coed being ordered to strip and crawl naked across the floor to taste the passion between her roommate's legs. About the softball coach who trains the catcher to take a dildo in the ass.

I ache to be them. To bring your sexy scenarios to life. I long to please your pussy like you've pleased mine over the last three months since I discovered your work. You've fucked me senseless with your raw words and vivid imagery, giving me orgasm after delicious orgasm. You've left me breathless but always craving more of you.

I want to return the favor.

We've never met, but you already own me, Mistress. My body responds only to you. Just thinking your name makes me wet. Your passionate prose hardens my nipples and clit, leaving me in a constant state of arousal.

Before you, I masturbated about once or twice a day. Now it's more like ten times...at least. You dominate my every thought and fantasy. When my hand circles my clit, it's you I see in my mind's eye. It's your words echoing in my head, pushing me closer to the edge.

I imagine you're like the respectable math teacher you write about, and I'm the principal who needs to be taught a lesson. You're all business in your glasses and power suit. But after school, your navy-blue skirt is hiked up and your thong pushed aside while I give in to your demands. You sit in my chair and I'm under my desk furiously sucking on your lips and clit until you come so hard your body shakes. You tell me what a good girl I am and pat my head before you pull your skirt back down and go on your way.

I climax thinking that one day you'll make me yours, and it won't be a fantasy anymore.

I feel like I already know you and what makes you happy. You write about women who seem hesitant to accept their submissive roles. That would never be me. I would never require your punishment or discipline—or resist it.

I know you like to be in control. I want to submit to your every command. Allow my body to be used in any way you desire. My mouth, hands, tits and cunt are yours to do with—and to—what you want.

Blindfold and handcuff me. Fuck me with your toys. Finger me, suck me, lick me till I can't take any more. Make me plead for every touch.

I know you like a woman who is willing to please you no matter the circumstance. Please let me taste you in your car, at work, in the shower. Please cover my face and hands with your juices while I'm on my knees before you.

I know you like an audience and you like to share. I want your friends to watch while you take me to new heights of ecstasy. My body is tense with wanting as I see the lust in their eyes. I want them all to devour me as you have, and I want to lick each pussy in thanks.

I know you've awakened my libido like no one ever has. I want to be yours.

Please, Mistress.

STACKED

Reina Sobin

T his is so wrong."

"Excuse me?"

I gestured at the seller's T-shirt. STACKED FOR YOUR VIEWING PLEASURE. The row of books across each of her breasts had immediately drawn my gaze. I distracted myself by thumbing through the book closest to me, trying not to stare at the way her fingers slid over a novel's thick spine.

"Ah, well, nothing like a double entendre to make the kids drool." She handed an old man his purchase and a few singles. "There you go, sir."

A young man stepped up, his eyes glued to the woman's breasts.

"Okay, three graphic novels. That'll be twenty dollars, just for you." She gave him a coy smile but otherwise didn't react to his leering.

"Uh, okay." The kid shoved the money at her and darted away, comics in hand.

"I think that guy was drooling all right."

She laughed and flipped a dark strand of hair out of her eyes. "Whatever gets them buying. The men come to stare and the dykes come to ask me out. It's fun for both parties so I don't mind."

She tapped the book I was holding. "Are you interested in that one? Chapter eight is particularly interesting."

I hadn't looked at the title until now: *Banging Your Way through History: A Tale of Two Women.* Oh, god. I flipped to chapter eight. "Private Acts in a Public Forum?"

"I remember one story in there where a woman dressed as a man, fake cock and all, and proceeded to seduce as many women as she could—wives, sisters, prostitutes—in alleys, at parties, you name it. Supposedly, she was never revealed until a relative found her journal after her death."

I stared at the cover. "Is that true?"

"I have no clue, but it does give a person fun ideas." She tapped the book. "Tell you what, I'm due for a break. How about we get a bite to eat and we can discuss your prurient taste in literature a bit longer?"

"Share a meal with a beautiful woman with wit and brains? You may have to drag me kicking and screaming."

"Oh, shut up." She turned to the girl next to her. "Hey, Sarah, can you watch the booth? I'm taking a break."

"No problem. I'm going when you get back though."

"All right. Thanks." She clasped my free arm and ushered me toward the makeshift café in the back of the convention hall. Lucky for us, it was quiet, since most of our fellow book-lovers chose the fried-food cart next door.

The menu was limited—simple soups and breads—quick to serve, without being messy to eat. We sat close to each other, at a table barely designed for two.

"I'm Erin, by the way." She held out a hand.

"Rachel."

I met her clasp and took a spoonful of soup.

"Have you always had an interest in fucking women in public?"

I coughed and somehow avoided spitting bits of clam across the table. "I, um…no."

"You don't sound too sure about that."

"Well, I've never tried—"

"Honey, we need to broaden your horizons." She tilted her cup and drained it. "Let's get back to your book. The woman I told you about—Anne—would strap on a faux cock, get dressed up in all her male finery, and attend one of the many dances that her town held. She would see a young woman that interested her and ask her to dance. While the woman was in her arms, Anne would use nothing but words and casual touch to seduce her. She must have said something right because there were several times when she was caught pleasing her dance partner right outside in the gardens."

My food forgotten, I scooted my chair closer. "Was she using her...cock...on them?"

Erin bit her cheek. "Sometimes, although she wrote, 'I enjoy climbing under my lover's skirt, putting my mouth to her until she screams her woman's pleasure.' 'Their joy filled my lips and often my clothes were wet from their excitement long after I had returned to the dance.'"

"Have you ever done that?" I was immediately embarrassed. "I'm sorry. That's none of my business."

"I don't mind." Her hand touched my knee under the tablecloth. "Are you asking because you want to know or because you want the experience?"

"I don't know..."

"Oh, I think you do."

I shifted in my seat at the knowing tone.

"I bet your panties are wet just thinking about what I could do to you."

I looked around to see if anyone could hear her, but no one was close enough to listen in. "I don't—"

Her fingers eased up my skirt. "You don't what? Want me to touch you? Tell me that you don't want this and we'll go back to our boring little meal."

"No, I want you to...touch me."

Erin reached my panties and I spread my legs a little to accommodate her. She teased me through the fabric, her fingers light and quick against my center. "My, my, you *are* wet."

I bit my lip and rested my head on one hand, focused on the table as if it were of particular interest. My other hand pulled my panties aside so she could stroke me.

"This is so wrong."

"Yet so delightfully right."

One finger dipped into my moisture and spread it over my clit. She circled me, delicate strokes designed to torment me. "Anne's journals were published, you know. The graphic detail was quite astonishing the first time I read it."

I kept my head down, afraid that someone would see my arousal. "Harder."

I pressed closer, seeking a firmer touch, but her fingers pulled away and continued to fondle me lightly.

"Let's see if I can paraphrase. 'I climbed under her long skirts and touched that most willing body. My tongue tasted her heat and I knew rapture.'"

"Oh, god." I panted shallowly, hoping no one would notice my state.

"Shhh…" Erin continued as if I hadn't spoken. "'The lady spread her limbs across the bench as a man would, her wetness covering my chin and cheeks as I lapped at her. She gripped my head in a gloved hand and pulled me tight against her womanhood. She whimpered as I pleased her, my fingers deep where few had been.'"

I gripped the table with both hands now, sweat along my hairline and the warning tingle of my climax in my belly. Erin's movement against my clit turned rough, the slippery juices of my sex smearing across my thighs.

"'I ate the lady as I would a fine feast, savoring the sweet dessert under my tongue. Her thighs closed about my head, trembling in her need for release. I had thoughts of sending her to heaven and brought her center into my mouth.'"

I came under those delicious fingers, her words doing just as much to bring me over. Somehow I managed not to cry out, not to shake apart at the seams. Erin grinned at my reaction as her hand eased away.

She stood, wiped her hand on a napkin, and pushed the book toward me.

"Come back when you get to chapter eleven."

SNOWBOUND

Sacchi Green

Will we be able to breathe?"

"You'd better hope so. Keep digging."

Icy pellets whipped across my face. Good. Pain prodded anger, and anger might distract Katy from panic. It was hard to stay mad as she burrowed into the white mound, her sweet little tail in stretch ski pants twitching like a chipmunk's.

As she scooped snow out behind her, I used it to extend our space. "Okay," I shouted above the wind. "Enough! Now pack the inside surface as firmly as you can. Use your round butt for something besides flirting." The storm stole the last words. Just as well.

Three skis including her broken one leaned against the opening of our improvised cave, giving us a bit more room once I'd packed snow over them. The fourth, bright red, I planted upright for searchers to see, after the storm let up. Hollow ski poles, tips and handles hacked off with my utility knife, went through the walls at angles to keep them from being plugged by falling snow; we'd have a little air supply—unless the accumulation topped three more feet.

"Coming in!" I wriggled through the remaining narrow slit. Katy curled to one side, making room. The space was wide enough to roll over in and high enough in the center to sit up.

"Good job." My tone was still brusque. "Help me spread this out." Ski-patrol equipment around here includes one of those thin Mylar "space blankets," big enough for one body to roll up in. Better now as a shield between us and the packed-snow floor.

In the dim light I saw Katy eyeing my buttpack, probably wondering what else was in there. Better not to mention the energy bars and chocolate yet. She didn't ask.

"Raf, I'm really, really sorry I got you into this."

A sincere apology. No petulance, no sly flirting now. Might be more to her after all than a cute face, a tantalizing body and a rich Daddy.

"What the hell were you doing taking off on a closed trail?"

"I knew you'd follow. That was the plan, to get you off alone with me." Katy lay back, an arm across her eyes. "I thought the trail would curve back to the base lodge eventually. I just didn't know the storm would be so bad, so fast. Idiot!"

"And you didn't know you'd crash into the rocks."

That body crumpled on the ground when I'd found her...
the broken ski...but she was okay. And mad enough at
herself for both of us.

I eased off. "The getting alone together part worked,
anyway."

"There is that. For as long as we survive." She
couldn't quite control a tremor.

"We'll survive. I'm an old hand at this."

Katy's body language shifted subtly. "In that case, if
you really think we'll be okay...maybe I'm not so sorry
after all."

"That's the spirit." When she'd asked for private
lessons, skiing clearly hadn't been the only sport she'd
had in mind.

"I suppose," she said, "we'll have to keep each other
warm. Conserve body heat."

"Not yet. We're still warm from digging. Wait until
we need it." Time for the distraction of an energy bar.
Katy ate her half and kept still after a wriggle or two,
even when I had us unzip our parkas and snuggle close.
Even through my flannel shirt and her fleece one, her
breasts against mine tempted me to wriggle, too, but I
resisted, and after a while, she dozed.

Snow rose above the entrance. Wind howled across
the tops of the ski-pole tubes, its unearthly sounds
becoming almost soothing. I dozed too.

"Raf..." Katy woke shivering with more than the
cold. "What time do you think it is?" Not quite panic.

I checked my watch with a penlight. Midnight. "Only

about seven hours until daylight. And the wind has died down. We'll be fine."

"I could sure use more body heat now," she said plaintively, panic subdued.

"Show me where you're cold." I groped under her shirt and sports bra. "Pretty warm here."

She gasped. Her nipples reached out for more as I tweaked them, but she managed to pull one of my hands down to her crotch. "Don't stop, but how about...how...ahhh!...how about...here?" She arched into my touch. I paused to pull her ski pants down for easy access.

"Nope, regular steam bath here." I slid my fingers along her warm tender flesh, then underneath her. She squealed in frustration. "Your poor little seat is definitely chilly, though. Too bad there isn't room in here for the spanking you need." I made do with a few firm pinches.

"Ow! Can I have a rain check—a snow check—on that? Right now I need more, please. More!"

In the confined space of the cave her scent was maddening. I struggled to keep a grip on my own needs. "No kicking or thrashing. There's nothing in here to tie you to."

"I'll try..."

And she did try, while my left hand kept on with all the torment her breasts demanded and my right worked her slick cunt lips and clit with hard strokes that made her beg for even more.

"Deeper Raf, please!"

So I obliged, but not as deeply as I wanted to. The ski-patrol supplies didn't include latex gloves. There was no resisting getting my tongue on her clit, though, and giving her every intense stroke she needed to make her scream at a pitch as unearthly as anything the wind had managed.

"You now, Raf," she managed to say at last.

"Make that a snow check, too. I kick and thrash enough to bring this whole place down."

I wasn't at all sure about there being enough air to breathe if I got going, either. "Try to sleep some more now."

Katy did. I didn't.

The pulsing of the helicopter penetrated our snow walls about when I'd expected. The pilot, a buddy of mine, would have seen the red ski.

I shook Katy awake. "Rescue time." She clung to me all the closer, but I gently disentangled her and made sure her ski pants were well up. "Now we get to kick the snow walls all we want."

I did the kicking. By the time we emerged into early morning sunlight, Katy's father was struggling through the deep snow to meet us.

"I'm fine, Daddy," Katy called. "Rafaela saved my life!"

Once they'd hugged he gripped my hand and shook it fervently. "How can I thank you enough? They told me you'd take care of her. I insist on a big reward...I'll write a check..."

"Daddy, I'm a grown woman," Katy said firmly. "I'll take care of that."

"Oh. Right. Of course." They'd clearly had similar issues before. He turned back to me. "Well, you have my sincere gratitude. What a good thing Katy's ski instructor was so competent! And...well..."

"And a woman?" Katy filled in. "Since we had to spend the night together?" She took my hand, with more of a squeeze than a shake. "I couldn't agree more." A swift, relatively chaste kiss on my cheek gave her a chance to mutter in my ear, "Snow checks are the best kind."

And they were. A reward that keeps right on giving.

WRITTEN ON STONE

Toby Rider

Bernadine stood naked against the red sandstone wall. *What would the priests and nuns think?* These river-carved canyons, all smooth curves and jutting angles and secret crevices, were as familiar and yet mysterious as her own body; she had never thought before how like a woman's body they could be. Like Janet's body.

The cleft in the rock face had seemed no more than a crack until Janet pulled a tangle of branches aside to reveal an opening wide enough for a slender girl to squeeze through. Inside, the walls opened into a small chamber, with room to walk about, then narrowed again. A shaft of sunlight slanted from the patch of blue sky far above onto the sandy floor, where a stream would flow in the wet season, leaping from the ledge outside and down over the cliffs to join the great river below.

"Forget the mission school." Janet knew Bernie's mind. "There are no priests here, or even gods, only shadows of whatever was sacred to the Old Ones. No one had found this place before I did, no rafting tourists or rock hunters or even our own people. No one, since the Old Ones left their marks to defy time." She traced, without quite touching, a spiraling line chipped into the stone. Above it, a shade darker than the red rocks, was the painted print of a hand. "See?" She held up her own hand, darker still than the rocks or the ancient paint. "The size of a woman's hand. Our hands."

For the touch of Janet's hand Bernadine would risk damnation—or, worse, cease to believe in it. Still... "How can you know what rituals they used?"

Janet didn't meet her eyes, gazing instead at other figures on the walls, animals and birds and shapes beyond guessing. "I saw it in a dream."

Bernie didn't entirely believe in dreams, either, in spite of the old traditions of their people. With Janet solemn before her, naked but for the deerskin pouch dangling between her breasts, it didn't matter. If Janet needed a sacred ritual to mark the bond between them before they could have more than stolen moments to touch and tease and press together in unfulfilled longing, so be it.

She raised her arms at an angle—*NOT like a crucifix!*—and spread her legs slightly for balance. When Janet opened the pouch and drew out a stick of compressed charcoal wrapped in corn husks, Bernie dipped her head. *Yes.*

Janet rolled the rough cylinder along Bernie's bronze skin, raising a flush. Across her collarbones, down to the stiffened peak of each breast, over the curve of her belly and lower it went, thrusting gently between her thighs until wetness darkened the pale corn husks. Bernie caught the scent of her own arousal.

Janet withdrew the packet, touched her tongue to the wet places, then tore at its covering with strong teeth. When enough of the charcoal was unwrapped, she pressed a hand into Bernie's belly and traced around it, leaving her own five-fingered mark on the tender flesh. Then she knelt and drew a black line on the rock down along Bernie's inner thigh.

Bernie tensed with the need to clamp her thighs around that hand, urge it into the secret places where the need was becoming a pulsing ache. Past calf, ankle; around foot; upward again along hip, waist, arm, shoulder—each moment, each touch of Janet's hand tracing her silhouette onto the canyon wall, was a torment and pleasure so intense it verged on pain.

"Don't move," Janet warned, as the final line inched upward again between Bernie's thighs, but her other hand slid downward, pressing into flesh now slick and hot.

It was a challenge. Bernie, close to bursting, still did not move. Even when the charcoal lines met at last, and Janet leaned abruptly forward to thrust her tongue into that wet heat as though she too had barely resisted, Bernie stayed rock still. But when Janet grasped at her hips, then dug demanding fingers into her buttocks to bring her harder against tongue and lips and teeth, Bernie clutched at her hair to force her even closer and met that hunger at last with writhing body and cries that echoed through the sandstone cavern.

When the sounds died away and their breathing slowed, Bernie fumbled for the husk-wrapped charcoal and nudged at Janet. "There's just room for your shape on the wall, if it overlaps with mine. And time together to etch them both into the rock, bit by bit, however many years it takes. Time to mark our place in time."

So Janet stood against the stone, one arm and shoulder across Bernie's outline there, while Bernie took charge of marking, and tracing, and tantalizing, and riding Janet's thigh at the last, until the canyon rang again with cries from both of them.

They lay spent on the sand, wrapped close together. At last Bernie found her voice.

"It was a true dream, then?"

Janet pulled her even closer and looked deeply into her eyes.

"It is now," she said.

HERE AND BACK AGAIN

Shanna Germain

The ferry goes from the island to the bay twice a day. I ride it to work a couple of mornings a week.

Annie rides it too. Not to work, not to anything. She just rides out to the bay and then back to the island. I'd like to think she's riding it for me, but I know that she was riding it long before she ever met me.

I met Annie at the little library on the island, where we were both looking up books on suicide by diet. Namely, how to bake ourselves to death with too much butter and too much sugar and not enough vegetables. It's the sweeter, tastier version of putting your head in the oven. We both put our hands on *Pastries and Pies: Full Flavor, Full Fat* at the same time. I thought she might fight me for it, but she offered it up to me instead. We laughed it off. But dying housewives can always spot each other.

It's in the too-easy laugh, the slightly haunted look in our eyes, that bit of gathered fat around the midsection.

Annie's got blonde-red hair, full of wild curls that whip in the salt wind. Her sunglasses are too big for her face, but they're not so dark that they hide her green-green eyes. Or the circles under them. She smokes—not at home, she says, just on the ferry—rolling her own cigarettes on the deck, not even noticing all the tobacco that floats away.

I sit with her outside on the front of the ferry, watching the waves splash up and get left behind, watching the island fall away and the mainland come closer, sipping my black coffee—burnt and astringent, but it keeps the cold out of my mouth. It's nearly an hour out and another back.

We talk for the first half of the trip, about nothing at all. We don't talk about home. Not about our kids or our husbands, not about the in-laws or the bills. That would bring them with us, out onto the wild sea, and the whole point is to leave them behind.

We say things like, "Look at that bird!" and "Water's rough today, isn't it?" and "Wonder what the weather's like across the way." Annie's long leg accidentally touches mine when she turns away from the wind to light her cig, and she leaves it there, knee to my knee. I hand my coffee off to her, take it back to find it's covered in her scent of tobacco and lanolin. She picks something random out of my hair, and I'm so glad for her touch that I almost forget not to lean into it. These are our rituals, fallen into by habit, by fear, but they give us the steps to keep moving toward the thing that we want, toward each other.

When my coffee's empty and she's rolled a fourth cigarette and tucked it into her shirt pocket for later, she faces away, across the water. Her profile is sharp everywhere except her cheeks, which are like big, soft scoops of ice cream. I want to lick her skin, taste the sea salt and wind.

"I'll be right back," she says. Another part of our ritual. Part of our denial. Or maybe acceptance. Sometimes they look the same when the land has been left.

"Okay," I say, and I lean back as though I'm going to keep sitting here.

The bathrooms have funny doors—magnetic, so they don't accidentally swing when the ferry tilts. I pull it open, feeling the resistance.

Annie's leaning against the sink, watching me close and lock the bathroom door. She says something, but I can't hear it over the liquid pounding in my veins. I go to her, waves of wanting streaming off me, powering me forward.

We don't kiss, not on the mouth. I don't know why. Maybe that's too real, too close to something. But we put our mouths everywhere else, on necks and shoulders, on palms and the hollows of throats. We are rough and tumble, grab and pull, closed eyes and open lips.

We have learned how to fuck without getting naked, without looking too closely, with our backs to the mirror. She grabs the bottom of my shirt and pulls it up, her nails scratching my sides. Her hands are down my pants even as mine are opening hers. She doesn't wear underwear, and my fingers are caught between the soft of her skin and the rough of the fabric before they sink into her, into that deep wet that comes of waiting for pleasure. She scrapes my clit with her thumbnail and I see a bright spot of pain behind my eyes. It makes me want her more, this thing I feel, this ache and pleasure and forgetting all twisted up. We fuck each other hard and fast, leaning in, holding each other up with the weight of our desire, with the rocking of our bodies and of the ferry. We fuck until I feel like I'm all the way inside her, filling her, and her me and then and only then can I come, a wet crash of power that drowns me soundless, breathless.

When we're done, we're both panting, disheveled, grinning without being able to really look at each other. Annie pulls the cigarette from her pocket, clears her throat. Her smile is like a wave that can't stop rising.

"See you on the water?" she says. She slips out before I can even think about answering and I lean against the sink, my turn now, trying to let my heartbeat go down to something like normal.

We can't do this forever, hiding here. Leaving our husbands and families and lives temporarily behind. I can feel it coming into its own, this thing between us, like a rising storm. Unstoppable. Fearsome in its rolling power. It makes me nervous and dangerous and wet. The dry land of my life is far away and everything here is liquid.

And next time I'm going to kiss her.

I WISH
I KNEW YOU

Cheyenne Blue

I wish I knew you like she does.

It's Sunday morning and I'm sitting on the rear deck with my husband. He's reading the paper and grunting about some perceived incompetence in the Obama administration. It's spring and the Rocky Mountains look so damn beautiful in the sun that I want to hold the picture in my head to look at when life moves back to winter.

Jed doesn't see the Rockies; he doesn't see me.

After I've served breakfast, I sit opposite him sipping a coffee. I'm not drinking in the mountains now; I'm looking east, toward the house across the narrow lane.

I sneak a glance at my watch; it's nearly 9:00. Jed rustles the paper, makes another derogatory remark about Obama.

The house opposite abuts the lane, so when the upstairs drapes twitch and slide back, I can see clearly into the bedroom—your bedroom.

I've never been able to strike up a casual conversation with you, but I've driven past your house a few times and I've seen you and your partner working in the front yard. You, my secret obsession, are stocky and the singlet you wear in the yard shows off fine tanned shoulders. A tattoo wraps over one bicep. I'd love to know what it's of. Your cropped black hair hugs your head, but there are small curls in the nape of your neck.

Your partner is curvy and feminine. Someone cruel would call her fat, but I'm no pot calling the kettle anything. Her breasts swell out under her T-shirt, and her belly folds into rolls when she bends to pull a dandelion from the lawn. *Plumpy,* I call her, to myself.

You look happy together. You touch, kiss openly. Jed would not approve.

Sunday mornings are my time for watching. When Jed goes off to church, I'm alone for nearly two hours. Jed doesn't like me staying behind, but I'm adamant. I don't like Jed's God; I don't like the things he says. So instead of church, I sit on the back deck and watch you going about your life through the windows of your house: cooking breakfast, folding laundry, just living.

I sneak a glance at my watch again. Jed turns to the sports section.

"You'll be late for church, honey," I tell him.

"Not going," he grunts. "Pastor's away. Some liberal

new fella. Not gonna listen to his shit."

Damn. Outwardly, I stay serene. "More coffee?"

Jed doesn't answer, just holds out his mug.

I refill our mugs and sip, gazing at the house across the lane. You're there, standing at the window, staring in my direction. Not at me, I don't fool myself about that. The Rockies are behind me and you're probably drinking in their beauty as I like to do. Plumpy comes up behind, slipping curvy arms around your waist. She nuzzles your neck, and I imagine her making a teasing remark about those little black curls that are growing so long.

You turn and take Plumpy in your arms. You bend. Kiss her. My hand tightens on my mug, for now you're kissing, really kissing. I can see your mouth slanting over hers, your hand cupping her ass, the other winding around her shoulders to draw her close to your body. I've never seen you kiss this intensely before. Something tightens in the pit of my stomach at the sight.

After long minutes, Plumpy breaks the kiss, spins away. I'm disappointed, but then she twirls, her mouth wide and smiling, and her hands draw the loose dress she's wearing over her head. It sails to the ground behind her and oh, my god, she's naked. Naked and beautiful. You're not smiling. When I see your face, it's intent, fierce, and even though there's distance between us, I can sense your lust.

I hardly dare breathe. I'm afraid my breath will catch in my throat, expel with a gasp that will alert Jed.

I concentrate on remaining silent, even as my heart is jumping in my throat. I sip my coffee and keep my eyes fixed on you. You're still dressed, but Plumpy's hand is tugging at your singlet. But you step away. I'm disappointed; you're not in the mood, you want coffee maybe, or you're late for something.

You drop to your knees, hold out your arms. Plumpy doesn't hesitate. She walks forward and your arms rise and wrap around her waist. Plumpy's hands are raking through your tight, black curls and you stare up into her eyes for a moment. Then you bend and kiss the curve of her belly. And then...

This time I do gasp, and my breathing is so tight I can't get air into my chest. Because you're kissing her again, but kissing her there, on the place I can't say aloud, even to myself. My hand shakes and I put my coffee down so abruptly it sloshes on the table. I don't care, and I can't look away: from both of you, but mainly you. It's always been about you.

You tilt your head, slouch a little, and Plumpy lifts a leg and places it on your shoulder. She's wide open, and I see there's no hair between her legs. Then your face moves in and I can see your tongue. There. You're kissing her there.

I'm flushed, I know I am. My face must be as red as sin and I'm burning all over. Burning for you, burning for what you're doing to her. If Jed looks up now, I'll be in trouble, but I don't care. There's a low ache in my own body, a yearning, a need. I haven't felt desire for so long, and never like this. Jed's paper rustles, but I ignore it.

You're pulling her even closer, and she's writhing. Your hands are grasping her hips now, but your face is still there.

Hurry, I think, *hurry,* before Jed looks up from the paper, before he realizes what I'm watching...before he drags me inside, protects me from... From what?

There's a tremor in my hand as I watch you, see how you pleasure Plumpy, see how she comes with her head thrown back, and those curves jiggling. And you're so strong and in control, and you wrap your arms around her waist and your face is pushed between her legs and I can imagine her howl of pleasure.

I'm shaky inside, but it's not with shock, even though Jed's God says I should be horrified. No, I'm shaky with feelings that haven't stirred me for years. My nipples are engorged and there's an ache of something low down in my belly, a pulse of desire down there. You're on your feet again, and you're in her arms. She so unashamedly naked, you so protective and proud. You look at your watch and smack Plumpy on the bottom, give her a quick kiss. You're probably telling her she has time for a shower before you have to go wherever you're going.

Plumpy moves out of sight, and you come to the window and gaze toward the Rockies. I wonder what you're thinking?

I wish you knew me like you know her.

HEAT
LIGHTNING

Sommer Marsden

I can't take my eyes off her skirt. Okay, so it's not so much her skirt as it is the long expanse of tanned thigh that disappears underneath the hem. A flesh-colored road I'd love to follow to its end.

I shake off the thought as my brother says, "...do you?"

"What?"

Dan grins. He knows what I've been thinking. But hey, he should cut me some slack; it's been a long while since Jessica and I broke up. And here sits his brand-new neighbor Maggie—who likes rare steak and '80s music according to our conversation—showing off thighs that would make any sane woman weep. Or man, for that matter.

"I said you don't like heat, do you? My sister would

live in the Arctic if she could figure out how to make money."

Everyone laughs.

He's right. I hate heat. Hate sunburn and humidity, shorts and tank tops. I hate swimming pools and having to smear myself in SPF anything. I always get some in my mouth and sunscreen tastes like shit, thank you very much.

"True story," I say.

"Oh, really? I love heat," Maggie says, leaning forward, touching my leg.

Talk about heat. Lord. It shoots through me like heat lightning, zipping and dancing under my skin. Way hotter than any fever, way steamier than anything August in the city can dish up. I turn my eyes to Dan's new pool to gather my thoughts.

If I were a guy, I'd have a hard-on right now. I am once again thankful I am not a guy. She cannot see my sudden and violent arousal.

I catch her watching me. A certain look in her pool-water blue-green eyes.

Maybe she can.

I clear my throat and take the beer that Dan offers. It's cold and bittersweet going down. My brother wanders off to chat with others and I am left sitting there with Maggie. Maggie whose hair is the color of raw honey. Whose breasts are full and very much *not* on display in her summer blouse, but they are *there*. Round and prominent and my eyes want to return to them again and again.

"Want to swim?" she asks.

"Swim?"

"Yeah, you know. Get in the water, get cool. Move around in a swim-like fashion so you don't drown."

The laugh she's provoked rips out of me and is almost embarrassing in its giddiness. "I don't swim."

"Well, you could stand out there."

"I don't have a suit," I say.

"Well, you have shorts and you have a tank and you'll dry fast enough in this heat."

It's still eighty-some degrees even though it's full dark and the lightning bugs are out. "But—"

She doesn't let me finish. She stands, pulls down the skirt and yanks off the blouse and stands there in a bikini the color of buttercream. She watches me. I think she's daring me to say no.

"Please?"

"Okay," I say. I'll regret it, I know I will, but I follow her anyway, a lemming to the sea. Or a dumb-ass following a pretty girl. You can look at it either way.

We wander to the deeper end. The end back in the shadows where the other visitors to my brother's small party will not see us. We're not fooling anyone.

She turns so suddenly that were we not tits deep in water I would have fallen on my ass. "I saw you looking at me," she says.

"Yeah, I'm sorry. I didn't mean to leer. I just—"

"Dan says you've been alone awhile."

"How nice of him to share my most embarrassing

facts with the neighborhood." I want to be angry—well, part of me does—but she steps in closer and even in the water I can feel imaginary zips and pops of electricity coming off of her.

I could die here. Drop dead of the combined forces of her closeness and the water. "I asked him. I saw your picture and I...I asked."

"I see."

How stupid do I sound? I wonder.

"Can I kiss you?" she asks, cocking her head like she might expect the answer to be no.

I am so off guard. I am so off balance. This woman is making my head hurt and my heart swell and other parts of me pulse. I'm stammering but I'm also nodding like an idiot and she gives up, leans in and kisses me.

Her mouth tastes pink and sweet like that girly drink she was drinking. She steps into me, all the way into me, so I can feel her pointy hard nipples pressed to me and when I put my palm up I can feel her heart galloping.

I kiss her back, but I find my bravery and I suck her tongue too. And then I wrap my hands to the sides of her slim waist and haul her forward. "Touch me, will you touch me?" she's whispering. "I've been watching you watch me all night and I just can't—"

So I touch her. I slide my hand into the cool well of the darkened pool and nudge my fingers under the lip of her sugary-colored bikini bottom. She is so unbelievably warm under my fingers and then around them as I thrust into her. Her body, feverishly hot on the inside, clamps around me and her kiss turns so intense it borders on desperate.

I'm feeling a little desperate myself.

Her kiss is oscillating like a summer fan. Strong and needy…gentle and teasing. Back and forth, in and out, up and down, I can't keep time with my body or my head. I'm spinning, falling, flying.

I press my thumb to her clit and curl my fingers. Her little hands grip my shoulders as if she's holding on and she gives me her orgasm as sudden and sweet as an unexpected thunderstorm that is over before it's truly begun.

I keep kissing her and swallow her cries as I milk each flicker and spasm from her hot little cunt.

"God, god, god," she says.

"You can just call me Sunny." I laugh.

She grabs my neck, kisses me, tugs me under the cold water. All sound, all air, all light is gone for an instant and it is just me and Maggie in the echoing depths of water.

When we break the surface she whispers in my ear. "Come home with me, Sunny. I have dry clothes. I have wine. I have…an urge to reciprocate."

My body hums with arousal, attraction, joy. Some things I haven't felt for a while. And as we climb free I turn to her and say, "Oh and hey, what *else* has my brother said? About me?"

She shrugs and those hard nipples poke the pale fabric of her bikini top. I want to suck them through the wet fabric and then bare them and suck them dry. "Just that you are super smart and funny and talented and…"

"And?" I hand her a towel as Dan gives me a side-ways grin from across the lawn.

That shit. He knows. He's no fool.

"That he thought we'd get along. Really well."

"Smart man."

ABOUT
THE EDITOR

SACCHI GREEN is a Lambda award–winning writer and editor of erotica and other stimulating genres. Her stories have appeared in scores of publications, including seven volumes of *Best Lesbian Erotica*, four of *Best Women's Erotica* and three of *Best Lesbian Romance*. In recent years she's taken to wielding the editorial whip, editing or coediting seven lesbian erotica anthologies, most recently *Lesbian Cowboys* (winner of a Lambda Literary Award in 2010), *Girl Crazy*, *Lesbian Lust* and *Lesbian Cops*, all from Cleis Press. Sacchi lives in the Five College area of western Massachusetts, with frequent trips to the White Mountains of New Hampshire, and can be found online at sacchi-green.blogspot.com, FaceBook (as Sacchi Green,) and Live Journal (as sacchig).